MAIL-ORDER DECEPTION

EAGLE CREEK BRIDES
BOOK FIVE

KARLA GRACEY

This book is dedicated to all of my faithful readers, without whom I would be nothing. I thank you for the support, reviews, love, and friendship you have shown me as we have gone through this journey together. I am truly blessed to have such a wonderful readership.

CHARACTER LIST

- **Jane Brown – seamstress; former maid to Marianne Denny, Eagle Creek**
- **Peter Algood – ship owner, New York**
- Mark Algood, his brother – bookkeeper, New York
- James Denny – schoolmaster
- Marianne Denny (née Delaney, first husband Gerry Wilson) – widow
- Macey Green – cook
- Mr. and Mrs. Denny – James' parents
- Mr. Delaney – Marianne's father
- Aston Merryweather – Eagle Creek's postmaster
- Helen Merryweather – his wife
- Nate Hale – sheriff of Eagle Creek
- Clara Hale – his wife

- Tom Greening – dairy farmer
- Elise Greening – schoolteacher
- Bailey Greening – Tom and Elise's son. Owner of Quinto the performing dog, delivers telegrams
- Aidan O'Shaunessy – rancher
- Meredith O'Shaunessy – his wife. Owner of Fliss (another talented dog)
- Many Birds – Crow tracker
- Walks With The Sun – Many Birds' son and Jonas' apprentice
- Chief Plenty Coups – revered Crow leader
- Strikes The Iron – his wife
- Alfie Pinchin – postboy at the postal office
- Jonas Gilpin – smith, in charge of the public stable
- Geraldine Gilpin – his wife
- Teddy – their young son
- Mr. Hemsley – owner of The Eyrie
- Bartholomew King – maître d' at The Eyrie
- Mrs. Effie Albert – seamstress and dressmaker
- David Albert – her deceased husband
- Hannah and Kathy – her apprentices
- Edwin Graham – Eagle Creek's master carpenter
- Jake Graham – his son and Jonas' apprentice
- Marla Dawes –actress. Adopted daughter of Marianne and James Denny

- Algernon DeVries – theater impresario and her husband
- Sister Margaretta – nun at the orphanage
- Harry and Ellen Parker, and their children – Peter's oldest friend and his family. Ellen was Peter's former fiancée
- Mr. Kingshott – Peter's shipping agent
- Cable Poole – unorthodox shipping magnate and philanthropist
- Marston – shipping magnate
- William Jesson – one ship trader, like Peter
- Father Timothy – Catholic priest
- Captain Jones – captain of *The Madelaine*
- Albert Beddington – powerful shipping magnate
- Arthur Albert – Mrs. Albert's brother-in-law
- Sarah Albert – his wife
- Mr. Frome – desk clerk at the hotel in New York
- Mr. and Mrs. Padget – a couple Peter meets at The Eyrie
- Aldwin – ship's boy
- Wilbur – deaf-mute who becomes Peter's protégé

PROLOGUE

MARCH 5, 1884, LONG POINT, TEXAS

Jane Brown's sixteenth birthday had gone unnoticed by everyone but her. Why would the nuns in the orphanage think to remember such a thing? She had no friends, only tormentors among her peers there and at school, so nobody who loved her enough to take a moment to think of her on her special day. She could barely remember a time when anyone had made a fuss over her. She had been so very young when her mother had passed away, and she had no memories at all of her father, who had been lost to influenza before she was born.

Yet, she was happy today. Because she had finally turned sixteen, she could leave school, and she couldn't have been happier about that. She'd hated every minute of her young life. Always being teased and bullied by the other girls at the fancy school she'd won a scholarship to attend. They were all so much prettier than her, and they were all from wealthy families and knew that their lives would always be easier than hers. At best, they had taunted her, telling her she might one day be a maid, or perhaps – if she excelled in her duties as she did in her studies – she might rise to become a housekeeper in one of their homes. They had ensured that she remained painfully aware of that.

She had often wished that she had never gained her place at the elite church school in Houston, and that the the church elders had passed her by when looking for clever orphan children to bestow their scholarship upon. But they had taken note of the quiet, rather bookish girl and been impressed by her intelligence. She had tried to be grateful for the opportunity that they had given her – it was the kind of chance that girls like her could only dream of – but she was glad that she was free of it all now. After all, what could she do with her fine education? Even the wealthy girls in her classes could only really look forward to a good marriage and babies.

She was lucky, though. One of the nuns had recommended her for a position. Sister Margaretta had not been particularly kind to Jane over the years. In truth, Jane was sure that she had received more beatings from Sister Margaretta than from any other nun at the orphanage. Jane wondered if she had gotten her the job out of some kind of need for atonement, for Jane had never been a badly behaved child. Her beatings had been for reading quietly in the dormitory, rather than playing outside with the other children. In Jane's mind, that should have garnered her some kind of reward rather than punishment.

So, now she stood outside the grand house in Long Point that was to become both her home and place of work, praying that things might be better here. She was glad to be away from the city. It was too busy and chaotic for her, and too full of bad memories. It was quiet here. Perhaps even a little too quiet, but Jane would soon get used to that. This was a new start for her, and she would do her best to make her new mistress happy.

She glanced at the piece of paper that Sister Margaretta had given her with the address of her new employers on it. At the bottom of the page, in large capital letters, was an instruction to call at the back door. Sister Margaretta had clearly been concerned that Jane might forget her place and would knock on the imposing front door upon her arrival. Jane shook her head and made her way around to the back of the house.

She walked through the well-ordered kitchen garden, noting the little slate placards with neat chalk writing telling her what would be found in each bed. Herbs were closest to the door, root vegetables the furthest away. She wondered if she would be permitted to work out here sometimes. She enjoyed gardening and had learned a lot about it, thanks to the lay brother who had tended the gardens at the orphanage. When she'd been banished outside, working under his tutelage had offered her a quiet activity and a chance to both learn new things and stay away from the raucous games of the other orphans. No doubt, the Wilsons had a gardener to keep their impressive gardens in hand. She wondered if he would be kind enough to let her help him.

She rang the bell at the back door and waited. The door was opened by a large black woman wearing a perfectly starched, pristine white apron. "You must be Miss Jane," she said, her thick Southern drawl as rich and sweet as honey. "My name is Macey Green, but most folks just call me Cook."

"Yes, Ma'am. Jane Brown. I'm here to be a maid."

"I know what you're here to be, chile. Now, you come on inside and tell me all about yourself."

Jane was bustled into the kitchen and sat down at a large pine table towards the back of the huge room. Cook placed some iced tea and a large slice of cake in front of her. She was very thirsty, so she took a sip of the tea. It was sweet and cold and had more than a hint of lemon to it. "This is delicious. I've never had tea like this before."

"I doubt you've had much, livin' in that orphanage."

"Do you know it?"

"Not the one you've come to us from, no, chile. But I know places like it. They're all much the same, don't you think? But that is all in the past. You have a family now and we'll take care of you."

Jane hadn't expected to feel welcome here, at least not for a while. Yet here she was, sitting with this warm and wonderful woman, being told that she had a family at last. She smiled a little awkwardly at Cook, who grinned back.

"I know I'm a lot to take, on first meeting," Cook said gently. "But I think that you and me are going to be good friends. Now, eat up and I'll show you to your room. You'll start work tomorrow. Today, just find your way around the house and the gardens. Get settled in."

Jane smiled. "Thank you." She took a bite of the cake. It was rich with butter and sugar, with a hint of vanilla in the thick buttercream frosting. She'd never tasted anything so delicious in her life, though she'd often stared at the cakes in the bakery window on her way home from school, dreaming of being able to buy something so decadent. She was wiping the plate with her finger to be sure she'd got every crumb when a beautiful lady swept into the kitchens.

"Cook, where are you?" Marianne called out. "I need you."

Cook emerged from the larder. "Keep calm, I'm here."

"Gerry's decided that we must have a ball for Easter. I don't know what he thinks I'll be able to arrange with only a month to prepare. People will already have invitations to go elsewhere, and I'll never be able to get flowers ordered in that time. Why don't men ever notice the planning that goes into such things? And it will be my fault if everything goes wrong and nobody comes."

"Calm yourself, chile," Cook said. Her gentle voice calmed the rather irate lady almost immediately. "We've managed with less time, and we'll manage now. I can pull out the menus from the last ball we had here and make some changes. I'll have them to you by tonight so you can place the order. And I'm sure people will come for my cooking, if nothing else."

Mrs. Wilson seemed to be soothed by Cook's calm practicality, but then a thought struck her. "But the new maid isn't even here yet? How will I get her trained and do all of this? I need someone who knows what they're doing, not a girl just out of school."

"The new maid is here." Cook nodded to where Jane was sitting, just out of Mrs. Wilson's line of sight. Jane jumped to her feet and hurried forwards. She bobbed a curtsey. Cook chuckled. "And I have a feeling that she'll do just fine without you having to show her everything."

"Mrs. Wilson, I learn fast and I'm a hard worker," Jane assured her new employer.

"You're going to have to be," Mrs. Wilson said, looking her over. Jane obviously passed muster as Mrs. Wilson smiled at her. "Neat, clean, and polite. Excellent. Now, do you read and write?"

"I do, Ma'am."

"Then take your coat off and come with me. We have invitations to write."

Jane glanced at Cook, who nodded reassuringly. It seemed that she wasn't going to get her day to become acquainted with Long Point after all, but she was actually glad of that. She liked to be busy, and helping Mrs. Wilson with something so important would help her settle in far more quickly than meandering around the house and garden. She pulled off her coat and followed Mrs. Wilson up the stairs, across a hallway that was even grander than the one in her old school, and into a sunny drawing room.

"I'm sorry you've not had more time to settle in," Mrs. Wilson said as she handed Jane a list of names and addresses. "But you are all I have to help me. I gave my housekeeper leave last week to tend to her sick mother, and our last maid left to get married just yesterday. I cannot tell you how glad I am that you are here."

"I shall do my best, Ma'am," Jane assured her. "And I like to be busy."

As they settled down together to write out the hundreds of invitations, Jane felt happy. She could be useful here, and she had been made welcome. She was clearly not intended to be just a maid, someone to clean and tidy up after her employers. She was to be a member of a family. There was already a sense of connection between her and Cook, and even with Mrs. Wilson. Jane sensed that her life had changed

7

for the better, and that from now onwards, her life would be good.

$$\sim$$

MAY 15, 1887, NEW YORK CITY, NEW YORK

Peter Algood stood at the altar. His twin brother, Mark, stood at his side. "She'll be here shortly," he whispered. Peter pulled out his pocket watch and looked at the time. Ellen was already over an hour late. He'd moved past feeling nervous about forty minutes ago. As more time had passed, he'd grown angry, humiliated, and now he was simply broken-hearted. She wasn't coming.

Peter turned to the priest. "Father, I think it is time to accept that my fiancée is not coming. I am sorry to have wasted so much of your time."

"Just give her a moment or two more," Father Algernon said, looking at him anxiously. "I've known brides to be more than two hours late before."

"No, Ellen is never late for anything. She despises tardiness. If she were coming, she would be here by now."

"What if something terrible has happened?" Mark asked anxiously. "Don't be so quick to judge her."

Peter shook his head, walked swiftly out of the church, and ran around the back, determined that nobody would see him cry. Once out of sight, he bent over double, the pain of her betrayal slicing through him like a knife. Why had Ellen not come? How could she do this to him? If she'd had doubts, why had she not mentioned them before today?

What if Mark was right and something had happened to her? What if she was lying in the gutter, injured and fighting for her life? But surely, if that were the case, someone would have come to the church to tell him? She should have been accompanied by her father and mother, her sister, and the coachman. Could something terrible have happened to all of them? He doubted it.

As he struggled to catch his breath, he glanced up and saw Mark coming toward him. He stood upright and wiped his eyes roughly with the sleeve of his jacket.

"I sent everyone away," Mark said softly. "I'm sorry, Pete."

"I shouldn't have left that for you to do," Peter said as he let his brother embrace him. "You've never been one for speaking in front of large crowds."

"Or small ones," Mark admitted. "But I'd do anything for you. You know that, don't you?"

"I do. And I hope you know that I would do the same for you."

"I do."

Peter shook his head, perversely amused by their use of *I do*. "Let's go home," he said. "Perhaps we might find a bar along the way, so I might drown my sorrows a little."

"Is that wise?" Mark asked. "Neither of us is much of a

drinker. Last time you had even a sip of whiskey, you were nauseous."

"Perhaps not, though if a man were to get the taste for that horrible stuff, there are no doubts in my mind that such a moment as this would be it. Just home, then."

They waited until all their friends and family had departed. Peter tried not to listen to their conversations as they left. He didn't want to hear if they thought it amusing or, even worse, that they pitied him. Once the church yard was finally empty and even Father Algernon had left and locked up the church, they made their way home.

A letter had been pushed under the door. Mark picked it up and handed it to Peter. "It's from her."

"I wonder what she has to say for herself," Peter said. He ripped open the seal and skimmed through Ellen's letter.

"So?" Mark asked. Peter handed him the letter.

Dearest Peter,

I know that I am a coward for sending you this letter today when I should have told you all of this so long ago. I know that you probably hate me now, and I do not blame you for that. I deserve your hatred and your anger. I should have done everything so differently, but I didn't, and so I have no choice but to do this.

I could not go through with it. I could not marry you. You deserve better than me. You deserve a woman who adores you, who would be at that church, by your side, proud to be your wife.

I should have told you months ago that my feelings had changed, but I could not bring myself to hurt you – and so I have probably hurt you even more. Please forgive me?

I didn't mean for it to happen, but I fell in love with someone else. And Harry didn't mean for it to happen, either. I don't even know how it happened. I thought him weak and silly, a man with no depths, but as I got to know him better, I saw that he was so much more than anyone gave him credit for being.

But you can rest assured that you need not ever see either of us again, for we left for Colorado this morning. Harry has taken some land there, and we hope to make something of it. It will be hard work, and I will need to learn how to cook, and sew, and to grow vegetables and fruits, but I will be with him and that is all that matters.

I am so sorry. I truly never wanted this to happen, and I hope that you find someone to love you as much as you loved me, and that you will be happy.

Yours, most regretfully

Ellen

"She's gone with Harry Parker," Peter said, shaking his head in disbelief. "That dolt. That lumbering idiot. She ran away with my oldest friend, of all people. And she thinks he'll be able to farm or raise cattle? She's even more of a fool than I thought him to be."

"I never liked him," Mark said angrily. "How could he do such a thing to you?"

"I only wonder how long it has been going on."

"I never noticed a thing. They always seemed to despise one another."

"A fine disguise, I suppose. Hide the strength of their affection for each other with an equally strong emotion. What a fool I've been."

"No," Mark insisted. "She holds the blame here. Don't you dare blame yourself. I won't let you grow bitter over this – for I know well enough how you can hold a grudge."

"I'll not grow bitter," Peter assured him. "I shall wish every man and woman well with their love affairs and pray they have happy marriages. But I shall never marry, Mark. I will never be able to trust another woman the way that I trusted her. I will not let myself fall in love ever again."

CHAPTER 1

*A*fter the excitement of yet another wedding, Eagle Creek had begun to settle back into its own somewhat sleepy rhythm once more. Everywhere except the dressmaker's shop, that was. Because the excitement would begin all over again in June, when the theater troupe came back to town and Marla Dawes married Algernon DeVries, surrounded by family and friends. Jane Brown and Mrs. Albert had been charged with making the gowns and suits for the entire wedding party, and they had been told that they should be as creative and colorful as possible.

Jane smiled to herself as she hemmed Marianne's gown for the wedding. Her old mistress still liked to have new dresses almost every week, and Mrs. Albert and Jane were glad of it. Marianne always ordered the finest silks and satins, and though they were sometimes difficult to work with, Jane loved the way each outfit looked once it was finished. Marianne had a fine figure and wore clothes very well indeed. But this gown was to be even more special than anything even Marianne had owned before because she wanted to look her very best as her adopted daughter walked down the aisle.

"Jane, dear, could you fetch me some azure cotton?" Mrs. Albert called from the sewing room at the back of the shop.

Jane stood up and stretched her back. Bending over the new sewing machine that Mrs. Albert had recently purchased could make her a little stiff. She took a spool of cotton from the drawer under the counter and took it through to her employer.

"Thank you," Mrs. Albert said, taking it from her. "This suit is altogether the most flamboyant thing that I have ever made. I cannot imagine anyone from Eagle Creek wearing it."

"It is for Algernon, is it not?"

"It is."

"Then it is probably not flamboyant enough," Jane said with a chuckle. "A young man of the theater needs to stand out, don't you think?"

"He should have asked a tailor," Mrs. Albert grumbled.

"But there is no tailor in Eagle Creek," Jane pointed out. "And he trusts us to make him something perfect for his wedding."

"How are you getting on with Mrs. Denny's gown?"

"Well. It is going to look lovely."

"We need to make a start on Miss Marla's gown," Mrs. Albert said with a heavy sigh. "She'll be horrified if it's not finished when they arrive."

"I'll have finished Marianne's by tomorrow, and I can start to cut out the pattern for Miss Marla's gown then," Jane assured her. "We will have everything done on time. We always do."

Mrs. Albert smiled. "I don't think I tell you often enough, my dear, but I am so glad that you came to work with me. You have made my life so much easier – and calmer. I used to get into a terrible panic when big events required new gowns for half the town, and Eagle Creek is so much bigger now than it was then."

"We should think about taking on an apprentice or two," Jane said. "That would make things even easier for us both."

"Some of Mrs. Denny's students?"

"Perhaps. I can ask if she has a young lady or two that she thinks might be suitable."

"Just good girls who can hem in a straight line will suit us. They don't need to be young ladies," Mrs. Albert said, grinning.

Jane went back to the vast Singer sewing machine. Mrs.

Albert insisted on keeping it in the shop so that prospective clients could see that they used the most up-to-date methods to make their gowns. There was more room in the shop than in the sewing room out the back, which helped a little when making particularly voluminous gowns, but mostly, Jane felt a little awkward working in the window with all of Eagle Creek able to watch.

But it also meant that Jane could watch Eagle Creek, and that was a pleasure. She enjoyed seeing her friends as they went about their business. She smiled when she saw newly-weds kiss on the street, unashamed of their love for one another, and she often laughed out loud at the antics of Bailey and his dog, Quinto, as they performed for anyone who'd stop and watch. Watching the young people of Eagle Creek was a particular delight, as they rode their bicycles and played ball in summer, and threw snowballs and raced down the mountain on their sleds in winter. They all seemed to grow up so very quickly, though, and that made her wonder if Bailey would stop his little shows now that he was almost a man grown.

The clock struck five. Jane heard Mrs. Albert as she tidied things away out the back, puffing and groaning as her arthritic joints creaked back into life after so long sitting in one place. She started to put away her own things tidily.

"Can you lock up?" Mrs. Albert asked, coming into the shop as she pulled on her coat. "I need to go to the clinic to get some more of that tincture they gave me for my joints."

"Of course," Jane said happily. She wiped down the counters and sewing tables, swept up the bits of cotton and ribbon on the floor, pulled down the blinds, and then locked the back door. She did a quick tally of the money in the till, checking it against the day's orders and collections. Satisfied that everything added up, she made the necessary entries in the large accounts book, then let herself out and locked the front door behind her.

As she turned to go home, she spotted Marianne waiting outside the school with a large perambulator. She waved and hurried over to her friend. It seemed so strange, even now, that she had followed this young woman across the entire length of the country to come here, and that everything had worked out so well for them both. When they had left Texas, after the death of Marianne's first husband, Jane had not expected them to find a new home so easily. She had thought she might miss Texas, at least a little, but she hadn't, not even a tiny bit.

"How is my gown?" Marianne asked with a grin as Jane peered into the perambulator and gently caressed the cheek of the baby inside. "I have to look better than all of those theater people, or at least as fine."

"You will look wonderful without even trying," Jane assured her.

"I do hope so. We went to see them perform in Chicago a few months before Elliot made his appearance, and they

17

were all clad in fancy silks and velvets even for a meal after the show. I felt positively dowdy."

"And that will never do," James Denny said, coming out of the school gate to join them. He bent over the perambulator and kissed his son, then kissed his wife's cheek.

"You must both be so excited," Jane said. "To have Marla here for an entire month and see her married to her young man. I can hardly wait myself."

"We will be glad to have time with her," James admitted. "Flora-Rose will be happy to see Marla, and she'll have the time to get to know baby Elliot, too."

"Has she even met him yet?"

"Not yet," Marianne said. "I can't wait for them to meet."

"I am glad that I caught you," Jane said, remembering the conversation that she'd shared with Mrs. Albert. "We would like to take on two apprentices at the shop. Do you have any girls at the trade college that you think might suit?"

"I must confess that I don't know," Marianne said. "But I'll ask my father. Since Elliot arrived, I've barely had a moment to go up there, but he's there every day. I cannot tell you how glad I am that he came to live with us. His expertise in running a successful enterprise has been a godsend."

"He seems to really enjoy it, too," James pointed out. "I think he's found his niche, though a little late in life."

"He was an excellent lawyer, too," Marianne pointed out.

"I know," James said. "But did he ever really enjoy that

as much as he does running the college? He's even been taking his own apprentices, training them to be law clerks and for other administrative positions."

"He does seem very happy," Marianne agreed.

Elliot began to cry. James bent down and soothed him with a quiet lullaby. "I should let you get Elliot home," Jane said as James took the perambulator from his wife and began to push it gently back and forth. Elliot did not seem soothed by either his father's song or the gentle movement of the perambulator.

"Come with us," Marianne insisted. "Stay for some supper. I know Flora-Rose would be delighted to see her Aunt Jane."

"If you're sure I'd be no trouble?"

"Jane, you are welcome whenever you wish," James said with a warm smile. "You don't ever have to wait for an invitation."

"Then, thank you, I would like that very much, though I would prefer to go home and get changed out of my work clothes first."

"Then we will see you shortly," Marianne said, looking delighted.

Less than an hour later, Jane arrived at the Dennys' large house on Main Street. Flora-Rose was toddling happily, wearing out her doting grandfather as she led him from room to room. "She's leading me on a merry dance," Mr. Delaney said with a besotted smile.

"Would you like her to lead me on one for a while?" Jane asked him.

He nodded eagerly. "I must confess that it has been a long and hard day, and a brief moment of respite would be most welcome."

He started to go into James' study, then paused. "Marianne told me that you are looking for apprentices. I have just the girls for you. Would you like me to send them tomorrow?"

"I would. Perhaps around lunchtime?" Jane suggested.

"Perfect."

Flora-Rose took her hand and led her into the parlor. Marianne was sitting on the sofa, feeding the baby. James was perched on the arm of the sofa beside her, reading to her aloud.

Marianne smiled. "This is the only way I get to read now," she said. "Being a mother to these two is exhausting, but wonderful."

"You do seem very happy now."

"Things are very different here, aren't they, to the way they were in Texas?"

"For us both," Jane agreed. But as she watched her friend and her family that evening, she couldn't help feeling that her life was missing some of the joy that her old employer now enjoyed.

Once Marianne had put her children to bed and James

and Mr. Delaney had retired to his study to smoke cigars and drink port, Jane got up to go home.

"Don't go," Marianne said, handing her a cup of hot chocolate. "I thought we might talk for a while."

"I should go, really," Jane said. "I have to be up early for work, and we have so much to do for Marla's wedding." But she took the cup of chocolate from Marianne and took a sip. The taste brought back memories of sitting around the big kitchen table in the house at Long Point, the three women talking together first thing each day, planning all that needed to be done.

"I know it is supposed to be a breakfast drink, but I find it soothes my nerves after a day with the children," Marianne explained. "I don't make it as well as Cook did, but I follow her recipe as closely as I can."

"You are very close," Jane assured her. "Perhaps a little more cinnamon might make it perfect."

"I admire your ability to do that. To taste something and know what is or isn't in it."

"I don't know where it came from, but she certainly encouraged me to use it. I miss her."

"I do, too. I write and beg her to come to us most weeks," Marianne said.

They talked about Elliot and Flora-Rose and Jane's work at the shop for a while, and Jane assured Marianne that she truly was happy in Eagle Creek. Marianne gave her a searching look. "Are you? I know you are content, but there are times when I think you wish you were somewhere else. You don't want to go back to Texas, do you?"

"Never," Jane insisted. "I never want to leave here. I am so grateful to you for bringing me here."

"But there is something missing, isn't there?"

Jane wondered whether she should confide in her friend. It wasn't as if there was anything Marianne could do to change things. But she needed to tell someone. "I just wish that I had what you have with James," she admitted. "A good, loving husband and a family of my own."

"I can understand why you would want that," Marianne said. "You would make such a wonderful mother."

"But I am plain and dull, and no man is ever likely to even notice me, much less want to marry me," Jane said sadly.

"Whoever told you that you are plain?" Marianne asked angrily. "You are quite lovely, Jane. Perhaps you might pin your hair a little differently, you're not a maid anymore after all. If you did, and if you wore a gown more like those you sew for other people, I am certain that many men would notice you."

"Why must I try to be something I am not, though?" Jane said softly. "Can I not find happiness as myself?"

"Of course you can," Marianne said. "But you have to actually seek it out, you can't hide away in the dressmaker's and expect it to find you there."

"I wouldn't know where to start looking."

"Then why not place an advertisement in the newspaper? You know as well as I do how many people in Eagle Creek have found love that way."

"I don't think I could," Jane said shyly. "What if nobody replied?"

"You'll only know if you try. I dare you to do it. You'll not know unless you do."

CHAPTER 2

"You have to actually reply to those," Peter teased as he found his twin poring over the matrimonial advertisements again. Mark had been reading them more and more over the past few months. As a shy man, his brother wasn't good with women, or anyone he didn't know well, but Peter was sure that he would make a loyal and devoted husband to a woman who could see beyond that and notice the kind man beneath.

"I don't know if I should," Mark said. "I can't imagine I'll be any better at talking to women by letter than I am in person. It's unfair that you got all the confidence and have no intention of using it."

"Oh, I use it," Peter said with a grin. "Just because I don't intend to fall in love, doesn't mean that I don't enjoy the company of pretty young ladies."

"And don't I know that," Mark said a little bitterly. "You are getting quite a reputation."

"I know, and I am glad of it. As long as people know I have no intention to wed, my behavior hurts nobody."

"You're starting to become a challenge, though," Mark noted. "I know of at least three women of your acquaintance who are sure that they are the ones who will win your heart."

"Can't win what doesn't exist," Peter said firmly.

"Your heart is still there. You'll find that out someday."

"Never. I am happy as I am. I do not feel the lack of anything – unlike you." He bent down over the newspaper and read a few of the advertisements. "What about this one?"

Mark pulled the newspaper toward him and bent down over it.

"You truly need to get some spectacles, brother," Peter told him. "You're as blind as a mole."

"I keep meaning to," Mark said. "I will go this afternoon. I promise." He began to read out the advertisement slowly.

Young lady of Montana seeks a man who wants a quiet life in a small town. Must want a family and have a warm heart. Interests include reading, theater, and spending time with loved ones.

"She sounds dull enough to be perfect for you, Mark."

"She does not sound dull to me. Just because she does not seek adventure and excitement the way you do does not mean that she is dull. You're right, she could be just what I have been looking for. I shall write to her as soon as I have got some spectacles."

"If you don't get them first, she'll only receive a piece of paper that looks like an ant with inky feet has been crawling over it," Peter teased.

"Go away, Peter," Mark said with a sigh. "I'm not in the mood for you and your nonsense. I know that you don't wish to find love again, and I understand why. But I am not you. I've never given my heart away, not even once. I want to find a wife and have a family – even if you think such pursuits are beneath you."

"I'm sorry, Mark. You are right. It is not fair of me to impose my feelings and wants onto you. You have every right to find out that women cannot be trusted and will only ever let you down on your own. Heaven forbid that you should learn from my mistakes."

Mark shook his head. No matter what his brother said, Peter would not change his mind. He had taken a vow and he had no intention of breaking it. He could understand that his bullheadedness was infuriating for Mark, just as Mark's desire to seek out what Peter avoided at all costs infuriated Peter. Since Ellen, Peter had not met a single young lady who had changed his view of the fickle nature of women. In truth, he doubted if there was a single woman in all the world who was deserving of his trust.

"Just try to be supportive," Mark said, picking up the newspaper and getting to his feet. "Even if you cannot be happy for me, try not to think less of me for wanting what most people want in life."

When he left the room, Peter sat down in the chair he had just vacated. Mark was miserable, he realized. He had nothing in his life, other than rows and rows of figures to add up each day. His work as a bookkeeper was not just robbing him of his eyesight, but his sense of humor as well. Mark was becoming boring. If he did not find a wife soon, he probably never would as even the dullest girl would not be able to bear living with a walking ledger.

He picked up a book and tried to read it but found little pleasure in it. Unlike Mark, he'd never been able to lose himself in literature, though he was never entirely sure if his brother actually enjoyed reading – he suspected Mark did it simply to have something to talk about with others. But to Peter, no matter how beautiful the prose, it was all just words on a page. He wished that he did not feel that way, but to him, books were just a way for people who had no life to feel as though they had one. He would much rather live the things written on the page than simply read about them. He felt much the same way about the theater and the opera, though he enjoyed the music of the latter at least.

Feeling frustrated, he got up and let himself out of the

house. He walked around the back to the stables. King, his beloved black stallion, nickered at the sight of him. Peter approached his stall and slapped his strong neck affectionately. "Want to go for a ride?" he asked him. King responded with an impatient nudge against Peter's shoulder. "Let me get your saddle, then."

A few moments later, the two of them were cantering out of the gates of the stable yard. Peter gently guided King along the street, dodging other riders and carriages without slowing down until they reached the park. At the sight of the green grass, King extended his stride, and they galloped fast, racing the wind. Peter loved to ride and often wished that he didn't live in the city. He longed for wide-open spaces with glorious views all around, where he and King could race to their hearts' content.

But he could not imagine a life outside of the city. New York was where everything happened. Living in a place with the kind of space that he dreamed of would be too quiet, too parochial. He and Mark were not part of New York Society, and neither wished to be. They both found the ridiculous rules laid out for the rich to be stifling and unsatisfying. But Peter longed for the kind of money that they had. If he was that wealthy, he wouldn't waste his time attending the theater or the opera, going to endless balls and soirees, he would travel the world and experience everything that he could.

But he was not rich, and so he stayed in New York,

living as exciting a life as he could manage. He doubted that a small town in the country would ever offer him the diversions that New York could – even if it would offer him the chance to ride and race. Yet he could imagine his brother living such a life and being utterly content. It never ceased to amaze Peter how different the two of them were, despite them being identical to look upon. Even their mother had struggled to tell the two of them apart when they were younger, though it had become easier for her once their personalities developed.

And if he'd needed any more convincing that such a life was not for him, he'd heard that Ellen was living in a small town in Colorado, married to a failed dairy farmer, with four children and a whole heap of misery – and he had to confess that it brought him a lot of happiness to know that. It seemed that Harry had proved to be just as incompetent as a farmer as he had been at everything else, and their romantic elopement had been the last joyful moment in her life. Once, he had hoped to forgive her, to be glad that she was happy, but forgiveness had never arrived. His anger at her had only grown, and that she had received her comeuppance seemed a just punishment to him.

But if it was what Mark sought, even if it was a desire that seemed to have come peculiarly out of the blue, Peter vowed to do all he could to help his brother. Mark had stood by him through everything, though Peter had done all he could to push almost everyone in his life away. He did not trust anyone except Mark anymore. He would miss his brother if he left New York, but he wanted him to be happy and find the love he seemed intent upon finding.

King began to slow. Peter leaned down and patted his neck. "Good boy," he said softly. "I needed that. I think you did, too." He turned the stallion's head, and they began to walk back to the entrance of the park slowly. Peter nodded politely to people he knew out walking in the park and made his way home. A messenger was waiting for him in the stable yard. He handed him a note. Peter read it and cursed under his breath.

He put King back in his stall, leaving him in the capable hands of the stable lad, and hurried inside. He stripped off his riding clothes and had a quick wash before pulling on a smart suit and shiny boots. He tied his silk cravat as he ran down the stairs and out onto the street, where he hailed a hansom cab. He promised the driver extra if he could get him to the port quickly.

Impatiently, he tapped his fingers on his knee as the driver drove them swiftly through the traffic. True to his word, Peter paid him double his fee and hurried into the offices of Kingshott and Walker, shipping agents. "She's not come in?" he asked the clerk at the front desk. The poor lad looked completely bewildered at his question.

"*The Madelaine*? I received word that she hasn't come in as expected."

"Oh," the lad said. "One moment. Mr. Kingshott sent that."

He disappeared into the back office, and Mr. Kingshott emerged a few moments later. A large man, with broad shoulders and a thick, graying beard, he was an old sailor who had done very well for himself. His knowledge of shipping was unsurpassed, and Peter was grateful that Mr. Kingshott acted as his agent in the port, where captains and merchants wished to work with men who understood their trade as well as they did. Peter had not sailed anywhere, though he longed to do so, but he knew that shipping was where he would make the fortune he needed to travel.

"*The Madelaine* is late. She's missed her slot."

"She can't dock, even if she comes in?"

"Not at the moment. The port is the busiest I've ever known it," Mr. Kingshott said with a shrug.

"And I presume we've still had to pay?"

"Of course, nobody else could use her slip."

"Has there been any word of her?"

"None, which is unusual."

"Nobody has seen her? Not throughout the entire passage to Bristol?"

"Not anyone who has come back to New York, Mr. Algood."

A pregnant pause followed his words. Neither of them seemed to want to utter the words out loud, but the fear in

Peter's heart grew with each passing moment. "Do you think she's lost?"

"I think it is possible," Mr. Kingshott said, his words measured, his voice calm. "But she is only a week late. I've known ships come in weeks, even months after they were due. It doesn't take much of a storm to push a ship off course, and without good weather it can be hard to get back on course."

"Do you think she will come in?" Peter asked anxiously. "Every penny I have is tied up in her, and barely half her cargo was insured as I couldn't get enough people to take shares in her."

"All we can do is wait and hope," Mr. Kingshott said simply.

"That is easy for you to say. You'll demand your share whether she comes in or not," Peter said. He immediately regretted it. Mr. Kingshott was a decent man, a good man. He deserved every penny that Peter paid him. "I'm sorry, I'm just worried."

"I know. You're not the first man to bite at me in a situation like this. You'll not be the last, lad. Do you want me to lease a new slip in case she comes in?"

"Yes, if you can. And you send me word if you hear anything about her at all?"

"Of course."

CHAPTER 3

JUNE 4, 1892, EAGLE CREEK, MONTANA

The day of Marla's wedding had arrived. Jane rose early and made her way to Marianne's house to help the two of them dress, and to be on hand if any last-minute alterations were required to either of their gowns. She wasn't surprised to find everyone up in the Denny house, but she was impressed by how calm they all seemed. Marla bounded to the door to let her in, flinging her arms around her in an exuberant hug.

"Thank you so much for my beautiful gown," she gushed. "When Mama described it to me, I thought I knew how lovely it would be, but seeing it myself brought tears to my eyes."

Jane felt a little overwhelmed by her fulsome compliments. Jane was naturally rather reticent about how she felt about anything, but she supposed that, as she was an actress, it was easier for Marla to express herself fully. "Thank you," she said a little awkwardly. "I am so happy that you like it, for there would have been no time to change much about it now."

"I tried it on as soon as we arrived last night," Marla said happily. "I think it may need a little nip and tuck. I do hope there is time for that, at least?"

"Let us go upstairs and see," Jane said with a smile.

Marianne was in Marla's chamber, clad in her nightgown. She looked so happy. "It is so wonderful to have everyone here," she said, tucking her arm through Marla's.

"I am so glad that you made me a part of your family," Marla said happily. "I would still be struggling to survive if it weren't for you and dear Papa."

"We couldn't be more glad that you burst into our lives. You've brought us so much love and laughter – you and Flora-Rose," Marianne said. She pressed a kiss to Marla's cheek.

A baby cried in one of the rooms nearby. "If you will excuse me a moment," Marianne said. "Elliot is hungry."

Jane picked up the gown she had so lovingly sewn for this special day and helped Marla into it. The girl was right, the bodice needed to be taken in just a little. "It is so hard to make a gown for someone who isn't here," she said, pinning it and then helping Marla back out of the dress carefully, so as not to prick her. "Usually, we'd do three or four fittings for a dress like this."

"You've done a wonderful job, but I fear I lost a little weight since I sent you my measurements. This last tour has been so draining."

"We were expecting you to arrive last week. What happened to delay you? Marianne didn't say."

"We were asked to do extra nights in Deadwood. All our shows were sold out and there was so much demand. Algernon didn't want to refuse as the theater there alone often makes us enough money to pay for the next production. It was a difficult decision for us, knowing that it would mean we had so little time here before the wedding, but there are so many traveling companies now that you simply can't upset any theater en route."

"I don't know how you do it, spending your life always on the move," Jane said. "I vowed never to go anywhere again after your mother and I traveled here."

"Being with Algernon helps," Marla said. "And I don't think I was made to stay in one place. I like knowing I have a home here, but that just makes it easier for me to go wherever the work takes us."

"Your mother is so proud of you."

"I know, and that helps, too. She and Papa have offered

me so much more than I could have ever imagined. My dreams were big, but my hopes of making them come true were so small before they found me and took me in."

"And look at you now," Jane said. "Now, I will need to get this done or you'll not make it to the church on time."

"I'll go and play with Flora-Rose," Marla said.

Jane began to make the adjustments to the gown. Luck had definitely smiled upon Marla, thanks in no small part to Marianne and James. But their family would not be whole if it weren't for Marla. If the young and foolish girl that she had been had not left baby Flora-Rose for James to find, things would have been so different for all of them. Jane couldn't help thinking that they had perhaps pushed their luck to its very limits. She wished she could enjoy even a smidgen of their good fortune.

She could not imagine finding so much love and happiness, though she had accepted Marianne's dare to place an advertisement in the newspaper. She did not hold out much hope of receiving even a single reply. She knew that there was little about her that was exciting or interesting. She was just a quiet person with simple tastes. She did not crave money or prestige, nor did she believe that she could expect a romantic or handsome husband. She simply wanted a warm home and a family to share it with, someone she could imagine growing old with in peaceful companionship.

Marianne came back into the room, bouncing Elliot on

her hip. "He is such a happy baby unless he is hungry," she said.

"He's a bonny lad," Jane noted, surprising herself a little at her use of the word her Scottish grandmother had used to describe pretty infants.

"Yes, that is it exactly," Marianne said. "He's a bonny boy."

"I placed an advertisement," Jane said quietly. "I wasn't sure if I would go through with it, but I did."

"Have you had any replies?" Marianne asked excitedly.

"Not yet, and I'm not sure if I will. When I saw the advertisement in the newspaper, it looked terribly dull. I can't imagine why anyone would respond."

"Jane, you are not dull. You are simply not as flamboyant as Marla."

"It would be hard for anyone to be that flamboyant," Jane joked. "She is rather like an exotic bird of paradise, isn't she?"

"She is, though it would have been hard to imagine that when we first found her. She was such a quiet and scared little thing."

"The power of your love."

"Perhaps," Marianne agreed. "But my point is that, once she had some love in her life, someone to support her no matter what, she blossomed."

"I know I have that from you, but I've not changed

much. I fear I may always be the girl who was teased and bullied for not being good enough."

"Nonsense. You are and always have been good enough, Jane. You are the kindest and most hard-working person I know. You are generous and sweet, and any man would be blessed to make you his wife. Someone will see you for who you are – the person I saw on that very first day that you came to work for me as a young girl. Someone clever and smart, with so much potential. You just need a little more courage."

"Perhaps I can borrow some of Marla's," Jane quipped. "She has more than enough to share."

"She does, and this will be the most extravagant wedding I think Eagle Creek will ever see."

Jane finished the alterations and watched over Elliot in his crib while Marianne took a bath. He was a good baby and gurgled contentedly as he played with his own toes and beamed up at Jane. She rocked the crib with her foot and occasionally bent to stroke his cheek or to let him hold tightly to her finger. She imagined what it would be like to have a child of her own, a son who would grow up with Elliot, or a daughter who he might one day fall in love with. It was a pretty dream.

When the gown was ready, Marla tried it on again and it fitted perfectly. "You are so clever," she said to Jane, happy tears in her eyes. "I cannot imagine being able to do something so intricate. All this beading and embroidery must have taken you so much time."

"And a few pricked fingers," Jane said with a shy smile. She had put everything into making this dress special for Marla and was so happy that she loved it.

"We should take you on tour with us," Marla joked as she took off the gown and hung it carefully on the armoire while she finished getting ready. "We'd have the finest wardrobe collection of any theater in the land."

"I'd be happy to make costumes for you here, but I've no desire to travel," Jane said. "Eagle Creek is my home. I'm happy here."

"I wish that you didn't feel that way," Marla said. "But I do understand. And I am glad that you are here, for Mama and Flora-Rose. And baby Elliot, of course."

"I would do anything for your mother," Jane said. "She gave me my first job and my first real home and family. I am honored that she still thinks of me as a friend."

"You are her rock, Jane. Don't ever forget that."

Marianne emerged from her dressing room, clad in cotton undergarments. "Can you pin my hair for me, Jane?" she asked.

"I've not done that for you in years," Jane said with a smile. "I hope I still know how."

"It's not something you forget," Marianne assured her. "I sent James to pick some flowers from the meadow. I hope he's brought them."

"I'll go and check," Jane said.

She went downstairs and found a basket of flowers on the kitchen table. After taking it back upstairs, she carefully pinned Marianne's hair and started to fix some of the flowers into the elegant knot she'd created at the back of Marianne's head. Marla watched, perched on the edge of the bed. "Will you do mine, too?" she asked.

"If you want me to," Jane said. She felt at ease among these people and thought of them as her family. She had been honored when Marla had insisted that she make her gown and when Marianne had insisted that she be a part of their preparations this morning. It made her hopeful that they felt the same way about her.

Marla took the seat Marianne had just vacated at the vanity table. While Marianne dressed, Jane brushed out Marla's long hair carefully, removing every knot, then began to twist and plait, curl, and pin until something spectacular emerged. As she had with Marianne's, she affixed flowers to Marla's hair, but she also added some tiny seed pearls that caught the light when Marla moved her head.

Marla picked up the hand mirror and admired Jane's work. "You truly have the deftest fingers of anyone I know," she said, marveling at the intricate hairstyle that Jane had created for her. "I didn't realize that I had such a long neck, or that my cheekbones were so pronounced."

"She is a genius," Marianne said. "Why else do you think I never let her go?"

They all laughed, which brought James to the door. "What am I missing?" he asked.

"Nothing," Marianne assured him as Jane helped her into her gown. "Is the carriage here?"

"It is, and you'll be terribly late if you don't hurry," James said, trying to look stern.

Marianne and Jane helped Marla into her gown for the final time. James sighed. "You both look perfect," he said. "What a lucky man I am."

"Jane, I have a surprise for you," Marianne announced. "I know you probably forgot to make a gown for yourself, so I asked Mrs. Albert to make you one." She went into her dressing room and emerged with a gown in a floral silk that echoed the color of her own violet gown. "You are part of our family, and you should be a part of the wedding party."

Jane felt tears welling up inside her. She had never been so happy. She let Marianne take her into the dressing room, where she put on the gown and Marianne did her hair, then they all went downstairs and took the carriage to the church. Marianne hugged her husband and Marla before she and Jane went inside. The church was a riot of color with the actors and actresses' flamboyant outfits, and the bright flower arrangements.

They took their seats in the front pew. Marianne grinned at Algernon, who looked a little nervous standing at the altar clad in a vivid purple suit. But his face softened, and a smile lifted his lips as he saw Marla arrive at the back of the church. Jane longed for someone to look at her that way, his face filled with delight at the sight of her. She couldn't help feeling a little envious that Marla had found someone who loved her that much, and she prayed fervently that God might be kind enough to send her someone who could love her perhaps half as much.

CHAPTER 4

JUNE 6, 1892, EAGLE CREEK, MONTANA

*T*he sun had risen hours before Jane woke. She stretched languorously in her bed. It was such a treat to have the morning off on a Monday. With Marla and Algernon's wedding over, things would be quiet at the shop for a while – and both she and Mrs. Albert were grateful for it. It felt like they'd been working themselves to the bone for months. She was tired, but it had all been so wonderful. Marla had looked so lovely, and Jane had been proud to be considered a part of the family.

But it had reminded her, yet again, how much she longed to have what Marianne and James had found, and what Marla and Algernon shared. She wanted to love and be loved, to give herself to someone who adored her, and to have a child, or perhaps two. But there had been no replies to her advertisement, even though it had been in the newspapers for more than a month now. But she had to remember that the advertisements were placed in newspapers all over the country, so it could take some time for a reply to reach the newspaper's office, and then they would have to send it on to her. She should not give up so easily.

Reluctantly, she got out of bed and opened the drapes. Eagle Creek was busy going about its business. She smiled. She had not expected to find a home. She'd been raised in an orphanage, where kindness had been hard to find, and she had attended a school where she had been an outcast because she was not wealthy like the other girls. She had always known that she would need to work hard and had resigned herself to a lifetime in Service. But her first job, working for Marianne, had been nothing like she had expected it to be.

She had presumed that she would be just another face, invisible to her employers, an unimportant cog in a big household. But she had found a family, of sorts, in Marianne and Cook. She had learned her trade and been good at it, but Marianne had never treated her like a servant. She'd been more of a friend and mentor to Jane than an employer. And Cook had been the mother she'd never had. She was the only person Jane missed from her life in Texas.

It was a beautifully sunny day, so she decided to dress and go for a walk by the creek. She would stop at the bakery and buy a pie and something sweet and delicious so she could enjoy a picnic by the water. She didn't often treat herself to the bakery's delicious cakes and pastries, but she felt like she deserved something special after the weeks of hard work on Marla and Marianne's gowns.

She took a small knapsack with her and placed her purchases in it. She walked slowly along Main Street, stopping to talk to friends and neighbors. It was a pleasure to have the time to do so. A line of people was spilling out of the postal office. She walked past, glad she didn't need to wait in line today. She was about to turn onto the path that ran down the side of the church when Alfie Pinchin caught up with her.

"Ma'am, Mr. Merryweather asked me to deliver these to you." He handed her a small pile of letters, then hurried back to the postal office.

She flicked through them, only recognizing the handwriting on one of them. She smiled at the sight of Cook's sprawling hand. She tucked the letters into her knapsack and walked along the path through the woods. She kept her eyes peeled as she walked, searching in the cool darkness for signs of deer and other animals. Further into the woods, she saw a small family of deer. Two does and a magnificent male, with two young ones. She held her breath and crouched down, watching as they made their stately way through the trees. She waited until they were out of sight, then continued along the path, out along the side of the creek.

The crystal-clear waters of the creek glistened in the sunlight and made a soothing sound as they bubbled over the stony creek bed. Jane peered over the bank, looking for the flick of a fish's tail or the swoop of a dragonfly. It was quiet here today. It wasn't warm enough yet for the children to want to swim in the pool, and they were in school anyway. She settled down on the shingled beach by the pool and pulled out her letters.

Cook was unhappy in her new household. She felt that she wasn't respected, and she missed Marianne and Jane so much that she was considering leaving everything behind to come to Eagle Creek. Jane knew that Marianne had made Cook an offer of both a job and a home if she ever wanted it, and that everyone would be delighted to see the elderly lady if she truly did decide to come. But she was wise enough not to get her hopes up. Cook liked to complain, but she rarely did much to change her situation.

She looked over the envelopes of the other letters and realized that they had all come from the newspaper office. People had actually replied to her advertisement. She opened the first letter carefully.

Dear Young Lady of Montana

I read your advertisement and wanted to reply. I am a quiet, home-loving man, and I am searching for a good woman who will be my wife and raise my children.

I don't read much. As a farmhand, I don't have much time to myself – and there wasn't much money to send me to school when I was a boy. I can read and write a little, but not much.

I'd very much like it if you'd write back to me.

Yours, most sincerely

Albert Pickles

Jane had to admit that he hadn't said much to inspire her to write back. He seemed a simple man, and though she didn't want a complicated one, he was a little less educated than she had perhaps hoped for. She loved to read and truly wanted to be able to talk about the books she read with her husband and perhaps share the experience by reading to each other in the long winter evenings. She knew that was probably romantic nonsense, something that she was unlikely to find, but she had to remain hopeful this early in the process.

The second letter was similar, though the writer was a hansom cab driver in Philadelphia. He had no intention of moving from his home, and that automatically made him unsuitable. Jane never wanted to live in a busy city again, and though she knew that she might need to consider leaving Eagle Creek if she found someone she came to care about who had work he couldn't leave, she wanted a man who would at least consider the fact that she had a job that mattered to her and a home and friends that she did not wish to leave behind.

She opened the third letter, feeling a little deflated. She

was beginning to doubt whether she would find anyone to love her this way. But as she started to read this one, she found herself smiling a little.

Dear Young Lady of Montana

I admire your courage in placing an advertisement. I have been trying to convince myself to do so for some months and keep talking myself out of it. I kept thinking that all I could say about myself would sound dull.

I was born and raised in New York, but I would give up city life in a heartbeat for I long for small-town life, with a wife who loves me and two or three children to raise. I enjoy reading, and my favorite stories are the tales of Tom Sawyer and Huckleberry Finn. They remind me of my boyhood and the games my brother and I played – and the trouble we got ourselves into. And I actually attended the theater just last night. The company performed one of Shakespeare's plays, and it was magnificent.

I am not an exciting man. I have always been good at sums, so my father found me a position working for one of New York's finest bookkeepers. I love my work, though I know many might find it dull. To me, finding the patterns in numbers is fascinating.

I also like to walk in the countryside. My grandparents lived about fifty miles outside of the city, and I loved visits to them as a boy. We would help make hay and care for their sheep and chickens. My brother and I would cycle the lanes and ride horses across the fields, and I'd rather like to live at least a little of that life every day.

Please, do tell me more about the place where you live and what you love about your work?

I hope you will write back soon

Yours, most hopefully

Mark Algood

He sounded perfect. Jane was surprised. He wasn't flashy or conceited, and he seemed straightforward and spoke plainly. She liked that. She put his letter to one side. She would definitely write back to Mr. Algood. There were four other letters. She quickly skimmed through them. Two were definitely not men she wanted to write to, but the other two were, like Mr. Algood, possibilities. She did not get much information from their letters, but there was enough to intrigue her. She did not think much would come of responding to any of them, but she knew that she had to be patient. As they built up a rapport, it would hopefully get easier to confide in one another, and then she might know if there was any hope for a future with any of them.

She took her lunch from her knapsack and began to eat the meat pie she had purchased for herself. The thick gravy spilled out onto her blouse. She wiped at it with a handkerchief, but it only made the stain worse. She dipped the handkerchief in the water of the creek and tried again. This time, the stain shifted a little, but she would have to wash the blouse as soon as she got home. She finished the pie, feeling a little annoyed at herself, and considered heading home.

She had planned to enjoy her day, not spend it doing laundry. The sun shone brightly high in the sky, the air was warm; she had cake to eat and a book to read. She would not let a tiny smudge of gravy upset her. She pulled out her book and began to read. She was soon lost in a world of pirates and intrigue, following the adventures of Jim Hawkins and the dastardly Long John Silver. She was so caught up in the tale that she didn't hear Father Timothy walking along the path toward her. She only noticed him when his body blocked the sun, leaving her in shadow. She looked up.

"Good day," he said, smiling down at her.

"And to you, Father," she said.

"I'm sorry, I didn't mean to startle you."

"I was a little caught up in my book," she said, showing him the cover.

"Ah, Mr. Stevenson. He writes a fine adventure. I can understand you not noticing me when your head is full of pirates."

"It is a wonderfully vivid story. Have you read it?"

"I have, and I enjoyed it very much," the priest said. "I know that there are many who think that a priest should keep his reading to the Bible, but I rather enjoy escaping into wonderful worlds and visiting new places the way you can when you read such stories."

"I do, too. I've done enough actual traveling to last me a

lifetime," Jane said with a smile, "but I still want to see more places, just without the discomfort of train carriages."

"The beds are particularly uncomfortable if you find yourself on a sleeper," he agreed. "Well, I shall leave you to your book."

"Thank you, Father Timothy," Jane said. She watched him walk along the creek, his long robes trailing on the path behind him. He was such a kind man.

She took out her cake and ate it slowly, savoring every rich bite, before she picked up her book once more. She wondered if any of the gentlemen she'd decided to write to had read this wonderful book. She hoped so. It would be nice to share their opinions on the characters and the situations they found themselves caught up in.

CHAPTER 5

*P*eter stood on the deck of *The Madelaine*, overseeing the loading of the ship ready for her departure on the tide. He'd been so relieved when she'd finally come in, almost two months later than she should have done, having been caught in a massive storm not long after setting out from Bristol that blew them up into the channel between Britain and Ireland. Captain Jones had explained that, with a broken mast and damaged sails, he had taken the decision to make port in Dublin so repairs could be made and the ship restocked. It had taken longer than he'd hoped. Dublin's port mainly serviced ships that sailed between Ireland and Britain, so there had been nobody New York-bound to send a message with.

The delay and the repairs to the ship had cost Peter a lot of money, but he had recouped most of it when she'd finally come in with a full cargo. Mr. Kingshott had recommended a shorter and safer trip to the Caribbean, the hold filled with salt cod and lumber and to return with sugar and molasses. It would make up the money lost and hopefully make a small profit.

Everyone had warned Peter about the months of anxious waiting and the ease in which a man could lose every penny, but it was that precarity that attracted Peter. If he did well, he would be rich. If he failed, he would lose everything. He knew that if the worst happened that he would be able to pick himself up. He was clever and adaptable, and not afraid of hard work. He'd made it through his first voyage, and though it had not been a success, it had not been a total failure. He was certain that he would make his fortune in due time.

Captain Jones emerged from the lower decks. "Sir, thank you for keeping your trust in me. I'll bring her home safely," he assured Peter.

"Just keep making sure that you do, and quickly this time," Peter cautioned him. "You're a fine sailor, and you took the right decisions. I'd much rather you come home late but with *The Madelaine* in one piece, with all of you aboard, than get word that she's gone down with every one of you and every penny of mine with her."

"Yes, Sir," Captain Jones said.

Peter climbed down into the hold and looked over the cargo one last time, then he went ashore. He entered one of the many coffee shops and took a table by the window. The maid brought him a cup of strong, hot coffee, and he ordered a meat pie. He would wait here until the tide took his ship out to sea. Most of the traders had a favorite place along the quayside, where they met to talk about their ships, insured one another, and played cards or chess to while away the time as they waited for ships to leave or come in.

"Algood, relief for you that she finally came in," Albert Beddington said, taking a seat opposite Peter. He was one of the most successful traders in New York, with a fleet of twenty ships that regularly traversed the seas. Peter did not approve of selling men, and he was determined not to be lured by the promise of easy money that the slave trade offered.

"*The Madelaine* is a good ship, and she has a fine captain, so I never doubted she would," Peter said firmly. He did not want anyone to think that he'd had even the slightest concern about his ship or the money invested in it.

"Jones is a good man," Beddington agreed. "But you wouldn't have lost a cent if you'd been able to insure the entire voyage."

"I know that, but I'm just starting out and you and your

friends don't like offering that to men like me. You wait until we fall on our faces and buy our ships at prices that you should be ashamed of offering a man."

"You don't like the way we do business? Then why join the trade?"

"Because I believe that it is possible to be a trader and still be an honest man," Peter said boldly. He knew that he was only making his life harder by insulting this man, but Beddington and his ilk made his blood boil. They were vultures, waiting to pick over the bones of those weaker than them.

"With an attitude like that, you'll never be welcome here," Beddington warned him.

"I'm not here to make friends, but to make money," Peter said starkly. "I'll make my way alone, or I'll fail – but at least I'll know that I didn't cheat others to do it."

Beddington stared at him, his face puce with rage. It was clear that nobody had dared to speak to him in that way in a long time. He got up from his chair, pushing it away so forcefully that it fell over, and stormed out of the door.

An elderly gentleman, with snow-white hair and clad in a perfectly tailored red wool suit, who'd watched their interaction got up, picked up the chair, and sat down on it. "You've done it now," he said with a grin. "Your name will be smeared and you'll struggle to get permission to tie up out to sea, much less get a slip now."

"He doesn't have that kind of power. He can't stop a man from trading," Peter said bravely.

"Oh, but he does," the man said. "I should probably introduce myself. Cable Poole," he offered his hand. Peter took it cautiously. "And you're Peter Algood. Everyone knows your name."

"Mr. Poole, would you please get to the point? You obviously have a reason for talking to me, given that you've just informed me that Beddington will make me a pariah."

"Oh, I do. I'll do anything to annoy that bloviating sack of lard."

"Why?"

"Because he tried to ruin my father, for being an honest trader like yourself. He almost succeeded until Papa decided that the best way to beat Beddington was to make sure that his threats could not affect his own activities. He bought a quarter of the port and ran it away from the likes of Beddington and his clique. I'm talking to you because I can help you. I can offer you a permanent slip of your own, with a warehouse large enough to hold all you can fit into *The Madelaine.*"

"And what is the catch?"

"No catch. You pay your rent on time, and I will ensure that your business becomes a success. I like that you don't deal in slaves. I like that you aren't prepared to bend to the likes of Beddington who have no morals and even fewer manners. And I think you'll like my side of the port. Come over whenever you like." He handed Peter a card. It was made of thick, smooth paper and had his name and address in elegant gold letters.

Mr. Poole stood up. "Please put Mr. Algood's bill on my slate," he called out to the young serving girl, who nodded and grinned at him as he gave her a cheeky wink and put on his red velvet top hat.

He was obviously well known here, and well-liked, though his popularity with the young lady may have had more to do with his handsome face and flirtatious manner than his actual character. Peter had not heard much about him. In truth, he'd heard nothing at all. That in itself seemed strange, if the man did indeed own a large part of the port. Peter obviously needed to ask around to find out more about him. He certainly wasn't going to make a business arrangement with a man he knew so little about.

He called on Mr. Kingshott on his way home. The wily old sailor laughed when Peter asked about Cable Poole. "You've been honored by New York royalty," he said. "The Pooles are infamous. Good people, honest, God-fearing. They stand by their word."

"So, I can trust him?"

"I'd trust no one more," Mr. Kingshott said. "He'll help you to trade the way you want to, and he'll get you your fortune."

"Will he want to act as my agent?"

"No, he'll let me do that for you. He trusts me, but I'm

the only agent he will let on his property. Thinks all the others are crooks."

"What if he wants more than I can pay?"

"He won't. If he's approached you, he already knows to the penny what you made and what you lost on your last voyage. He'll know what the current cargo should bring you, and he'll price you fairly. You have the kind of chance that most men would be prepared to kill a man for. You'd be a fool to turn him down – especially now you've offended Beddington. The man is furious and vowing to break you, I heard."

"Word travels fast," Peter said wryly.

"The docks are a small world," Mr. Kingshott said sagely. "And gossip is almost as valuable as the cargo in the ships."

Peter thanked him and went home. Mark had already returned from his work and was stirring a pot of stew on the stove. He turned and grinned at Peter. "She wrote to me," he said excitedly.

"Who wrote to you?" Peter asked. He had no idea what his twin was talking about.

"That lady in the newspaper. The one you showed me. She wrote to me," Mark repeated. He put down the spoon and picked up the letter from the kitchen table and handed it to Peter.

Dear Mr. Algood,

Thank you for your letter, I was glad to receive it.

I have read Mr. Twain's A Connecticut Yankee in King Arthur's Court, *and I liked it very much. I keep meaning to read* The Adventures of Huckleberry Finn, *but I haven't done so yet. I have been reading* Treasure Island *recently. It is such a fun story, with pirates and intrigue. I think Long John Silver is one of the most dastardly characters I've ever read.*

My dearest friend's adopted daughter Marla, is an actress and her theater troupe was in town recently. They performed some wonderful plays, and Marla married the impresario while they were here, too. It has been the most wonderful but tiring time. I made her dress, and it was the hardest thing that I have ever done. But she looked so beautiful, and it was the most wonderful day.

The place where I live is a small town, surrounded by mountains. As you may have guessed from its name, we have many nesting eagles in the area and a beautiful creek. The water is so clean and fresh, and it is lovely to walk along the banks and see the fish swimming. I like to take long walks up into the mountains and through the valley, but I don't get as much time to do so as I would like.

I shall read Mr. Twain's book, and perhaps we can discuss it when you write next time?

Yours, most happily

Jane Brown

"She sounds terribly boring," Peter said dismissively. "But perfect for you."

"I think so, and there is no need to be rude about her," Mark said angrily. "Can you not be happy for me? I do not expect you to find a woman I like interesting, or even to like her – given you find it hard to like any woman these days – but I do expect you to be respectful, Pete."

"I'm sorry, I've had the most peculiar day. I'm tired, and you know how anxious I was about *The Madelaine.*"

"I do, and so I will forgive you tonight."

"But not in the future? I understand, Mark, and you're right."

It was strange to see his twin so excited about a woman. Mark had never shown much interest in girls, though Peter suspected that his reticence was due to his shyness rather than a lack of desire. This new situation was a little worrying, though. Mark had only received one letter from this woman and knew so little about her, yet he sounded like he was already a little smitten. Peter would have to do all he could to politely keep Mark's feet firmly on the ground and ensure he didn't get hurt.

CHAPTER 6

AUGUST 19, 1892, EAGLE CREEK, MONTANA

*J*ane had received replies from all three of the gentlemen that she had written to. One of them, she would certainly not be responding to as he'd been rather improper, making lascivious comments about what manner of wife he wanted. The other two had been suitably polite. They'd engaged with her questions and made pertinent queries of their own. They seemed to be quite nice men, but she wasn't sure that they would ever be anything more to her than that.

She wasn't a silly young girl. She didn't expect to feel a spark of attraction from a single letter, but she had hoped that things would not feel so stilted. She thought about how easily she could write pages and pages to Cook without even noticing, and then how difficult it was to reply to these men. She simply did not know what to say to any of them to keep their interest. She had not been raised, as Marianne had, to flatter and please men so that she might make a fine match.

Jane had always known that she would work to support herself. It wasn't spoken of openly, of course, but there had been a tacit acceptance of the fact that marriage would be frowned upon if she wished to remain in Service. Most girls like her left their positions once married, to become wives and mothers. She had never wanted to do that. She had loved her work and had no wish to leave it just because she was wed. She didn't doubt that Marianne wouldn't have minded her staying on, but there would have been pressure on both of them for her to conform, had she found a suitable match. It had been easier to dismiss the idea of marriage out of hand.

She pressed the fabric Mrs. Hale had brought in for them to make into drapes for her parlor, ready to hem it. It was a straightforward task, but one that brought Jane a lot of plea-sure. Unlike a gown, which could take weeks of hard work depending on how much embroidery or beading a lady required, curtains could be made in less than a day with the Singer sewing machine. The fabric was usually easier to manage than silks and satins, too.

"Jane, dear," Mrs. Albert said, waddling into the shop. "My knees are so bad today. I think I'm going to go and see

Dr. Walker. Hopefully, he can give me something to make it easier."

"Are you sure that you should be going to New York next week?" Jane asked, concerned for her mentor. "You can barely walk."

"Well, someone needs to. We need to order new fabrics, and I prefer to see and feel anything before I buy it – and it is so much cheaper when you buy directly from the merchants in the harbor before they sell it to the shops. And it gives me a chance to see what the city ladies are wearing."

"Perhaps I should go instead," Jane said reluctantly. She didn't really want to go anywhere, much less to a city the size of New York, but Mrs. Albert was right. Their stock of fine fabrics was running very low.

"I'd not ask that of you. I know you don't like to travel."

"I'll go. It is part of our work, is it not? And you can't travel as you are."

"If you are sure, I would be grateful. I'm a little too old to be traipsing all over the country." She gave Jane a grateful smile and left, crossing Main Street slowly to the clinic on the other side of the road.

Jane put the iron back in the fire and sighed. She had hoped to never leave Eagle Creek, but perhaps it might work out well for her. One of the gentlemen she'd been writing to lived in New York. Maybe she would find it easier to write to him in the future if they met in person. At the moment, the fact that he was faceless made it too difficult for her to think she was talking with a real person.

She quickly wrote him a letter and ran down to the postal office to mail it. It would hopefully arrive ahead of her, so he would be aware of her visit. She didn't want to arrive on his doorstep unannounced. She wondered if he might think her too forward, just announcing that she would be visiting, but she couldn't help that. If he truly felt that way, it was better that she knew it now. She did not wish to marry a man who would tell her what to do or how to behave.

When she returned to the shop, Mrs. Greening was waiting for her. "I'm sorry, I had to run an errand," she explained as she took her place behind the counter.

"I don't mind. I saw you running down the street and assumed you wouldn't be long."

"How can I help you today?"

"I need a new gown," Mrs. Greening said with a shy smile. "I'm with child again and seem to be swelling up much more quickly than I did before."

"How wonderful," Jane said, genuinely happy for her. "Now, I am assuming that you will want something that you can let out as the baby grows?"

"Yes, please," Mrs. Greening said. "I'd love something that isn't tight over my belly if you can make something like that."

"It is a shame that the fashion now is for tiny waists,"

Jane mused, trying to think of something she could adapt. "They aren't really suitable for an expectant mother."

"I can't bear the idea of a corset, even now. I dread to think how uncomfortable I'll be when this little one is ready to make an appearance."

"You know, I've seen some pictures of lovely dresses that have a fitted bodice and then flare below the bust. I think they might be perfect for a lady with child," Jane said. "They were in fashion a long time ago, but I think they were quite lovely."

She rummaged in the large drawer of patterns that Mrs. Albert had kept since she had been a girl, looking for something that she could show Mrs. Greening. In the bottom drawer, right at the back, there were two. She pulled them out and spread out the sketches.

"Oh, they're quite lovely," Mrs. Greening said. "And they look just the thing. I'll take one of each."

Jane showed her the bolts of fabric she had enough of to make up the gowns. Mrs. Greening chose a pretty, floral cotton and a light woolen fabric that was as soft as a kitten's fur. Both would suit the styles well. "I shall get started as soon as I have finished these curtains. I'll call you in for a fitting in a few days, Mrs. Greening," Jane assured her.

"I knew you'd think of something, and given how long we've known each other now, I'd really feel much happier if you were to call me Elise."

"Elise, thank you. I shall try my best. I think I was a

maid for too long. I still struggle not to be so formal with people."

"I can understand that. We are so well-drilled to stay in our place and to show deference, aren't we?"

"I suppose we are," she agreed as she filled out an invoice and took a small deposit for the gowns.

Jane returned to the curtains. The iron was too hot, so she took it out of the fire and let it cool a little before she finished pressing the fabric, then sat down at the sewing machine. She threaded it carefully, then began to feed the fabric through, creating neat stitches in a perfectly straight line. Before long, both pieces of the fabric were hemmed all around. She took a thick cream woolen fabric and hemmed it before sewing it into the outer fabric, then attached hanging hooks at equal distances. She hung them up on the bar over the shop window, to check their length and how well they hung. They were perfect. She took them down and folded them neatly, ready to be collected.

Mrs. Albert did not come back all afternoon. Jane assumed that Dr. Walker had sent her home. After closing up the shop, she visited her employer on her way home. She knocked loudly on the cottage door and let herself inside. "Don't get up, Mrs. Albert. It's only me," she called out.

She found Mrs. Albert sitting in her armchair, her feet up on a footstool. "I'm sorry, dear," the elderly lady said. "I meant to just have a little nap, but I must have slept all afternoon."

"Dr. Walker gave you something for the pain then?" Jane knew her employer hadn't been sleeping well because of the pain.

"He did, but I'm to use it sparingly. I feel much better for a little rest."

"You should take a couple of days off," Jane insisted. "I can manage at the shop, and the girls will be in, so I'll have plenty of help. You get some rest so that you are well enough to manage when I go to New York."

"I couldn't," Mrs. Albert protested. "It's my shop. I should be there."

"You must, or you'll not be well enough to work at all," Jane said firmly. "You took me on to help, so you must let me do so. We're not very busy. There's nothing I can't handle alone – and I won't be alone, anyway."

"The girls aren't good for much other than sewing buttonholes," Mrs. Albert said.

"Then I'd best teach them a few more things so they can do more," Jane said with a smile. "I'll come and see you the night before I go to New York, but I don't want to see you until then. And I'll send you something to eat for supper tonight, too."

"You are a good girl, Jane. I'm so glad you came to Eagle Creek."

"I am, too."

Jane went home, where she quickly made and baked two chicken pies. She left one on the table to cool and took the second to Mrs. Albert. "Ooh, that'll see me through a few days," the older woman said, as she took a deep sniff of the delicious-smelling pie. "Thank you."

"It is my pleasure," Jane assured her.

"Won't you join me for supper?"

"I won't. I'm tired, and I need to make some arrangements if I am to go to New York in your stead."

"I understand," Mrs. Albert said, nodding. "I cannot thank you enough for everything."

"You don't need to. You gave me work, doing something I love."

Back in her own kitchen, Jane sat down and re-read the letter from Mr. Algood, searching it for clues that might indicate that he might become more than a friend, given time.

Dear Miss Brown

Thank you for your letter. I am so glad that you decided to write back to me. I was not sure if I would be interesting enough as I am quite a quiet and shy man.

On your recommendation, I purchased Treasure Island *and have started to read it. You are quite right about Long John Silver, he's a real piece of work, isn't he? Poor Jim has faced some difficult times, he deserves a true friend, and I fear that he has not found one in John.*

Your town sounds lovely. I've never seen an eagle in flight, it must be quite the sight. I was raised here in New York. It's busy and smelly, full of people, which oddly makes it easy to hide. A man can quietly go about his business without anyone much noticing because everyone is busy elsewhere. That can be a little lonely for some, but it doesn't worry me at all. I have my brother, so I don't need everyone to know my name and every detail of my life.

I can imagine that in a small town, everyone knows everyone else's business. While I can imagine that it is good to feel connected and a part of something larger than your-self, it must be difficult to bear at times? Do you not find that everyone has an opinion on all you are doing, whether it be right or wrong in their eyes? I am not sure that I could live with all eyes upon me. I know that not everyone wishes to live in the city, though I find its anonymity to be oddly reas-suring sometimes.

My brother and I will be attending the theater this evening. A troupe of players from Europe is here, and I am excited to see them. They've come from Paris, from the Comédie-Française. My brother assures me that it will be a night we would both rather forget, but he does not much enjoy the theater. I fear it may be a little too bawdy for me – though I doubt I will understand a word as I never learned French in school. But in New York, it is important to be seen to attend such things, and so we endure it.

I do hope that you will write to me again.

Yours, most hopefully

Mark Algood

Jane still wasn't sure what to make of him. He seemed

nice enough, if a little rigid in his tastes. And he didn't seem overly keen to live anywhere other than where he was now. He seemed to like living in New York, where he could be quiet and unseen. He certainly wouldn't find that in Eagle Creek. Everyone in Eagle Creek seemed to know everyone else – and have their ideas on how people should live their lives. But he would perhaps take her to the theater, even if he did not much enjoy it himself, and they would be able to talk about books together, at least, so she would not feel so alone on her trip to New York.

CHAPTER 7

SEPTEMBER 21, 1892, NEW YORK CITY,
NEW YORK

*D*ear Mr. Algood,
    *I do hope that you won't think me presump-
tuous, but I must make a trip to New York for my work and
wondered if you might perhaps like to meet while I am
there?*

*I won't have much time as I will be busy seeking out
fabrics, but my evenings will be free if you might perhaps
like to dine with me, or take in a play?*

*I'll understand if you think it's too early and would
rather not meet, but I would feel terrible if you found out I*

had been close by and not told you, and you were hurt by that.

I arrive on the twenty-sixth and will be staying at The Grand Hotel if you would like to call on me.

Yours, most sincerely

Jane Brown

"Pete, she's coming," Mark called out loudly, thundering up the stairs. "She will be here next week!"

"Who will be here?" Peter asked sleepily. He sat up in his bed and rubbed his eyes as his twin burst into his bedroom. "What are you making such a ruckus about so early in the morning?"

"Miss Brown, the lady I've been writing to, she's coming to New York next week." Mark's face was strained. Peter wasn't sure that it was the reaction that he'd expected from his twin, should Mark actually ever find the courage to meet with a complete stranger.

"Next week?"

"Yes, she wrote to tell me. She must have sent it before she set off for it to arrive before her." Mark thrust the letter at him.

Peter took it and read it carefully. "Then you will need to get a new suit and a haircut, and you'll need to think of things you can talk to her about when she gets here," he said. He handed the letter back to Mark, lay back down, rolled onto his side, and closed his eyes again. "And as that won't be for another five days, leave me be. I was up until three, playing cards with Kingshott, and that man is a cheat and a card shark if ever I met one."

"No word on *The Madelaine* yet?"

"She's not due for another few days," Peter said. "I think this will be my lot from now on: late nights and a knot in my belly from a week before she's due until she arrives."

"Why not do something more predictable to earn a living?"

"Because anything more predictable will not make me my fortune," Peter explained for the hundredth time. "You may be content staring at rows and rows of tiny figures all day, but I am not. I want more than the life we have here. There is a big world out there, brother, and I want to see it all."

"Yet you are not the one taking to sea," Mark pointed out. "You'll not see much of the world from the port of New York."

"But I will earn enough there so that I can. Now go away and get ready for your lady friend. No doubt you'll bore her to tears the first evening and she'll never want to see you again, and I'll be able to get some sleep once more."

"You think I'll bore her?" Mark asked anxiously. He perched on the edge of the bed, his head and shoulders drooping. "Of course, I will. I bore everyone. Even you."

"You don't bore me," Peter said. He sat up again. He was obviously not going to be permitted to get any more sleep. He put a supportive hand on his brother's hunched shoulder.

"And I was joking. You seem to have much in common with Miss Brown, so there is no reason why you won't find much to talk about together."

"But you know that I am not good at speaking to young ladies," Mark said awkwardly. "I've never managed to do so, not the way that you can."

"I only manage it because I don't care what they think of me."

"It isn't that. You're more confident than me, in every aspect of life."

"I assure you that when it comes to women, the best thing any man can do is to ask a single pertinent question and then listen to what she has to say. So many men talk over women, sure that their own ideas and pastimes are more important, that the ladies genuinely adore it when a man actually listens and makes out that he cares what she thinks."

"I doubt it is that easy," Mark said. "And how will I know which question to ask?"

"Well, in this particular situation, if I were you, I would ask about her work. It is clear that it means a lot to her. She is traveling for weeks, across the country, for it."

"But what do I know about fabrics and sewing?" Mark wailed.

"That is rather the point," Peter said, shaking his head. Mark truly was impossible at times. "By asking her, you will learn."

"I wish I were more like you."

"But you aren't, and frankly that is probably why this young lady actually likes you enough to meet you."

Mark stared at him. His expression changed from one of despair to a more pensive look. Then he beamed.

"What?" Peter demanded. "What is your ridiculous brain conjuring now?"

"You could meet her on my behalf," Mark said triumphantly. "You can meet her, make her like me, and then we could switch."

"Are you completely out of your mind?" Peter said, aghast at such an idea. "I'll not deceive her like that. It's not right. How do you think she'd feel if she found out? And she would. She'd have to be a complete idiot not to notice the change after spending a few days with me and then spending time with you."

"But you can pretend to be me. You've done it before."

"When we were boys, to get us out of trouble."

"To get yourself out of trouble," Mark corrected him.

"I won't do it. It isn't right," Peter said firmly.

"But I'll just make a terrible mess of it all. I'm so nervous that my palms are already sweating. Please, Pete, for me? I just need to know a little more about her before I actually meet her – and you can find things out. Women like you. They talk to you."

Peter sighed. Mark wasn't going to let this go. In his mind, it was the perfect solution to his painful bashfulness. No matter how much Peter argued that Miss Brown would still eventually have to meet the real Mark, it wouldn't make any difference. "I've not read that dratted book the two of you have been talking about," he said. "She'll work it out just from that."

"Not if you read it before she comes, and perhaps some of my Mark Twain books, too," Mark said, his eyes as wide as a puppy's. He looked so pathetic that Peter took pity on him.

"I've never read a book in a week in my life, much less two or three."

"There's a first time for everything, and it would distract you from thoughts of *The Madelaine*."

"No book is good enough for that," Peter said, shaking his head. "Bring them here. I'll try to read a bit of all the ones that you think I should. But if I don't enjoy any of them, then I'll not do it. I won't set myself up to fail from the outset."

"Thank you, thank you, thank you," Mark said. He hugged him and hurried out of the room, returning moments later with copies of *Treasure Island, The Adventures of Huckleberry Finn,* and *A Connecticut Yankee in King Arthur's Court.* "I've made notes in the margins about things I might discuss with Miss Brown if she wrote back to me."

"That might be helpful," Peter said drily. "Now get out of here. I've clearly got a lot of work to do – and you need to get to work."

Mark nodded and disappeared, clearly not wanting to run

the risk of Peter changing his mind. Peter collapsed back against his pillows with a heavy sigh. What had he let himself in for? He had read Miss Brown's letters, and she seemed as dull and uninteresting as his twin. Bookish and quiet, no doubt. And he worried that he might actually harm Mark's chances rather than improve them. He was most certainly not the intellectual type. He much preferred leaping before he looked and taking action rather than making careful, well-researched plans. If Miss Brown was more like Mark, as he suspected she was, then Peter's brash ways might be too much for her.

He picked up one of the books and began to read. Mark was right about one thing; he had a lot of time on his hands as he waited for *The Madelaine*. Perhaps a little reading might help to pass the time more quickly. He was surprised when he heard the clock chime eleven. He'd become quite engrossed in the tale of two boys as they grew up and the adventures they had together. He got up and washed and dressed quickly for a luncheon meeting with Mr. Poole. A last-minute impulse made him pick up the book and tuck it into his pocket.

He reached the port a little after midday. Mr. Poole was standing on one of the slips, watching as cargo was loaded into the hold. Peter hurried toward him. "Good day, I am sorry I am a little late."

"Not at all," Mr. Poole said as they shook hands warmly. "I have a few things to finish with here, I'm sorry. Not enough stevedores today for some reason, so I'm running a little late myself."

"I heard that there had been an outbreak of influenza in some of the slums around the docks," Peter told him. "I know many of the men live there."

"That would explain it," Mr. Poole said with a frown. "I wonder if there is anything we can do to help them?"

"Cleaner, better housing would be a start, I suspect."

"I shall look into it. Now, why don't you go ahead to the coffee shop? I shall be with you shortly."

Peter was constantly surprised by Cable Poole. The man had as much money as Midas, yet he didn't seem to have much use for it himself. All anyone around him had to do was to mention a cause that needed assistance and Poole would find a way to donate substantial funds to fix the problem. He seemed to not care how much money he spent on such things. He was a genuinely good man, and he paid the best day rates in the docks.

Half an hour later, Mr. Poole joined Peter in the coffee shop. "You know, I thought a little about the stevedores," he said, taking off his top hat and coat and hanging them on the stand by the door. "Do you think men would be happier to know they have work and a set wage rather than relying upon day rates?"

"I'm sure they would. A man can make plans when he knows his salary," Peter said. "But what happens on the days when there is little for them to do? You'd be paying them to stand around idle."

"There's always work to be done," Mr. Poole said. "Mending sails, repairing buildings, moving cargo. I'm sure there would be only the rarest of days when there would be no work at all."

"I'm sure the men would be thankful, but what of the others? Those not lucky enough to work on your dock?"

"Perhaps our example would encourage others to do the same. Staff who know they are valued work harder, don't you think?"

"I'm sure I don't know," Peter said. "But I would."

"I shall try it. And I will also look into building homes for them behind the dock. There's enough land to re-home most of those in the slums on the south side of the port."

"You are a good man, Mr. Poole."

"No, I am a man who wants men to be at work on time and put in a hard day's work for me," he said. "I can assure you that my interest is as mercenary as any man's."

"Well, I am certainly glad that you took pity on me," Peter said. "I hope that my ship will bring me enough to buy a second ship when she comes in this time."

"You'll need one of the bigger slips if you do," Mr. Poole said with a smile.

"I'm content with the one you've allotted me for now. But when I get my third, perhaps we will need to renegotiate our deal."

CHAPTER 8

SEPTEMBER 27, 1892, NEW YORK CITY, NEW YORK

*a*s Jane had expected, the journey to New York had been long, tedious, and uncomfortable. But a hot bath and a night in a comfortable bed had helped her to feel more like herself again. She had a busy day planned as she wanted to get home to Eagle Creek as soon as she possibly could. She dressed and made her way down to the breakfast room. Several well-dressed men were eating pastries and drinking coffee. She asked for eggs and coffee, which were brought to her quickly. The eggs were delicious, light, and fluffy with just the right amount of butter and salt. The coffee was excellent, dark, rich, and bitter.

As she was finishing her coffee, a bellboy brought a letter to her table. She gave him a couple of coins and then opened it.

Dear Miss Brown

I hope that this will be there to greet you on your first morning in New York. I hope that you won't find the city too overwhelming.

Would you perhaps consider letting me call upon you this evening? We could dine in the restaurant at the hotel and get to know one another a little better.

Yours, most hopefully

Mark Algood

"Could you fetch me a pen and some paper?" she called out to the bellboy. He turned and nodded, then hurried off. Jane took a couple of deep breaths. Her stomach was suddenly filled with fluttering butterflies and she felt a little queasy. She took a sip of water and tried to calm herself. He was only asking her to spend time together, as she had planned for them to do when she wrote to him. He had suggested a place where they would be surrounded by others, so she need not fear that he might try to take advantage of her, and it was here in the hotel, so she would not have to find some strange place in the dark. In truth, it was as considerate a request as anyone could make.

Moments later, the bellboy returned with a small bottle of dark blue ink, a pen, and some thick cream paper.

"Wait a moment," she told him. "I'll need you to deliver

this immediately." She quickly wrote a reply and watched the bellboy leave to take it to Mr. Algood. She wanted to meet him. She hoped that he would be a little more forthcoming in person than he had been in his letters. She wanted to know him – not just which books he enjoyed.

Out on the street, she was almost run over by a racing hansom cab as she tried to cross the road. She wasn't naïve – she'd spent her childhood in Houston, which was a very busy city – but New York was so much bigger, faster, and noisier than she could ever have imagined. After the peace and quiet of both Long Point and Eagle Creek, she wasn't quite ready for just how many people lived and worked here.

She asked a shopkeeper who was standing in his doorway calling out his special offers for directions to the fabric merchants Mrs. Albert had told her to call on. He smiled at her and took a quick look at the addresses, then took a pencil from behind his ear and quickly drew a map underneath them. "It's easy enough, but it is quite a walk to the docks from here. You might want to take a hansom," he warned her.

"I'm happy enough walking," Jane said. After four weeks on four trains, she was simply glad to be on stable ground once more. It would do her good to get moving.

She followed his directions and was standing outside one of the fabric merchant's warehouses about an hour later. There was a small door cut into a much larger one. She knocked on it and opened it cautiously. "Good day," she called out.

She stepped inside and stood by the door. In front of her were row upon row of wooden crates, piled up to the ceiling of the vast warehouse. "Is anyone here?" she called out a little more loudly this time.

"One moment, Ma'am," an elderly sounding voice called from somewhere above her. She looked around, trying to see if there were stairs to an office anywhere, but all she could see were more crates.

A minute later, she saw some legs appear, then a torso, and finally a white-haired head from behind some particularly large crates. She moved closer and saw that there was a ladder. The man turned and smiled at her. "Good day. How may I help you, my dear?"

"Mrs. Albert sent me," she explained, hoping that the name would mean something to him.

It obviously did as he smiled gently. "How is Effie?" he asked fondly.

"She is well, though her joints give her some trouble," Jane said.

"You must be Miss Brown. Effie wrote to tell me to expect you. I'm Arthur Albert."

"Albert?"

"She didn't tell you that I'm her brother-in-law?" Mr. Albert said, a twinkle in his eye.

"No, she did not."

"It's the sort of thing she forgets to tell people. Now, I'm to help you find the very best fabrics. Effie gave me orders to look after you as if you were my own daughter."

"Well, I must admit that I will be grateful for your assistance," Jane said. "I've not purchased fabric in bulk like this before."

"Effie said as much. But her name's well known here, and there are few men brave enough to try to take her for a fool." He beckoned her to follow him. "Now, I've picked out the best of what I have right now for you to look over. They're laid out in the office."

Jane followed him gratefully. It would have been a much less anxious journey had she known that Mrs. Albert was still, in her own way, looking out for her. The tiny office was tucked away right at the very back of the vast warehouse. A large rack hung on the wall, with at least fifty fabrics draped over the rods. Jane moved toward them without waiting to be asked. She reached out and let her fingers trace along the weave, her eyes closed. She knew that her fingers would tell her whether a fabric would be easy to sew, how it would drape and fold, and how it would feel against the skin far more than her eyes. Any manufacturer could make something that looked good.

Mr. Albert stood behind her. "You're just like her," he said with a chuckle. "She's got the wisest fingers in the land, I swear it."

"I'd not argue with you about that," Jane said with a

smile as she opened her eyes. "She has forgotten more about sewing and fabrics than I will probably ever be able to learn from her."

"I think you know more than you think already."

She returned to her inspection of the fabrics. Within an hour, she had chosen eight that she was sure would be suitable to have shipped to Montana. "Excellent choices and, of course, I shall give Effie her usual family discount," Mr. Albert assured her. "Now, would you like to get something to eat before I take you to Jenkinson's?"

Jane's stomach growled its answer. "I think that something to eat would be a fine idea," she agreed.

After a hasty lunch of steak pie in a nearby coffee shop, Mr. Albert took Jane to the next fabric merchant's warehouse on her list. He talked quietly with the owner while she looked over the fabrics on offer. He had some excellent voile, some nice tulle, but his velvets and satins weren't as fine as Mr. Albert's had been, though they had particularly pretty designs. She negotiated a price with him and arranged shipping.

"It's a little late to go to anyone else today," Mr. Albert said, "but I can meet you at ten o'clock in the morning at Georgiou's? He often has things nobody else does as he trades with his family in Greece. They get fabrics from Turkey and Northern Africa. Some of them are quite spectacular."

"I'll look forward to it," Jane said, shaking his hand. "Thank you for your help today."

"It has been my pleasure. After all, you're part of the family now, aren't you?"

"Well…" Jane said cautiously.

"And because you are, I know that Sarah would be most angry with me if I don't invite you to dine with us tonight."

"I'm afraid that I can't," Jane said regretfully. "I already have other plans. But perhaps tomorrow night?"

"That would be perfect. I know that Sarah will want to hear all about how Effie is. They were the closest of friends. And she'll want to hear how her beloved Eagle Creek is."

"Your wife used to live there, I presume? I know Mrs. Albert has lived there all her life. However did you meet?"

He chuckled. "I used to be a traveling salesman. I had a little cart and a sturdy pony, and I sold whatever I could get my hands on. I met Sarah in Eagle Creek and fell in love with her the moment I saw her, but she had no intention of living a life on the road. When I left town, I promised that when I returned that I would have a proper business and a fine house for her to live in – if she'd just wait for me."

"That is so romantic," Jane said with a sigh. "And you returned for her, and she had waited?"

"Well, it took me a little longer than I had hoped. Five years, in fact. So, when I finally went back, she had married already," Mr. Albert said with a smile. "But she had been widowed and was glad to see me. Effie and my brother met at our wedding and fell head over heels. Sarah moved here, and David moved there."

"What a wonderful story, and how wonderful that it worked out so well for everyone."

"I know David and Effie were very happy together, and I hope I still make Sarah happy," Mr. Albert said. "Now, I shall see you tomorrow."

Jane went back to the hotel and fussed with her hair for an hour before pinning it in exactly the way she always did. She had rather hoped that she would be able to pin it the way that Marianne had done it for her, for Marla's wedding. It had looked so pretty, but she wasn't entirely sure how to do such a hairstyle on her own head. It was so much more awkward than doing someone else's hair. She took out the blue velvet gown that Marianne had given her for her last birthday and put it on. The style suited her well, but its low-cut neckline exposed her full breasts and made her feel a little self-conscious.

As the clock struck seven, she picked up a shawl and made her way down to the lobby. Several people were sitting at the little tables in the grand hallway, talking animatedly to one another. A tall, gray-haired man stood by the door, holding it open for a tiny, white-haired older lady who beamed at him lovingly. She couldn't see anyone who looked like they were waiting for someone.

Mr. Frome, the desk clerk, beckoned her over to the

counter. "There is a gentleman waiting for you in the drawing room," he informed her.

"Thank you."

Jane crossed the hall to the drawing room. It was a light, bright, but comfortable feeling room. There was a wall of books on her right-hand side and large windows that overlooked the pretty gardens to the rear of the hotel in front of her. Paintings of country landscapes and seascapes filled the wall to her left, above elegant pieces of wooden furniture with intricate marquetry or lacquer designs upon them.

A gentleman was standing by the windows, looking out over the gardens. He had a fine figure with broad shoulders and slim hips. At the sound of her footsteps, he turned and smiled warmly at her. Jane felt her breath catch in her chest. He was deliciously handsome with his square jaw and aquiline features. His skin was lightly tanned, and his chestnut brown hair was slightly tousled. His eyes were the brightest blue. "Miss Brown, I presume?" he said, moving toward her gracefully.

She held out her hand. "Yes, and you are Mr. Algood?"

"I am," he said. "And it is truly a pleasure to meet you."

CHAPTER 9

SEPTEMBER 27, 1892, NEW YORK CITY,
NEW YORK

*P*eter was a little surprised by the elegant young lady standing a little nervously in front of him. Her gown was as fine as anything he'd seen in New York, and she held herself with poise. Her face was lovely, and she had soft brown eyes and a tiny smattering of freckles over her nose. But what was merely lovely transformed into real beauty when she smiled. Her eyes lit up, and she had tiny dimples in her cheeks. He was transfixed.

And he shouldn't be. He reminded himself that he was here on Mark's behalf, to make a good impression on this young woman that Mark cared for. He was not here for himself. He smiled and offered Miss Brown his arm. "Shall we go through?" he asked.

"Why not?" She tucked her arm through his and laid her hand on his arm. Her fingers were long and slender, and her nails were short and neat. Unable to stop himself, he placed his free hand over hers. Her skin was soft and warm. He felt a frisson of electricity surge through his body at the innocent touch and knew that he should never have agreed to any of this.

A waiter showed them to their seats. Peter held out Miss Brown's chair, and she sat down. The waiter draped her napkin across her lap while Peter sat down opposite her. They watched silently as the waiter poured water into their glasses and then asked if they would like anything else to drink. "Nothing, thank you," Miss Brown said quietly.

"A small whiskey, please," Peter said. He needed it. He'd not expected to be attracted to Miss Brown.

"I've never tried whiskey," Miss Brown said once the waiter had brought it over and left them with the menu.

"Would you like to?" he asked.

She nodded. "If you wouldn't mind? Everyone I know seems to drink it but me."

He handed her the glass. Their fingers brushed lightly, and again there was that surge of sensation flooding through him. Peter had never felt this way. Even holding Ellen's hand and kissing her had never created such feelings in him – and he'd intended to marry her. He watched as Miss

Brown licked her lips and took a tentative sip. She certainly hadn't meant it to be, but it was one of the most sensuous things that he'd ever seen. But the seductive image passed quickly when she spluttered as the fiery liquid hit the back of her throat.

"People drink that for pleasure?" she asked. She took a couple of large gulps of water to try to ease the burning feeling.

"You get used to the fire." He chuckled. "It is an acquired taste."

"One I think I may continue not acquiring," she said with a chuckle.

"A wise decision." Peter toasted her choice.

She raised her glass of water, and they clinked them across the table. "I do like wine, though. Perhaps we might have some with our meal?"

"Of course," he said. "They have an excellent wine list here. Do you prefer white or red?"

"I don't mind. Red gives me a terrible headache, though, so perhaps white would be best? I have more work to do tomorrow, and I can't afford to make any mistakes."

"You're here for work, you said," Peter said, suddenly remembering that she wasn't here just to meet his brother. "You're a seamstress, I believe you said, so what is it that you are doing here?"

"Buying fabrics and watching people," she said. "Buying directly from the importers here in New York saves us a fortune." She pointed to the fine linen tablecloth. "For example, this grade of linen would cost me four times more if I were to buy it from a merchant in Billings as it does to arrange for a merchant here in New York to send it to us directly."

"Goodness," Peter said. He'd never much considered that the cost of fabrics, or anything, might be so different in other parts of the country. "I suppose it is because of the cost of shipping it?"

"Yes. Every link in the chain from New York to Billings has to make a little profit, so the price continues to rise. My employer Mrs. Albert has a brother-in-law here who is a fabric merchant, and he's been helping me to get the best deals for all that we need for the next year."

"And he'll arrange one large shipment straight to you."

"Exactly."

The waiter approached them and asked if they were ready to order. Jane flushed prettily. "We've barely even looked at the menu," she said as she picked it up and started to flick through it.

"What would you suggest?" Peter asked him.

The young man smiled. "Well, the roast duck is particularly good tonight," he said. "And I'd suggest the chicken soup to start and the chocolate gateau for dessert."

"Then I shall have those," Miss Brown said, putting her menu down again, looking delighted that the decision had been taken for her.

"I shall have the same," Peter said. He opened the wine list and scanned it before pointing to one.

"Where were we?" Miss Brown said a little awkwardly once they were alone again.

"Talking about your work."

"And I have probably bored you quite long enough."

"Not at all," Peter assured her. She was clearly very passionate about her work and had spoken most animatedly about it. He'd never thought he'd be interested in fabric, yet he was hanging on her every word. "But you also mentioned that you are here to watch people, why do you need to do that?"

"Well, as a dressmaker, it is important to keep abreast of the current fashions. Young ladies, no matter where they are, wish to be well turned out and to wear the most current patterns. By seeing what ladies wear here, I can go back and recreate something similar for our customers in Montana."

"I suppose that makes sense. But could you not just buy the patterns?"

"There is a small business in buying patterns, but most dressmakers prefer to make their own. If you've not seen anyone wearing a particular style, it is quite difficult to see how it should look when finished, and all ladies' bodies are a little different, so you're always making adjustments to ensure that the gown suits the figure anyway."

"That makes sense. Your dress is lovely, by the way. I should have said so when we met in the drawing room."

"Mrs. Albert made it especially for me," Jane explained. "My former employer, Marianne, asked her to make it for my birthday in April."

"That is very generous of her."

"She is a good friend now. I am so blessed to have her and her family. They treat me as if I was one of them, not just a poor orphan who turned up on the doorstep."

"I'm sure you have earned that love and trust. People don't just give such things away easily in my experience."

"No, they don't," she agreed. "But what of you? You told me so little about yourself in your letters. I enjoyed sharing thoughts about books, but what exactly is it that you do, and do you enjoy it as much as I enjoy my work?"

Peter grinned. "I don't think I do. I don't think many people are lucky enough to be as passionate about their work as you seem to be. I spend my days poring over ledgers, adding and subtracting, trying to make sense of other people's accounts."

"And do you enjoy it?"

Peter wanted to say no. To him, Mark's work was possibly the dullest occupation he could think of. But he had to remember that he was not himself tonight. Thankfully, Mark often spoke of how much he enjoyed his work and why, so it wasn't hard for Peter to speak about it, though it felt oddly uncomfortable to be lying to her. Up until then, he'd not had to lie. "I do. I get great satisfaction when the totals tally and there are no crossings out on a full ledger sheet. But I know such things are dull to most people, so we need not talk about it."

"Then what else makes you who you are?" she asked innocently.

"I am a twin," he said, wanting to say something that was true. "I suppose that has shaped who I am more than anything."

"And are you like your brother? To look at, I mean?"

"We definitely look alike, so much so that there are few who can tell us apart," Peter said. "But our personalities are very different."

"So, I'd know it wasn't you if I met your brother?"

"I hope so," Peter said cautiously. What he really hoped was that he could do a good enough job of acting the part of his twin tonight so she wouldn't notice the difference when she did meet Mark.

Their food arrived, and Peter was pleased to see that Miss Brown did not pick at her food. She ate with gusto. It was rather refreshing. So many young ladies in New York seemed to eat like birds, but Miss Brown ate every bite and talked about the flavors and textures with delight. He was sad when they finished the last bites of the deliciously rich dessert. It meant that they would soon have to part.

"When do you return to Eagle Creek?" he asked her.

"In three days' time," she said.

"Might I see you again, before you leave?"

"I'm busy tomorrow, but not the day after," she said, seemingly happy that he had asked.

"I could try to get tickets for a play or the opera?"

"I would like that very much. I told you, didn't I, that Marianne's daughter is an actress. Well, she's not really her daughter, but that's a long story, one I could perhaps tell you another time. But her troupe comes to Eagle Creek often, and it is always so wonderful."

"I shall see what I can do," Peter promised her.

"I should go now." She put her napkin down on the table and started to stand up. Peter jumped to his feet and moved to pull her chair away. When she smiled up at him, he felt his heart skip a beat.

"I shall see you on Thursday evening. I am looking forward to it already."

He watched her leave the dining room, then sank back into his chair. What a fool he'd been to agree to any of this. Now he would have to go home and tell Mark how well everything had gone and then watch his brother ruin everything when he took her to the theater on Thursday. He only hoped that Miss Brown would forgive them both for the deception.

With regret, he paid the bill and walked home. Mark was waiting up for him. "So?" he demanded.

"It went very well. She is a charming young lady. You're very lucky," Peter said flatly.

"So, why are you so down about it? Did she want to see me again?"

"You're taking her to the theater on Thursday. She likes the man she thinks you are. I did my best to be like you, but she isn't like her letters. She's fascinating in person. Very charming, witty, and sweet. Don't ruin the good work I've done for you tonight."

Mark blanched. "That is a little unfair."

"Brother, I love you, but you did the wrong thing tonight. As I sat opposite Miss Brown, I felt worse and worse about lying to her. It didn't feel right, and she deserves better. If you truly wish to get to know her better, you need to actually do it yourself."

"But I can't on Thursday," Mark said nervously. "I've got to attend a soiree at the senior partner's home. It isn't something I can take someone I barely know to. Please, take her out again on Thursday. She's only in town for a few days, and you said I'd take her to the theater. I don't want to disappoint her."

Peter glared at him. "I'll do it this time, but only this time. After this, you are on your own."

CHAPTER 10

SEPTEMBER 29, 1892, NEW YORK CITY,
NEW YORK

*J*ane frowned at her reflection in the mirror.
She wasn't sure if the gown she'd purchased
really suited her, but there hadn't been much
choice in the store that was ready and would fit at such short
notice. She hadn't expected it to go as well as it had, so she
had only brought one gown suitable for evening wear with
her, and she couldn't possibly wear the same dress to meet
Mr. Algood twice. Well, there wasn't time to make any alterations, so it would have to do.

She brushed out her hair and pinned it carefully. Mr.

Algood hadn't seemed to mind the way she'd worn it the other night, but she wanted to try something different tonight. She took it down and re-pinned it five times before she was happy with it. She wanted to make a good impression on him, to leave him with happy memories of the times they had spent together. She had not expected to like him as much as she did, and she had certainly not expected him to be as handsome as he was.

All through their meal, she'd had to keep pinching herself to check that she wasn't dreaming. He was clever and funny, and a true gentleman. He'd made her feel like a real lady. She could hardly wait to see him again and had been counting down not only the hours but the minutes, much to Mr. and Mrs. Albert's amusement the previous night. They'd teased her a little about her being away with the fairies, and she'd had to admit the truth of it.

She'd done her best to ensure she was not distracted while making her deals. She and Mr. Albert had overseen the arrival of all her ordered fabrics that afternoon and then packed them carefully for their journey by rail to Eagle Creek. She was happy with everything she had chosen and prayed that Mrs. Albert would be when it arrived a few days before she did.

Deciding that she was as ready as she ever would be, Jane pulled on the jacket that she'd bought to match her new dress and hurried downstairs. Mr. Algood was waiting for her by the front door. His face lit up at the sight of her and it made her feel as warm inside as the tiny sip of his whiskey had done – and took away her breath just as much.

"Good evening. You look lovely," he said as he offered her his arm.

"You are looking rather handsome yourself," she said with a smile. "So, is it a play or the opera?"

"Neither," he said with a sad shrug. "I could only get tickets to the ballet. I do hope you won't be disappointed."

She stared at him. "I have never been, but I always wanted to. How wonderful."

"You aren't just saying that?" he asked a little nervously.

"No, I truly mean it. I used to watch the girls at my school running around with their ballet slippers and talking about their lessons. I couldn't afford such things and have no grace anyway. I always envied them that."

"You are very graceful," Mr. Algood said gallantly, making her blush. Jane raised a hand to her hot cheek and ducked her head away from him a little. "I am sorry that you felt left out as a girl. I do hope that you don't feel that way any longer?"

"I do a little," Jane admitted shyly as they stepped outside. "All of my friends are married and having babies now, and again I am the last to do so."

"Hence your advertisement?"

"Indeed."

They climbed into a waiting carriage and sat quietly for a few moments before it pulled away. "And do you think that you might be interested in marriage with anyone you've been writing to?"

"I wrote to two other gentlemen in the beginning, but their letters told me that they weren't for me," she said cautiously. She didn't want him to think that she was pinning all her hopes on him.

"I'm glad that you aren't writing to them anymore," he said softly.

He didn't say anything else for the rest of the journey across the city. Jane wasn't entirely sure what to make of him. He had been so much more talkative the other night. But being able to talk in the privacy of a crowded dining room was a little different from the close quarters of a carriage. They were still virtually strangers, after all.

When the carriage came to a halt, he jumped out and offered her his hand to help her down. She took it gratefully, but the heel of her boot got caught in the hem of her gown and she stumbled, almost landing on top of him. He caught her and held her tightly against his strong body. She could feel the warmth of him through the soft velvet of her gown. "I'm sorry," she whispered.

"Are you hurt?" he asked, putting her away from him and looking her up and down.

"I'm quite well, just a little clumsy."

"We should go inside."

She followed him into the grand theater. She had never seen anything quite like it before. The red, plush carpet underfoot, the gold bars holding it in place on every stair, the elegantly carved railings of the banisters, and the gilded moldings on the walls were quite magnificent. She stared open-mouthed at the opulence on display.

"It's all fake," Mr. Algood whispered to her as they were shown to their box. "Just plaster and paint, all of it."

"It looks real," she marveled.

"That is the miracle of the theater, the ability to hide the truth from our eyes. We step inside these temples and willingly give up our disbelief. We don't see actors, dancers, or singers, we see the characters they play. We lose ourselves in all of it, willingly."

"I never thought of it that way. But you're right. I am prepared to lose myself in whatever is put before me on that stage tonight. I want to be caught up in it all, to forget myself and my dreary life, to be a part of something bigger and more beautiful than my life could ever be."

He smiled at her, his eyes twinkling in the semi-darkness, and they took their seats. The orchestra in the pit began to play, and the curtain rose. The real world fell away, and Jane lost herself in the music and dancing. At times she laughed and at times she cried, but it was always mesmerizing and beautiful. The grace and strength of the dancers were remarkable, and their flowing movements were barely marred at all by the sound of their shoes against the hard stage. As the curtain fell, Jane clapped louder and harder than anyone else.

"That was quite beautiful," she sighed as the lights went up in the theater.

"I'm so glad you enjoyed it," Mr. Algood said happily. He helped her into her jacket and put on his own coat before they left their box and made their way downstairs. "I wanted to make your last night here special so you would want to return someday."

"I'm not sure I'll ever want to return to New York. I do so hate traveling, but I shall not dread it so much knowing that there are such wonderful things to see and do here."

"And that I am here?" he asked tentatively.

"And because you are here," she agreed.

PETER SLAMMED the door loudly upon his return. He had been determined to stay at least a little aloof and keep his distance from Miss Brown. He'd hoped that by attending the ballet, which he usually despised, he would find it easier to do so, but she had looked so lovely and had been so enthralled by the ballet that he had found it impossible not to enjoy the evening as much as she had – especially when he'd had to catch her to stop her from falling face first onto the dirty street. She had fitted so perfectly into his arms, and he had not wanted to ever let her go.

Mark wasn't home yet, and Peter was strangely grateful for that. He had no desire to see his brother and recount every moment of the evening for him so he would know what to write about in his next letter to Miss Brown. Peter was angry with Mark for being such a coward, for putting himself and Miss Brown in a most peculiar position. She thought that she was being courted by Mark. He was pretending to be his brother, though he had failed quite miserably at that much of the time.

And what of his own vows to himself? He'd sworn never to love again, yet this young woman had managed to steal his heart. How could he ever admit that to Mark? He was not supposed to fall in love or to have any manner of feelings for Miss Brown, yet there they were, complicated and fierce, gentle and tender, all at once.

He stomped up the stairs to his room and sank down, fully clothed, on his bed and lay staring at the ceiling. What a mess! In that moment he realized that he loved Miss Brown. What a torture it would be if she and Mark eventually met and decided to wed. What if she went into that marriage thinking Mark was the man she'd met over the past few days? Did she have feelings for him? From the way she'd looked at him at times, he was sure that she must have, but she'd not said anything. How he'd longed to kiss her when he'd held her so tightly against his body.

But she believed him to be Mark. What would she say if she knew the truth? Would she still want either of them or would she never wish to speak to either twin again? He felt awful for deceiving her. He hated Mark for making him do so. And he didn't know if he could bear it if she and Mark married one day. It would break his heart. Mark was the other half of himself. They had been so close. But if the day came when Mark took Miss Brown to be his bride, Peter was certain that he could not be there to witness it.

The door downstairs creaked open. Peter quickly undressed, jumped into bed, and turned off the lamp. He feigned sleep when Mark whispered into the darkness of his room. "Are you awake? How was the ballet?"

Thankfully, Mark did not persist and closed the door almost silently. Peter heard him padding along the landing to his own room, then the click of the door and the creak of the bedsprings as he sat down. He waited in the darkness until he heard the sound of Mark snoring, then turned on his lamp once more. What could he do? What should he do?

He decided to write a letter to Miss Brown. He wouldn't send it, but there were words he needed to say. He felt like he might burst if he kept them inside. It seemed so peculiar that, after all this time, he should fall so hard and so fast for her. She was perfect. She was lovely to look at, but more importantly, she was easy to talk with, to be with. She enjoyed life with a quiet passion that was infectious. He was in love with her, and he was certain that there was nothing he could ever do that would change that.

But he had agreed to meet her for his brother's sake.

Mark was so painfully shy, and utterly inept when it came to talking with women. Peter had promised Mark that he would do all he could to ensure that she left New York with a good impression of Mark. He was sure that he had at least managed that. Now it was up to Mark to keep that up, to make her happy. And if he didn't? Would Mark be upset if Peter then courted her himself, as himself?

Sadly, he couldn't see a way that anyone would come out of this ridiculous situation happily. If Mark married Miss Brown, Peter would never see either of them again. If things did not go well between Mark and Miss Brown, she might realize that she had never actually met Mark and then she would be angry and would want nothing more to do with either of them. But if perhaps it ended without some kind of revelation, Mark would no doubt be unhappy if Peter were to pursue Miss Brown. How had such a simple and innocent thing become so complicated – and potentially incendiary?

He got out of bed and paced up and down. He had to do as he had done with Ellen before. He had to banish Miss Brown's memory. He had to forget his own feelings for her. He would not lose his brother. No woman was worth that. But a nagging voice in the back of his mind kept telling him that Miss Brown was worth whatever sacrifice was necessary to make her his own.

No!

He had vowed never to trust any woman. He could not let himself do so again. He would not hurt as he had over

Ellen, not for a woman he'd only met twice. He could do this. He could banish her to the very depths of his mind. He'd done it before. He could do it now. He did not love Miss Brown. He was simply infatuated. It would pass. It had to.

CHAPTER 11

OCTOBER 28, 1892, EAGLE CREEK, MONTANA

It was good to be home. Jane was glad to wake up in her tiny cottage and look out and see the mountains and the big sky that made her feel so free. She was keen to get back to her work, to see if Mrs. Albert was happy with the choices she had made, and to start making some of the dresses that she'd been sketching on the train on her way home. It had been a real blessing to see a number of ladies on the train leaving New York as she'd barely noticed anyone in the theater or the restaurant. All she'd been able to see had been Mr. Algood.

Sketching had kept her mind from wandering to thoughts of him, at least until she'd made her way to her sleeping compartment each night. She was still surprised at how easy he had been to talk to and how much she had enjoyed his company. She could hardly wait for his next letter to arrive. She had not gone to New York with thoughts of love and marriage, but she had certainly returned with them. She could think of nothing she wanted more than to become Mrs. Mark Algood.

Hannah, one of the new apprentices, was in the shop when she arrived, hemming a sheet on the sewing machine. "That is looking very good," Jane said, looking at the neat stitches and perfectly straight line. "You've been practicing while I was away."

"Mrs. Albert has had us practicing two hours every day," the girl said, obviously proud that Jane had noticed how much she'd improved. "She says my buttonholes are finally straight, too."

"Well done. Is she out the back?"

"She and Kathy are unpacking the new fabrics. They're lovely, aren't they?"

"They certainly are. I hope Mrs. Albert thinks so, too."

"Oh, she does. She is impressed with how little you got the merchants to charge you, too."

"I had a lot of help from her brother-in-law," Jane admitted.

She went through the shop and into the workshop. Mrs. Albert beamed at her. "Oh, it is wonderful to have you home. You have done very well, my dear."

"Thank you. I didn't want to let you down. Why did you not tell me that one of the merchants was your brother-in-law? By chance, I went to him first, but if I had not, I doubt the prices I got would have been as good."

"Dear Alfred, he's a good man."

"I had dinner with him and his wife."

"How is dear Sarah? I must write to her. It has been too long since we last saw each other."

"She sends her best wishes and hopes you will be well enough to undertake our next buying trip."

"I do, too, but my knees are getting worse, not better," the elderly woman said sadly. She looked down at her gnarled hands. "My fingers, too. I think it may soon be time I admitted that I cannot carry on working so hard."

"We need not think about that now," Jane said, putting an arm around Mrs. Albert's narrow shoulders. "There is time yet. You have the three of us to do all the tricky bits, but we're not ready for you to leave us yet. You have so much still to teach all of us."

"Perhaps that is the answer. I shall buy myself a comfortable armchair and just teach you from a place by the fire."

"We would be content with that," Jane said with a smile, knowing that Mrs. Albert was not ready to retire even if her body wished to make her do so. She loved being in the shop, talking to their customers, and seeing the girls learn and become competent seamstresses.

Jane and Kathy insisted she sit down as they unpacked

the fabric and stored it carefully on the huge rollers in the fabric store so they wouldn't wrinkle. When they were done, the room was a riot of color and texture that would bring happiness to the women of the town for many months to come. Mrs. Albert sent the two girls home and sat down with Jane. "So, did you bring back some patterns, too?"

Jane pulled out her sketch pad and showed her mentor her ideas. "I did these on the train, and I think there are several ways I can adapt them for the women in Eagle Creek. I'd like to cut out a pattern for each of them and make them up to see what I can do. Is there some old fabric I can use?"

"Use whatever you think will suit them best. I'm sure we'll be able to sell them. Your work is always beautiful. And if not, then you should have them. You work hard, and I owe you for going to New York for me."

"That is too much. I know exactly how much those fabrics cost now."

"You took two months out of your life to do something you never wanted to. And there will be times you'll need to do it again, no doubt. You didn't even hesitate to offer to go. I was blessed beyond measure when James brought you to me. You're like the daughter I never had."

Jane felt tears pricking at her eyes. "Thank you," she said, her voice choked with emotion. She'd never had a mother, though Cook had probably been the closest thing to one. But she and Mrs. Albert had been friends from the moment they'd met. Their shared love of sewing and beautiful fabrics had brought them together, and the old lady's kindness and generosity had kept them close.

"I'll fetch us some tea," Jane said a little awkwardly. She needed a moment.

When she returned with a pot of tea and two cups, Mrs. Albert was looking closely at her sketches. "These truly are wonderful, but more importantly, did you meet with your young man?"

Jane poured her a cup of tea and handed it to her. "I did."

"And?"

"And he was wonderful," Jane said with a sigh. "He's very handsome, tall with broad shoulders and chestnut hair. He was kind and funny, and he seemed to like me."

"Then he's a sensible man. Anyone who cannot see how lovely you are is a fool. Will he come and visit you here?"

"You only ask because you want to meet him," Jane teased.

"Indeed. I need to know he's good enough for you," Mrs. Albert said firmly. "I'm not letting you marry just anyone."

"I won't be leaving. You do know that don't you? Whatever happens, Eagle Creek is my home, and my place is here."

"I said the same thing. Luckily, I was blessed that my husband fell in love with Eagle Creek the first time he saw it."

"From what his brother said, he would have lived

anywhere because it was you he fell in love with at first sight. If you'd wanted to live on the moon, he would have found a way to make that happen."

"He did love me," Mrs. Albert said with a soft smile. "He was the finest man I've ever known. Every woman should be loved that much. You deserve to be loved that much."

"Well, we shall see," Jane said. She sipped her tea. "I cannot plan for that. If he loves me, he will let me know, don't you think?"

"I'm sure he will."

～

NOVEMBER 7, 1892, EAGLE CREEK, MONTANA

A letter had arrived from New York. Jane could hardly wait to open it, but she wanted to be alone when she did. She hurried the girls as they swept up and closed the shop and breathed a sigh of relief that resulted in a puff of steamy breath in the cold air as she showed them out and locked up. She hurried home, her coat flapping open as she ripped the envelope open. She took the letter out as soon as she'd closed the front door behind her.

Dear Miss Brown

I cannot tell you how wonderful it was to meet you while

you were in New York. I waited a little before writing to you but didn't want to leave it for too long.

I do so hope that you had a wonderful time and enjoyed our time together. I know that I did, very much. It wasn't what I expected it to be, but perhaps even better than I could have imagined. I was so happy that you enjoyed the ballet. It is not something I attend often, but I do enjoy the music.

I recently read Henry James' The Bostonians. *I must confess that I wasn't entirely sure I liked it, but it was definitely an interesting read. I would think that it might appeal more to a woman than it does to a man. I think I may return to one of my favorites and enjoy some Hardy for a while. I know many think him a little morose, but I rather enjoy his prose. His descriptions of places are some of the finest in all literature in my opinion.*

I do hope that you will write back soon.

Yours, most impatiently

Mark Algood

Something felt different about this letter. Not from Mr. Algood's other letters, but from the man she had met in New York. She supposed that not everyone was an excellent letter writer, but it seemed peculiar that a man who was as open as Mr. Algood had been in person should have reverted to just talking about books. Perhaps he would feel reassured that she still wished to remain in contact once she wrote back. He was probably just a little nervous. She quickly penned a reply, hoping that he would be more like himself when he replied.

She lit the fire, made herself some supper, and sat down in her armchair to read *The Adventures of Huckleberry Finn*. It was a fun set of stories, and she was enjoying the book. She'd read it because Mr. Algood had said that it was a favorite, but such a choice of book seemed unusual now she had met him in person. He'd not really seemed like the kind of man who read much at all, if she was honest, and when she'd asked questions about the books that he'd told her he liked, he'd been a little vague in his responses.

She took out the letters that Mr. Algood had sent to her and read all of them again. Something wasn't quite right, but she couldn't put her finger on what it actually was that felt wrong. She genuinely liked, perhaps even loved, the man she had met in New York, but she wasn't so sure about the man who had written these letters to her. It was like he was two different people. She supposed that she wasn't the same in her letters, either. But should she say something about it or just hope that things would get better?

She would be happy to give the man she had passed so many wonderful hours with the benefit of the doubt. He was all she could have ever dreamed of, and he seemed to genuinely like her. She could hardly believe that. Why should such a man care for her? What could he possibly see in her that he'd not seen in another woman before? She knew she should stop thinking so much about it. It wasn't as if Mr. Algood had ever written her a particularly warm letter, one that had made her heart sing with happiness – but his physical presence absolutely did, and that was surely more important?

There was a knock on her door. Jane looked up, perplexed. Few people would call so late, especially given how cold it was tonight. She opened the door to reveal Marianne, dressed top to toe in fur. "I couldn't wait any longer to hear your news. How did you find New York?"

"Come inside. I think you mean how did I find Mr. Algood."

Marianne grinned and stomped her boots on the mat before she came inside. Jane shut the door behind her as she peeled off her hat and coat. "Hot chocolate?" she asked.

"Ooh, lovely," Marianne said. She went through to the small parlor and started warming herself by the fire.

Jane heated some cream and melted the chocolate into it before taking it through to Marianne. As she sat down, Marianne raised an eyebrow at Jane. "So?"

"He was wonderful. A gentleman. We had a meal together and went to the ballet. Both evenings were magical, but then he sent me this." She handed Marianne the letter.

Marianne skimmed it quickly. "Well, that is a little perfunctory, isn't it?"

"It is, and it is so strange that a man be so different in person and in writing. I've been racking my brains to understand why."

"Some men just aren't good at expressing themselves, Jane. I know James wasn't. He didn't tell me how he felt when we were younger. So many things might have been so different if he had."

"You wouldn't have needed me to be your maid," Jane pointed out.

"Which is why it is best to trust that everything has a reason and purpose," Marianne said. "If James had asked for my hand, you're right, I would not know you. None of us would be here in Montana, and we may have all been more miserable because of it. Because James could not say how he felt, we now have Marla and Flora-Rose and our lives here, where we're all so content."

"Then I shall try to trust that Mr. Algood's reticence in writing does not mean that he does not have strong feelings, and that there is perhaps hope for the future," Jane said determinedly. "Because I think I fell in love with the man I met in New York."

CHAPTER 12

DECEMBER 17, 1892, NEW YORK CITY, NEW YORK

With Thanksgiving a month past and Christmas rapidly approaching, New York had an energy about it that only came during the holiday season. It seemed that there was a never-ending flow of parties to attend, and Peter enjoyed many of them. Some, though, he wished he'd stayed at home for. Mark ignored the festivities, as he did so many other things that brought other people joy. He buried himself in his ledgers and books and tried to ignore the extravagant spending going on around him.

"Brother, you need to take some time off," Peter begged

him. "At least come with me to Cable Poole's ball tonight? It will be fun, with lots of pretty girls to dance with."

"I don't want to dance with pretty girls," Mark grumbled.

"Why would any man not want to dance with a pretty girl? What is wrong with you, brother?"

"Miss Brown wrote back."

"Then what possible reason do you have to be so morose?"

Mark pulled the letter out of his pocket. It had obviously come some time ago as the paper was dogeared and ripped in places from being kept there and occasionally pulled out to be read.

Dear Mr. Algood,

Thank you for everything. I cannot tell you how much I enjoyed our time together while I was in New York. You were such wonderful company. I've rarely felt so comfortable with a stranger as I was with you.

And I must beg you to let me pay my share of our meal and the wonderful visit to the ballet? I know it is not usually for a woman to pay for such things, but it feels peculiar to me to not pay my way. I've been looking after myself for so long that I am just not used to it, I suppose.

But much as I loved my time in New York, it is so very wonderful to be home. I am not a traveler. I hate being away from my own bed for such long periods of time and never sleep well. My little cottage is small, just a tiny parlor with a kitchen and bedroom above, but it is all mine, and that feels like such an achievement given my start in life.

I did not ever expect much for my life, growing up in the orphanage. Nobody expected any of us to amount to much. But my life has been unexpectedly blessed and has led me here to Eagle Creek, a place I never wish to leave. I do wish you could visit me here. I think you would enjoy the wide-open skies and the feeling of freedom living here gives. The towering buildings of New York are impressive, but do you not think that they can sometimes be overpowering and oppressive?

But there is beauty there, too. You just have to look a little harder to find it, I suppose. I cannot tell you the emotions that the ballet brought out in me. I have never seen anything so beautiful, and I get to watch eagles soaring overhead every single day. Perhaps it was so wonderful because it was so rare for me? Would the eagles win your heart more easily than a ballet because they are different for you, I wonder?

I've not read the Henry James book you spoke of, but I did read The Adventures of Huckleberry Finn. *It is a charming collection of stories, though I rather felt that it may suit young boys and men more than most girls. I've not had much time to read since I returned as there was all that fabric to unpack and new patterns to make up. I sketched some ideas on the train on my way home and have made them up now. I'm rather pleased with them, to tell you the truth. I feared that I might not have quite caught the essence of what I saw in New York, but it seems my eye is better than I feared.*

Please do say that you will think about coming to visit me here? I so long to talk with you again, properly, face to face. It is so much nicer that way, don't you agree?

Yours, most hopefully

Jane Brown

"This is a perfectly wonderful letter," Peter said. "Any man would be happy to receive such a thing from such a woman."

"You mean that you would be happy to receive it. After all, she is talking to you, isn't she?" Mark said a little bitterly.

"You asked me to meet her because you were too shy," Peter pointed out. "I did not want to, remember?"

"But you got on well with her, didn't you? You liked her, and she liked you? And now she thinks she is writing to you, because – well, she's never written like this to me before. This is full of what she thinks and how she feels because that is what you talked about with her, isn't it? My letter to her must have seemed so stilted and strange after she had spent time with you. I should have just met her myself, even if it would have been a disaster. Anything but thinking that she wants you."

"She doesn't want me," Peter insisted. "We have nothing in common, unlike the two of you. You just need to write back to her in the same spirit that she has written to you."

"Didn't you read it? She wants me to visit her there, by her blasted creek."

"Then go. You might find that you like it there."

"I hate the countryside. You know that. I'm made for the city."

"You don't know that," Peter pointed out. "And you did used to enjoy visiting our grandparents. You may like it more than you think. As you said yourself, the noise and chaos here is often overwhelming for you. You might come to love the tranquility there. Write to her. Say you'll visit. Have an adventure for once in your life, Mark."

"But she doesn't want to ever leave, which means there is little point. If she won't leave Eagle Creek and I have no desire to leave New York, why should we bother?"

"Because one of you might change your mind. Love makes people do strange things, Mark. And believe me, you want to get to know her properly. She is quite lovely."

"Come with me, at least? I can't bear a trip like that alone."

"No, I can't always be there to rescue you."

"I need you there to tell me what to say and do. You know what the two of you talked about, and you know I will ruin everything if I am left alone with her. Please. You have to come."

Peter sighed. "I have things to do here."

"We'll go as soon as *The Madelaine* departs. You'll have months with nothing to do before she returns."

Peter had to admit that Mark had him there. Once his ship had set sail again, there would be little for him to do and nothing to keep him in New York. And though he would never admit it to anyone else, he did want to see Miss Brown and Eagle Creek even if Mark didn't. He missed her every single day. It was the strangest thing. He longed to see her smile, the way her cheeks dimpled so gently, and the way her lovely eyes shone when she was happy.

"I'll come, but we don't go until after Christmas. I'm happy to miss New Year's Eve balls, but I will not spend Christmas in a hotel, or even worse on a train."

"I shall write to her immediately."

"Tell her something real in your letters, something you feel – not just something you read or think you should say," Peter said. "Women like to know what's happening in your head, not just the bare facts of your life."

Mark nodded and disappeared, leaving Peter alone with his thoughts. He hoped that Mark would listen to his advice. He'd find things much easier with Miss Brown if he just gave a little of himself to her. He wondered what she would think about her suitor dragging his twin brother with him to see her, especially as she'd not been introduced to him in New York. If he were her, he'd think it strange. But Mark didn't seem to mind that his behavior made him seem peculiar. He just wanted to make the best impression he could, and Peter couldn't hold that against him.

JANUARY 30, 1893, EAGLE CREEK, MONTANA

"We're here," Peter called to his brother. Mark didn't move. Peter took his bag down from the rack above their heads and then shook Mark roughly. "Wake up, we're here."

Mark opened his eyes and yawned loudly. "Thank heavens. I think I'm starting to understand why Miss Brown doesn't like traveling. My backside is numb from sitting on these terribly uncomfortable seats."

"I don't think that is why she dislikes traveling," Peter said, pointing out of the window at the soaring, snow-covered mountains, "though it probably doesn't help matters much. I think she just found her home and hates the idea of leaving it."

"Brrr, it is so cold here," Mark said as he opened the door to the carriage and a blast of arctic air hit them. "I thought winter in New York was terrible, but this is beyond anything I could have imagined."

"Wrap up and stop complaining." Peter threw a fur hat and mittens at him, then climbed out of the carriage and looked around.

The station was small but busy. People hurried to get

their belongings from the train or to get themselves onto it. A young lad with a cart hurried toward him. "Got any luggage?" he asked cheerfully, his breath misting on the icy air.

"A trunk in the baggage cart. Name's Algood."

"Very good, Sir," the boy said before speeding off.

Mark clambered down from the train and skidded on a patch of icy snow on the platform. He landed on his backside with a clump. "Ow," he moaned, rubbing his derriere as he stood up. "Nobody sensible could truly want to live here, surely?"

"I'd move here tomorrow," Peter said happily as the lad reappeared with their trunk. "We're booked at The Eyrie. Can you give us directions please?"

"They'll send down a sled for you if they know you're coming today," the boy told him.

"How civilized," Peter said, looking pointedly at Mark.

They made their way out of the station, and as the boy had predicted, a large sleigh was waiting for them with a pair of pretty white horses in the shafts. "How much further?" Mark asked the driver as he climbed in and wrapped a thick woolen blanket around his knees.

"The Eyrie is about half an hour up the mountain," the driver said happily. Mark mumbled something incomprehensible to himself, but he was clearly unhappy.

Peter helped the driver with their trunk and climbed in beside his brother. "You might try to at least be polite," he said angrily. "These people are Miss Brown's friends and neighbors. You'll not win her heart unless you win theirs, too."

"Stop telling me how to win her heart. You've been schooling me every minute of the day on what she'll like and what she won't. You're hardly an expert. Your fiancée left you at the altar and ran away with your oldest friend, remember? You don't have much experience in predicting what women want."

"Maybe I didn't then, but much has changed since," Peter pointed out. "You were much nicer then, for a start. You've become a grumpy old man, and you're barely into your thirtieth year."

They didn't speak for the rest of the journey. Mark because his teeth were chattering from the cold and because he was too angry to say anything without shouting, and Peter because he was overwhelmed by how beautiful everything around him was. He'd found the town of Eagle Creek to be quaint and charming, but as they drove further away from it, higher into the mountains, he found himself understanding what Miss Brown had meant about the big sky here. It seemed to go on forever. It made him feel both very small and very free all at once.

The hotel was as luxurious as any in New York, yet Mark found things to grumble about there, too. Peter was furious with him. He'd not made even the tiniest effort to try to enjoy their trip here. He was rude and surly with the staff at the hotel, and he closed himself off inside his bedchamber and refused to come out even to eat once their bags had been brought up to their suite.

Peter went down to the dining room alone. He soon made friends with some of the other guests staying there and was invited to join an elderly couple from Chicago for supper. He had a most enjoyable evening listening to their stories of coming here in summer when the sky was blue and the meadows were in bloom with wildflowers everywhere. "I must come again," he said to them.

"Oh, you must. If we could, we'd never leave," Mrs. Padget said with a smile. "Perhaps we shall be able to when Monty retires from the bank."

"Well, I shall bid you goodnight and hope that we will meet again in the morning," Peter said.

"Good night, young man. It has been a pleasure meeting you," Mr. Padget said. "If you'd like to join us tomorrow, we're taking the sleigh further up into the mountains."

"I would like that, but I shall have to see how my brother is feeling. He's a little tired and overwrought from the traveling."

"We understand. Just let us know at breakfast," Mrs. Padget said, patting his hand affectionately.

Peter went up to the suite. Mark's door was still closed. He stood at the window and looked out into the darkness. He should never have forced Mark into the trip. He should have let him stay away. Because knowing that Miss Brown was barely half an hour away was half killing him. He longed to hurry back down the mountain, knock on her door, and beg her to give him her heart. But then he would have to explain everything, and he wasn't sure that he could.

Reluctantly, he went to bed, where he lay awake wondering what would happen when Mark and Miss Brown actually met. Mark couldn't put it off any longer. He'd come all this way. Surely, he would make the effort this time? For her sake, Peter wanted things to work out between Miss Brown and his twin. She had liked the man she thought was Mark enough to invite him here so he could meet her friends and see her world. He could not bear the thought that she might feel in any way let down, or hurt, by Mark's cowardice and deception.

CHAPTER 13

JANUARY 31, 1893, EAGLE CREEK, MONTANA

"*I* can't," Mark said firmly. "I've barely slept a wink all night. I've made the most dreadful mistake coming here. I thought I could do it, but I just can't."

"Mark Algood. Never have I been so ashamed to call you my brother," Peter said, shaking his head in disbelief. They had come all this way to see Miss Brown, and now Mark was refusing to join her for luncheon in the hotel's restaurant. "She's waiting for you. She has taken time away from her work so that she can meet you. The least you can do is join her for lunch."

"I know that. The bellboy just brought me the note

saying she'd arrived, remember?" Mark said sarcastically. "But it doesn't change the simple fact that she thinks she is meeting you."

"No, she thinks she is meeting you. She thought that in New York, and I did my best to make sure she met you even though you were too cowardly to face her."

"I know it. I am a coward. And I am sure you did your best to be dull and uninspiring, but you find that as impossible as I do to seem interesting and at ease with people," Mark pointed out. "I just don't want to disappoint her. She wants to stay here, to live here, in this arctic wonderland of hers. I despise it. I hate being cold. I hate mountains and all this space everywhere. It makes me feel insignificant, unnecessary, and as if all I have striven for has no purpose."

"Maybe it has none," Peter said with a shrug. "Perhaps we would all be happier if we acknowledged that so much of what we do is meaningless in the grander scheme of things."

"This is the difference between us," Mark said sadly. "You actually like it here, don't you? I saw your face as we drove up here yesterday. You're enchanted by it. I can't wait to get away, to get home."

"You have to meet her and tell her that, then," Peter said firmly. "She loves her home. She won't leave it for New York. You need to be honest with her and let her know what you are thinking."

"But what if she is my only chance at happiness?"

"How happy will you be if everything has been built upon lies?"

Mark frowned at him, his brow furrowing deeply. "Don't," he begged. "I know I should, but surely it would be easier to do so by letter? Once we are back in New York?"

"I'm sure it would be, but that does not change the fact that Miss Brown is waiting for you in the dining room now. You cannot leave her there indefinitely."

"Please, be me again," Mark asked, his eyes pleading with Peter. "You'll know what to say, how to be polite and kind. I'll only make her miserable if I go and meet her now."

"No, Mark. This is your mess. I'll not keep cleaning it up for you," Peter said firmly. "Miss Brown deserves better than this."

"So give her better, give her you. We both know that I don't have the way with words that you do. You'll charm her and make her memories of me happy, at least. Peter, you have to do this. She is expecting you anyway. She's never even met me."

Peter scowled at his brother and shook his head. He reached for his jacket. "I do this for her, not for you," he said as he let himself out of the suite.

Fuming, he stomped along the corridor. Mark was such a coward. Peter should never have agreed to meet Miss Brown on his behalf. If he'd not done that, they wouldn't be here now. No doubt, after meeting Mark in person, Miss Brown would have found some polite reason to stop writing to him.

As it was, Peter had been dragged across the country to help his twin try to woo a young lady that he himself had strong feelings for. Yet, he could never tell her that. Whatever happened between Mark and Miss Brown now, she would never forgive either of them for their deception if she ever found out.

He saw Miss Brown, sitting in the foyer waiting for him, as he ran down the stairs. She looked lovely. Her cheeks were pink from the cold air outside, and she looked a little nervous. She was fidgeting with her coat and hat in her lap. He hurried toward her. "Good day," he said, bowing to her politely. She looked a little flustered as she stood up and let him take her hand and kiss the air above it. "You look lovely."

"Thank you," she said, awkwardly tucking a stray strand of hair behind her ear.

"I'm sorry to have kept you waiting," Peter said. He offered her his arm and escorted her into the dining room.

"Don't worry," she said with a shy smile. "I was a little early. How was your journey here? It is quite draining, isn't it?"

"It wasn't the most pleasant time I've ever spent, but all discomfort was worth it to be here now."

"You probably didn't get to see much of the mountains. It must have been almost dark when you arrived."

"I saw enough to know I want to see more," he said. "It

was still quite light when the train arrived, though it grew quite dark very quickly as we drove here."

"I could arrange to hire a gig and could show you the most important places at the weekend," she said eagerly as he held out her chair for her. Peter felt a pang of guilt. He should be honest with her about that. Mark was probably already getting ready to leave the next day.

"That would be lovely, though I hope to do a little exploring of my own. I'm afraid I may not be able to stay for as long as we'd hoped for. Pressing business in New York calls me back sooner than I'd like."

"You can stay until the weekend, at least?"

"I certainly hope so. After all, with a four-week train journey, what would a few days matter?"

She beamed, and Peter knew that he would stay even if Mark did not. He could not bring himself to disappoint her. As they dined and talked endlessly about all manner of topics, Peter wished that things had been different, and he had been the one to encounter Miss Brown first.

She was such a lovely creature, sweet and unassuming, clever but not overbearing. She wasn't glamorous or refined as the young women in New York were. But though she was not naïve, thanks to her difficult upbringing, she was not hard about it. There was a softness to her that he had never encountered before, she was precisely who she said she was, and there was no pretense about her. She did not try to be someone she was not. It was most refreshing, and the more they talked, the more Peter thought his brother a fool.

When their meal was finished, Miss Brown got up to leave. "Might I escort you down the mountain?" Peter asked her. "I would very much like to see the town properly, and where you work."

She flushed with pleasure. "I would like that," she said. "Though I cannot tarry too long. There is always so much work to be done."

"I am grateful that your Mrs. Albert was able to spare you this long," Peter said as they walked through to the lobby. "If you will wait for me just a few minutes, I shall fetch my coat."

"I shall arrange for the gig to be brought around," she said with a smile. She crossed the lobby to the counter as Peter ran upstairs, taking the stairs two at a time.

Mark was staring morosely out of the window when Peter returned. "You have been gone such a long time," he complained.

"You tasked me with taking your place at lunch with a delightful young lady. Did you expect me to gobble my food down and hurry her out of the door?"

"I'm sorry. I just can't wait to get away from this place. You have told her that we are leaving?"

"I told her that I have pressing business to return for but a few days here will not much matter. If you wish to leave, then go. I intend to stay at least until after the weekend."

"I thought you didn't want to hurt her?"

"I don't," Peter said. "But arriving one day and leaving the next would be most rude. You'll be able to write to her after I return and say that you think you wouldn't suit after enough time to consider it."

"I don't want to say that, though," Mark whined.

"But you cannot bring yourself to even meet her, so unless you hope to have a marriage by correspondence, there is little reason to waste her time further," Peter said a little harshly. "She deserves a man who can respect her enough to be there himself, not send another in his stead."

"You agreed to it."

"I did, and I should not have done so. But after this week, I'll not be a part of this any longer. It isn't fair on her, or me."

He grabbed his coat and hat and left Mark alone again with his thoughts. Peter wondered if Mark had even considered what he was passing up with his petulance. He doubted it. His brother's social anxieties were so hard for him to bear, but he should not have gotten his own or Miss Brown's hopes up by writing to her. If he'd thought things through properly, before he'd sent that first letter, then all of this could have been avoided.

One of the bellboys had brought Miss Brown's coat just as Peter returned. He helped her into it, and they walked outside. It was a clear, bright day. The sky was impossibly blue. The snow had been cleared from the paths around the hotel but lay undisturbed like a thick white carpet over the meadows and mountain peaks. It was truly perfect. Unable to help himself, he smiled at the sights all around him and took a deep breath of the fresh, mountain air.

Miss Brown giggled. "I always do that," she said. "It doesn't seem to matter how long I live here, the sights still take my breath away and bring delight to my heart."

"It is spectacular," Peter agreed. "I'm not surprised that you don't enjoy traveling when you live here."

"I didn't enjoy traveling even before I saw this place. My journey here with Marianne was so long, and I hate being cooped up in such a small space. No matter how luxurious our passage, it was torture for me."

"I can understand that. We traveled first class, and I've never been so uncomfortable in all my life."

He helped her into the waiting gig and took the reins from the stable boy and handed them up to her. "I do hope you know how to drive this thing as I've never had to drive a vehicle in all my life."

She grinned. "I do. I can teach you if you'd like. It's easy enough."

He climbed up beside her. "I'll leave the reins in your capable hands for now, but perhaps you might give me my first lesson on Saturday?"

"I'd like that," she said, then clicked softly to the pony in the shafts.

They moved off steadily. "Is this your gig?" Peter asked her.

"No, I rented it from the public stables. You can hire almost anything there. I was lucky that there was no snow this morning and that the road had been cleared. I don't like driving the sleds, though they are much safer than a light vehicle like this when it is icy and the snow is thick on the ground."

"You drive very well," Peter remarked. "Your hands are so soft on the reins. The horse barely knows you're there."

"That is the secret, or so I'm told. Be gentle with an animal and it'll do what you want without you even having to ask. Percy is a dear, though," she said, nodding to the pony. "I can trust him to find his own way much of the time, he knows his job so well."

The time passed too quickly, and they were soon driving into the town. Miss Brown pointed out each shop and business, waved to friends, and even introduced him to a few people. She turned the gig into a large, gated yard opposite the station and brought it to a stop. "We're here."

Peter jumped down and hurried around the gig to help her down, but she had already descended and was handing the reins to a young lad. "Thank you, Jake," she said. "Perhaps you could arrange a suitable mount for my friend, Mr. Algood?"

"Will do, Miss Jane," the boy said with a smile. He

unhitched the pony from the shafts of the gig and led him toward the stalls.

"I must leave you, now," Miss Brown said softly. "Thank you for a lovely lunch."

"It was my pleasure," Peter assured her. "Might I call on you on Saturday morning? For that driving lesson you promised me?"

"I would like that," she said shyly. "I would like that very much."

CHAPTER 14

*J*ane had hardly slept, but she felt perfectly well. She dressed quickly and waited for the knock on her door impatiently. She found it a little hard to believe that Mr. Algood's letters could possibly have been written by the same man as the erudite and charming one that she had spent time with. She could only assume that he just didn't feel comfortable committing himself to paper.

Finally, he arrived. She opened the door before he'd even made his way up the garden path. He beamed at her, and she felt her breath catch. He was so unutterably handsome. She could hardly believe that a man like him could be interested in a plain girl like her.

"Well, it seems that we have the weather for my first lesson," he said happily as he bent to kiss the back of her hand. This time, his lips brushed her skin, ever so lightly. She felt a shiver course through her body that had nothing to do with the cold.

"Indeed, we have had such lovely weather for your visit," she agreed. "I am so glad that the sun has shone for you."

"I don't think I've ever walked so much, especially not in the winter," he said. "Mr. King gave me a map and marked out a number of trails that would be safe to pass despite all the snow. It was quite wonderful. I don't know if you've seen it, but the waterfall about a mile from The Eyrie was quite magnificent, swollen as it was with meltwater – but there were the most spectacular icicles that I have ever seen hanging from the rocks, too."

"I've not been to the waterfall," she admitted. "I must confess that I did not even know there was one. Perhaps you might show it to me before you leave?"

"I would be delighted," Mr. Algood said. "Perhaps tomorrow, after church? I assume you will be attending?"

"I shall," she said. "And you must join me for lunch at my friend, Marianne's. She has insisted that you do."

"She wants to check me out, no doubt."

"You may be right," Jane said with a smile. "She's my

best friend and the closest thing to an older sister that I've ever had. Are you missing your twin while you are here?"

"Not one bit," Peter said happily. "We are as different as chalk and cheese. It is nice to be away from him for a while."

"I'm sure you can't be that different. You're twins, after all."

"You'd be amazed," he said drily.

"I've asked Jake to have the gig ready for us for ten o'clock," Jane said. "I thought we could go to the bakery on our way there, to get something delicious for a picnic? You do like picnics, I hope?"

"I love picnics, though I don't think I've ever considered one in such cold temperatures before."

"We shall take blankets, too," she assured him. "And we can build a fire down by the creek to warm us."

"Then I am in favor of winter picnics," he said, offering her his arm.

There was a line coming out of the bakery. It only opened for a few hours on a Saturday morning, so the towns-folk could buy all they needed for the weekend. The smells emanating from the shop as they waited were mouthwater-ing. Jane felt her stomach grumble and willed it to be quiet. She'd not been able to eat breakfast because she'd been too excited.

Once inside, she made a selection of some pies and pastries that would travel well. Mr. Algood's eyes were wide, and he insisted on paying for everything – including some delicious treats for them to eat straight away. Jane wondered if he'd heard her belly rumbling. Perhaps he'd been as nervous as her and missed breakfast, too. They munched happily on flaky, buttery pastries with plump sultanas in them. "These are wonderful," he announced.

"I've not tried them before, but they are. I shall have to add them to my basket more often," she agreed.

Jonas Gilpin, the town's blacksmith, greeted them warmly at the public stable. "I was expecting to see Jake or Walks With The Sun," Jane said as he took their money for the gig rental.

"I let them have the weekend to themselves," Jonas said. "They work hard all week, but they're young and need time to enjoy themselves."

"You are a good master," she said.

"I try. But they are easy apprentices to teach, so I am blessed."

"How is Geraldine? And Teddy?"

"They are both well. Teddy is excelling in his studies, and we are all trying to get the house ready in time for when his grandparents move here next month."

"Is there much to do? I can help if you need an extra hand."

"I shall tell Geraldine. She will be glad of your assistance."

"It will be my pleasure."

He glanced over at Mr. Algood. "Good to see you again."

"And you, Mr. Gilpin."

"Are you enjoying your time with us?"

"I am. You are blessed to live somewhere so magnificent."

"We like it," Jonas said. "But I shouldn't keep you. No doubt you have much to fill your time with."

"Thank you, Jonas," Jane said, taking the reins from him.

Mr. Algood helped her up. Though she didn't need his assistance, she rather liked that he was so gallant with her. She'd never been treated that way before. As a servant for much of her life, she'd been expected to fend for herself. It felt a little strange to be treated like a lady, but she was not going to say anything to stop him from doing so. It made her feel very special and as though somebody cared about her.

He climbed up beside her, and they drove out of the yard. She guided the pony through the town and out to a quiet stretch of road just outside the town limits, then handed Peter the reins.

"It's not like riding," she explained as she adjusted them a little. She could tell that he found it strange as he kept slipping back to the way he'd hold them if he were on horseback. She smiled and corrected him each time. "Now, when you ride, much of your intention goes through your body. The way you shift weight tells the horse which way to go. You don't have that when driving. Everything goes through the reins," she explained. "In the beginning, you'll overcorrect, thinking they need an obvious signal, but just the lightest touch tells a pony all it needs to know."

She showed him how to click his tongue. He'd never tried before, so it took him a little while to master it, but when he did, he looked so proud of himself that she longed to lean over and kiss him. She did not, of course. "Why not try to get him to walk?" she suggested.

Mr. Algood clicked to the pony and slapped the reins gently across his rump, as she'd shown him. Percy eased into a walk. "Try to turn him a little," Jane encouraged.

Mr. Algood did so, using the right rein and then the left. As Jane had predicted, he was too generous in his directions and poor Percy almost took them off the road. "Gently," she encouraged. "Tiny, tiny movements. Remember, he knows his business better than you do."

Mr. Algood tried again. This time, he was able to get Percy to negotiate a pothole in the road and then assume a straight line again. He beamed. "I did it."

"Yes, you did. Now, why not try it at a trot?"

He slapped Percy's rump again with both reins, and the pony picked up his hooves and began to trot. They made their way around another bump in the road. "You're a natural," Jane said happily.

"Thanks to you," Mr. Algood said. "You're a good teacher."

"I think you'll find that much of it is down to how well

schooled Percy is," she said. "I'm not sure how many other ponies I'd be able to drive as well, myself."

"He is a fine animal, much better than most in the public stables I've come across."

"Jonas insists that his animals are the best quality," Jane explained. "And he takes good care of them. His apprentice, Walks With The Sun, is Crow. They are people of the horse, and Jonas is the first to admit that he's learned much from the boy."

"It is a rare man that admits he can learn from those younger than him."

"Jonas is definitely that," Jane said.

"It sounds as though you perhaps harbor feelings for him," Mr. Algood said cautiously.

Jane stared at him. "Oh, no, not at all. Not like that, at least," she assured him. "He is a kind and good man, but he is married to one of the loveliest ladies I know. And he's so tall and big. I always feel so tiny when I'm near him. I would be afraid of him if I didn't know him to be such a good man."

Mr. Algood smiled weakly. He didn't look convinced by her answer. Jane was secretly delighted. He was jealous. She'd never known a man to be jealous because of her feelings for someone else before. It made her feel oddly powerful, but she did not want him to think that there was anyone else before him in her affections. "I can assure you that I have no romantic feelings toward him, at all," she said quietly.

"Good," he said softly, staring deeply into her eyes. His gaze was soft, but it made her feel suddenly self-conscious. Her skin prickled as though she were hearing a heavenly choir. She gazed back at him, losing herself in the deep pools of his hazel eyes, and wondered if she would ever feel about any other man the way she did about him. Yet there was still so much left unsaid between them. She still could not make any sense of why he was so different in person from the way he was in his letters. And she needed to know.

"Why are your letters always so perfunctory," she said, pulling away and breaking the spell that had fallen between them. He stared at her, looking puzzled. "I mean, when we are together, you are so open and we have such wonderful conversations, but your letters are so stilted. It is as though you are searching desperately for something to say but have no idea where to start."

He shook his head and gave a wry chuckle. "You could say that I am two men, I suppose."

"But you aren't, so that is a silly thing to say."

"I just find it easier to talk to anyone in person," he said. "And you are so very easy to talk with. I have enjoyed our times together very much indeed."

"I have, too."

"I'm glad. But I must return to New York on Monday,"

he said regretfully. "I wish I could stay, but there is much that I need to do upon my return."

"I understand," she said sadly. "It will be hard for me to say goodbye to you again, but your life is there."

"And yours is here."

"Are our worlds perhaps too far apart?" she asked anxiously.

"I fear they may be. I cannot just leave New York, and I can understand entirely why you would not wish to leave this place now you have found it. I am not entirely sure where that leaves us if I am utterly honest with you."

She nodded. She didn't like his answer, but she understood it. He had said out loud the thing she had feared might happen when she'd posted her advertisement – that she would find the right man, but it would be entirely the wrong time for them. Right then, they needed different things. She could not bear the thought of living in New York and leaving her home here. He just could not up and leave all he had built in the city to live here. They would part on Monday, and she doubted if they would ever see each other again.

"I know that we are essentially saying goodbye," she said as she took the reins from him and drove them back towards the town. "But could we just enjoy the rest of today and tomorrow as if we have every intention of this friendship continuing?"

He took her hand in his. "I can do that. It will break my heart to leave you, but I have no choice."

CHAPTER 15

*P*eter was determined that today would be the most special day of Miss Brown's life. She had looked so sad when they had acknowledged the painful truth that their circumstances simply could not be reconciled at this time. He hated that he had not been able to tell her why, that he had spoken as Mark rather than himself, because the more time he spent with her, the more he longed to throw everything he had worked for in New York away, to come here and be with her. But she did not know that he was Peter. She still thought that he was the man who wrote terrible letters to her, and he did not ever want her to know about how Mark had deceived her.

As heavy snow had fallen overnight, he had arranged for a sled driver to pick them up and take them up the mountain to the waterfall after lunch at the Dennys' house. He hoped that she would love it as much as he had. It was such a special place, and he longed to share it with her.

All through this morning's church service and lunch with the rowdy Denny clan, he'd been anxious to have her all to himself again. He wanted to savor every moment, for he knew that it would be all he'd ever have. After Ellen had left him the way she had, he had never had any intention of letting anyone into his heart again. It had come as a surprise that Miss Brown had quietly let herself in and made his heart hers. And it was a travesty that nothing could come of it.

The driver of the sled knocked on the door at exactly three o'clock. "That's for us," he whispered to her.

She stood up. "I'm sorry, but it seems that Mr. Algood has something planned for us. Thank you so much for a delicious lunch, Marianne."

"It has been our pleasure," their elegant hostess said graciously. She gave Jane a hug and whispered something in her ear that Peter could not quite make out. "And I do hope that we will be graced with your presence at our table again in the future, Mr. Algood."

"I would like that very much," he said politely.

Mr. Delaney shook his hand. "Look after our Jane," he said with a stern look. "She's precious."

"I agree wholeheartedly."

Marianne slapped her husband playfully. "Stop scaring him, James."

Peter could see that both of them were concerned for Jane. He wanted to reassure them that he had no desire to ever bring her pain, but he could not as he knew that they would soon be saying goodbye and both of them would feel the wrench of their parting deeply. He shook Mr. Delaney's hand and kissed the air above Mrs. Denny's. "Thank you, again."

Outside, he tucked Miss Brown up in plenty of blankets in the rear of the sled before taking the seat beside her. "What did she whisper to you?" he asked as they sped through the town.

"That she hoped I wasn't making a terrible mistake, spending this time with you, knowing we are to say goodbye tomorrow."

"Ah," Peter said. "I thought it might be something like that."

"They are worried for me. They've never seen me with a young man before. They just want me to be safe and happy."

"And what do you want?"

"Am I allowed to say?" she asked lightly. He nodded. "Then I want you to stay."

"I only wish I could," he said, taking her hands in his. He peeled off her mitten and pressed a kiss to the very center of her palm. "I have never felt the way I do about you for anyone before."

"It is a shame we live so very far apart." She sighed as he put an arm around her shoulder. She leaned against him, her head fitting perfectly into the crook of his neck. It felt so right to sit this way, to be so close that she could feel his warmth through her thick fur coat.

He should tell her the truth. But he didn't dare. He didn't want to ruin the moment. This day had to be perfect. He wanted to leave her with a positive memory, a happy and loving memory of their time together. He wanted that for himself, too, because a lifetime without her was going to be the hardest thing he'd ever have to face.

The sled sped up the mountain, past The Eyrie, and up toward the waterfall. The driver brought it to a halt a short walk away. Peter nodded to him to wait, then helped Miss Brown out of her cocoon of blankets. He took her by the hand and led her along the path. It was more slippery today, thanks to the fresh snow, so they walked slowly. He lost his footing on a hidden rock, making her laugh. When she did the same thing just a few steps further on, he was enough of a gentleman not to laugh.

They could hear the sound of the water from some way away even though they couldn't see the waterfall itself. Miss Brown's face was a picture of excitement. Peter was glad he had brought her here. He tried to imagine Ellen's face if he had taken her to see a waterfall. No doubt she would be disgusted that he'd even think she might be interested, much less that she wished to get her gown muddy or have to wear a thick fur coat and go out in the snow to do so. The two women were as different as he and Mark, and he had been such a fool to think himself in love with Ellen all those years ago.

Now, he knew what love truly was. It meant sacrifice for the sake of the person you loved. He was ready to walk away so that Miss Brown would never know how badly she had been duped by himself and Mark. He hated that he had to do so, but Mark had not once considered anyone else's feelings but his own in this matter, so it was down to him to do so.

They turned the corner, and the waterfall was finally revealed. Miss Brown gasped audibly, even above the roar of the tumbling water. She raised her mittened hands to her face, covering her mouth as she stared wide-eyed at the phenomenal power of the water crashing down over hundreds of feet of rocks. "Thank you," she murmured. "I've never seen anything like this before."

"I'm just glad I was able to find a little secret pocket that you've not yet found," he said, delighted at her reaction. She turned back to the water but surprisingly leaned back against his body. Peter held his breath as he placed his hands gently on her hips. She pulled them around her waist and they stood quietly, her head on his chest, his arms around her, for the longest time. Her mittened hands kept his ungloved ones warm. He bent his head and kissed the top of hers without even thinking about it.

She turned her head slightly and smiled up at him.

Unable to stop himself, he claimed her lips for his own. They were soft and sweet, tasting faintly of the cherry pie they'd had for dessert. She turned fully and slipped her arms around his waist as he deepened the kiss, and she kissed him back fervently. He held her close, not wanting to ever let her go. "Oh, Jane."

"I wish you weren't leaving," she said sadly. "I didn't want to think about it today, but it is always there, isn't it? You are going, and this is the end."

How could he leave her? How could he not at least try to explain the truth and hope that she might forgive him and tell him she still wanted him to stay?

"There is something I should tell you," he said, extricating himself from her arms. "I swore I wouldn't, at least not today. I wanted us to have this one perfect day."

"What is it, Mark?" she asked, reaching out as if she wanted to pull him back and comfort him. He winced at her use of his brother's name. He'd emboldened her to do so by using her name.

He exhaled sharply and loudly. "Curse him," he said loudly, turning away from her for a moment as he tried to compose himself.

"Curse who?" she asked innocently.

"Mark," he said bluntly.

"Mark? But you're Mark." She looked utterly bewildered. He hated himself for doing this to her, but she had to know. He had to try to tell her how he felt, and he could not do that while she thought he was his brother.

"No, I'm Mark's twin, Peter," he said softly.

"His twin?" She looked aghast. "But, but you've, I've…"

"Let me explain, please, Miss Brown?" he begged her.

"Explain," she said curtly. "And quickly, before I leave in the sled and leave you here to make your own way back."

"Mark wrote to you. He was the one who replied to your advertisement," Peter said quickly, "but he wasn't who you met in New York."

"That was you?"

"Yes."

"What was I? A bet? A joke between you?"

"Nothing of the kind. He truly wrote to you hoping to find a wife, I promise you that."

"So why did he not come and meet me then?"

"Because he is shy and knows that he does not express himself well when there are pretty young women around. He begged me to go in his stead, to make a good impression upon you."

"Oh, how you must have laughed when you told him that you had, that you'd had me eating out of your palm," she spat at him angrily.

"It truly wasn't like that," Peter tried to assure her. "I liked you. I really liked you, from the first."

"But not enough to tell me the truth."

"I felt it wasn't my place to do so. Mark had trusted me. He knew I was safe because I took a vow years ago, never to marry, never to fall in love again. He trusted me to be him with you."

"And yet he sent you again, even after you'd made his first impression," Miss Brown said, her eyes flashing angrily. "Little wonder that you seemed like two completely different people."

"No, it is no wonder at all," Peter agreed. "He begged me to come here with him. He did at least come here, but he hated it and he was so afraid that you wouldn't like him, and he just couldn't meet you."

"So, what has this been about?" she asked, raising her arms to suggest the romantic setting of the waterfall. "If you have no intentions of falling in love, you have certainly done all that you could to ensure that I did. Did you do that for Mark, too? Or for your own amusement."

"Miss Brown, never for that, you have to believe me," Peter said, wounded by her words. "I liked you from the first moment I met you, and my feelings only grew as we grew closer. It got harder and harder to tell you the truth. I realized that I had fallen in love with you despite my vow."

"This is not love," she said, shaking her head. "I don't know what this is, but it is not love. It is as well that you are leaving tomorrow, for I don't think I ever want to see you again."

She marched away from him. "Jane," he called out. "Miss Brown, please."

She did not turn around. She could not. Tears were pouring down her face. She had trusted him. She had let him woo her, and he had won her heart, but he was not the man she'd thought him to be. She wasn't sure who he was anymore. He was not Mark Algood, after all. But who Peter Algood was, she had no idea, and she wasn't sure that she wanted to find out.

She half ran, half walked back to the sled. "Take me home," she said to the driver as she climbed in the back. He gave her a puzzled look. "Now," she said firmly.

Peter emerged from the trees as the sled began to pull away, but he didn't run and try to climb into it. He did not try to stop her, but stood and watched her go, his expression full of pain. She turned away. She would not pity him, not after all he had done to her. He had made a fool of her. He'd even allowed her to introduce him to her friends, the only family she had.

She wiped her cheeks with a mitten and sniffed loudly. She would not let him do this to her. She had not even liked Mark Algood before she'd met him. He'd been interesting enough to write to, but she was sure that their correspondence would have fizzled out as Mark's inability to share anything about himself had continued. She would have found his reticence too hard to penetrate. She had fallen in love with the man she'd met in New York. The one she'd taught to drive, here in Eagle Creek. The one who had just kissed her with so much passion that every cell in her body had tingled with desire for him.

But he was not Mark Algood. He was not who he had told her he was. And if he could keep up the pretense for this long, what else had he lied to her about? What else would he lie to her about in the future? He'd said that he'd tried to act like his brother. So how much of the man she had believed herself to be in love with was Peter, and how much was him acting as someone else? She could not trust his declaration of love for her. Who could in such circumstances? She could not trust anything he'd ever said to her.

CHAPTER 16

FEBRUARY 6, 1893, EAGLE CREEK, MONTANA TO NEW YORK CITY, NEW YORK

$\mathcal{P}$eter stood on the platform of the station, praying that she would come though he knew that she wouldn't. There was so much more he needed to say to her, but the more he practiced the words in his head, the less they made sense to him. There was nothing more he could say. She was right to hate him. He waited until the very last minute, hanging from the door of the carriage, ready to jump if she appeared, praying she would prove him wrong. The train had begun to move slowly out of the station before he gave up all hope and pulled himself inside the carriage.

He had been so sure that he would never love again after Ellen had left him at the altar all those years ago, yet Miss Brown had quietly crept into his heart. He was not sure if he would ever recover from the loss of her, even though she'd never truly been his. He stared out of the window but didn't notice anything outside, though the train was traveling through some of the most spectacular scenery that he had ever seen. He felt bereft and that there was nothing good left in his world to care about.

He had a compartment to himself, something he was extremely grateful for. It meant he could take his meals in private without having to make his way down the train to the elegant dining car. He imagined the other passengers, those who were excited about their journeys, chatting happily about where they'd been or where they were going, making new friends among the other passengers. He simply couldn't bear the thought of it.

As the miles passed, Peter realized that he didn't want to return to New York, either. He was disappointed in Mark. No, that wasn't the word. He was furious with his brother for the situation that he'd put himself and Miss Brown in. Why had he ever written to her if he'd never had any intention of actually meeting her? He'd wasted Miss Brown's time, as well as his own, and had made both of them miserable. Right now, Peter wasn't sure if he could forgive Mark for that.

But if he did not return to New York, where would he

go? He certainly wasn't welcome in Eagle Creek, which was the only place he actually wanted to be. He had no friends or family in other places that he could travel to. But he did have a ship, and that could take him anywhere. He bit his lip. Could he do it? Was he cut out for the life of a sailor? He'd never intended to become one, after all. His shipping business had only ever been intended to be a means to an end. But he needed a different life now, at least for a while.

He'd heard enough talk in the coffee shops about ship owners like himself going to sea and how dreadfully it had worked out for everyone involved, but Peter wasn't like those men. He wasn't afraid of working hard. In truth, he rather welcomed work that was hard enough to keep his mind occupied so he didn't think of Miss Brown too often. Captain Jones was a good man, one who could be trusted not to share Peter's true identity with the crew, so he could sign on as a hand, just like anyone else. He was sure that it would be better for everyone if they didn't know who he really was.

By the time he changed trains in Chicago, he had made up his mind. With a few hours to spare before his next train left the station, he sent a telegram to Mr. Kingshott enquiring whether *The Madelaine* was in port. She should be due at any time if all had gone well on her current voyage.

But Peter needed to delay her leaving again if he was to go to sea with her. He needed to find a reason for Mr. Kingshott to delay her departure, but he couldn't think of anything other than the truth – which he didn't want to tell his agent. On the other hand, he was the ship's owner. He could tell the man to do whatever he wanted. It was King-shott's job to do what made Peter happy, all Peter had to do was say that he wanted to see his ship.

The rest of his journey was unremarkable, and his resolve to go to sea was stronger than ever by the time he reached New York. He didn't even go home before heading to the port. He smiled a little when he saw *The Madelaine* sitting low in the water, clearly heavily laden and ready for her next journey. She was a sight to behold, even in port, with her tightly furled sails and high masts. Captain Jones was standing on the deck, looking a little anxious.

"Permission to board?" Peter called out as he began to walk up the gangplank.

"Permission granted, Sir," Captain Jones said with a smile.

"What is wrong? You look concerned."

"I was just worried about the weather. I feared that we might miss a chance for an easy passage if you didn't come soon."

"Then let us go as soon as you can muster the men."

"Us, Sir?"

"If you don't mind, I'd like to offer my services as a deckhand. I know nothing and I don't want the men to know who I am, but I need to get away and I want to work hard. I promise you that I'll not be dead weight."

"I'm sure you won't, Sir, but are you truly sure? The sea isn't for every man."

"Then it's as well that it is only a short sailing. If I am terrible and hate every moment, we can part ways as soon as possible," Peter said with a wry smile.

"I'll take you, gladly. We're three men short of the number I'd prefer. There's been another outbreak of influenza in the tenements, causing all manner of misery."

"I'm sorry to hear that. Is there anything we can do to help them?"

"Give money to the church, I suppose," Captain Jones said with a shrug. "They're the only ones doing anything to help. Poor people don't warrant worrying about, do they?"

"No, I suppose they don't," Peter said thoughtfully. "How long will it take you to muster the men?"

"An hour, perhaps two."

"And will we catch the tide?"

"It will be the perfect time to sail."

"Then I will meet you back here at seven o'clock exactly," Peter said, glancing at his pocket watch.

He unlocked the small door of his warehouse and let himself inside. He grabbed a kitbag from the stores and some items he knew that all sailors took with them to sea as he provided them for his men and quickly packed the few items from his luggage that he thought he might need. He locked the rest of his things away in his office, then locked the warehouse door behind him.

He hoisted the kit bag over his shoulder and hurried through the port, out into the many tenements that surrounded them. Never had Cable Poole's words about living in such conditions echoed so loudly in Peter's ears. The families lucky enough to have left these slums to move into Poole's clean, well-built buildings were blessed indeed. It was easy to see how outbreaks of illnesses could spread so quickly in conditions so bleak. Large families, often with seven or eight children, lived in single rooms with no sanitation and noises that seemed somehow louder here than they did anywhere else in the city. Children in rags, with no shoes played in the streets, trying to hold on to the tiniest scraps of their childhoods that they could. There were no doubts in Peter's mind that most of these children worked just to get some crumbs of food for their families, whether it was onboard ships like his own, in factories, or as newsies.

The church was the only solidly built building for miles. It looked imposing with its dark stone façade and high bell tower. The door was open. Peter wondered if it was ever closed. He doubted it. In a community like this, the support that the church could provide was so badly needed. Inside, he saw a few huddled figures in the pews. Two young priests were moving from group to group, offering consolation and baskets of food.

One of them saw Peter and hurried forward. "God bless you, Sir," he said. "You are welcome here."

"I heard about the influenza. How can I help?" Peter asked. He didn't have time for niceties. "Tell me how much you need, and I'll do what I can to raise the funds you require."

"That is good of you, Sir. Whatever you can afford to give." He beckoned Peter to follow him to the back of the church and led him down some stairs into the crypt. Peter gasped when he saw row upon row of beds full of sick men, women, and children.

"I mean it," Peter said emphatically. "I am not a very wealthy man. I have enough that I can make you a sizable donation, but I can raise more from the wealthy men I know. Tell me what you need. I'll make sure that you receive it."

The young priest fell to his knees and crossed himself a little dramatically. "Thank you for seeing us, my Lord, and sending this, your angel, to our aid."

"I'm no angel," Peter said wryly.

"You will be to these people," the priest pointed out. He quickly scribbled a few lines on a piece of paper. "This is what we need. Medicines are expensive, and though the nuns are doing all they can, we need real doctors and nurses, too."

"I'll do all I can," Peter assured him.

He left the church, hurried across town to Cable Poole's fine townhouse, and banged on the door impatiently. A smartly clad butler opened the door, his spine as straight as a poker, the expression on his hawklike face one of extreme disdain. Peter didn't care. "Is he in?" he demanded loudly, barging past the butler and flinging open the door of Cable's study.

"Yes, I'm here," Cable said, standing up behind his desk. The butler had followed Peter and was trying to protest that he'd had no choice but to let Peter in. Cable grinned. "Thank you, Waters, I'm happy to see this man."

The butler nodded politely but still looked ruffled by Peter's lack of manners as he closed the door.

"I've not made a friend there," Peter noted. "But I don't have time to please your man."

"My man is hard to please, even if people have the finest manners," Cable said. "How can I help you?"

"You must know of the influenza in the slums?"

"I do. I've been doing all I can, but it doesn't feel like it is enough."

Peter thrust the list of what the church needed. "Can you get these things to St. Mary Immaculate?" he asked.

Cable nodded. "I'll be happy to. I only wish that my hospital was already built and we had razed every one of those terrible tenements to the ground and got people into clean, safe homes."

"We'll have to work harder to do that," Peter said. "They're treating them in the crypt, hundreds of them. It's desperate."

"I know. But why is this so urgent for you now?"

"I leave on *The Madelaine* with the tide. I need to get away."

"But – correct me if I am wrong – you've barely returned from being away?"

"You are quite right, but I need to go again. I'll explain on my return. All I have time for tonight is to know that those people are in good hands."

"I'll do all I can in your stead."

"Thank you," Peter said. "I know I can trust you to do so."

Cable flushed, clearly flattered by Peter's faith in him. "Then I will wish you Godspeed, my friend. I will pray for your safe return."

Cable saw him out, and Peter hurried back to the dock. He went aboard and was shown his bunk and put in the capable hands of the bosun, Mr. Barratt, who would be responsible for teaching Peter his duties. He kept out of the way as the experienced sailors went about their tasks and prepared the ship to leave. A small tug towed them out into the main harbor, where the men began to unfurl the sails. He smiled as the wind began to fill them and the ship sped forward as if she were flying into the vast ocean beyond.

By the time New York had disappeared from view, Peter had already learned how to tie the sheets and was feeling much better about himself than he had in a long time. His hands were starting to blister and his head was full of so many new terms that he felt like he was learning a whole new language. His shipmates were, in the main, a jolly bunch and seemed to enjoy a good laugh at the expense of the newest man aboard. Peter was happy to be the butt of their jokes. He was the first to admit that he knew nothing about sailing and deserved their ribbing.

CHAPTER 17

MARCH 12, 1893, EAGLE CREEK, MONTANA

*I*n the first few days after Mr. Algood had left town, Jane had been buoyed by righteous anger. Why would anyone choose to take part in such deception and then claim that they did so because they cared for her and didn't want to hurt her? The only possible outcome of such a thing would be that she would be hurt at some point. It was such a ridiculous secret, one that would have become more and more apparent with time. She'd already noticed the difference between the man who wrote to her and the man she'd met in person. The differences between the two men would only have grown clearer the longer things had gone on.

But as the days had become weeks, she'd come to miss Mr. Algood – though she wasn't sure which one. It was ridiculous that she didn't know if anything about Peter Algood was real. Had he truly been trying to be like his brother? If so, he'd not done a particularly good job at it. Peter had been charming and gregarious in ways that Mark was not in his letters. She had slowly come to accept that she could not possibly have ever been in love with him, as the man she had met had never actually existed. He was neither Mark, nor Peter – and so she tried to reconcile her heart to its loss.

She threw herself into her work with even more passion and fervor than usual. She was glad that it was spring and every woman in town seemed to want a new dress. She helped them to choose from the array of fabrics she'd purchased in New York and developed patterns to flatter and suit each of them. For a small town so far from a big city, Eagle Creek would be one of the most fashionable places in America.

"Penny for them?" Marianne said with a smile, coming to help Jane with the dishes after another delicious Sunday lunch.

"They're not worth even that," Jane said with a sad smile.

"You're still thinking of him, aren't you?"

"I hate to admit it, but I am. I don't even know who he is. It is so silly."

"Our hearts are such difficult things to make sense of," Marianne said. "You know that I loved James for most of my life, but I spent many years happily married to another man."

"Mr. Wilson was a kind and good man. I doubt he ever lied to you or pretended to be someone he wasn't."

"He was, and no he did not. But he was often absent, and you know how lonely it could be at Long Point. I was a young woman, so very far away from everything I'd ever known. It was hard to settle, to be resolved to make the best of my lot."

"I should never have placed that advertisement. I was happy here. I had my work and my friends."

"But something was missing," Marianne reminded her. "That gap would have eaten away at you the longer you'd left it unfilled. You have such a big, warm heart, Jane. You deserve so much better than the Algoods offered you."

"Maybe that isn't true. Maybe I don't deserve a husband and a family. Perhaps I should learn to be content with my lot – taking care of others, helping them to be as happy as they can be."

"You are very good at that," Marianne said. "But you deserve to find the kind of love I share with James. Perhaps we should place another advertisement to try to find it?"

"Not yet," Jane said. "My poor heart isn't ready to try again so soon after this."

Marianne nodded. "I understand. But I'll not let you wallow for too long, Jane."

They finished the dishes and wiped down every surface in the kitchen, then went through into the sunny front parlor, where James was playing with Flora-Rose. Elliot was lying on his grandpapa's belly. Both were snoring gently by the fire. James looked up and beamed at them. "I am a tiger," he told them.

"He is," Flora-Rose said happily. "Like the one in the circus."

"My goodness," Marianne said, kneeling down to join them. "Are you the ringmaster? Can you keep the tigers under control?"

"I can," the little girl said proudly, puffing out her little chest. "Watch me, Mama."

Flora-Rose barked orders at her father, who happily did all she asked and even let her ride around the room on his back, crawling on all fours. Jane so longed to have all that her dear friends shared. She did not need their big house or the money they had in the bank, but she wanted the love they had in abundance for each other and their children. She especially longed to be a mother.

But she would not accept second best. She would not let herself be made a fool of – and the Algoods had made a fool of her. They had assumed that she would not notice that they weren't what they seemed. They had probably been laughing behind her back the entire time. Why would they do such a thing to her? She simply did not understand why anyone would reply to a matrimonial advertisement if they had no intention of ever meeting the person they were writing to. Mark Algood was clearly not a man meant for marriage, and she had no idea why Peter would agree to the subterfuge as he had. It simply didn't make any sense, any of it.

Why could she not just banish them both to the very depths of her mind and forget them altogether? Why did she see Peter Algood's handsome face, smiling at her as though he truly loved her, every single time she closed her eyes? She so wanted to purge his image from her mind, but he seemed to be permanently embedded there. No matter how busy she tried to stay, how much work she took on, he was there, almost as vividly as if he were in the room beside her.

She missed him. She hated that such a thing was true, but she couldn't deny it. She had fallen in love with the man she'd thought him to be, and she was not the kind of girl who could simply forget her feelings. She had dreamed of their future, and it had been a beautiful one, as full of love as the Dennys', with as much fun and laughter as they shared. And now it would never be.

"I should get home. I have to get up early for work tomorrow," she said to her hosts. "Thank you for a wonderful day."

"Thank you for coming," James said, grinning up at her as he did another turn around the room with his tiger-tamer daughter.

"I'll see myself out," she said to Marianne, who was now lounging on the sofa and looked so comfortable.

She walked along Main Street slowly. The air was fresh, but not too cold. Spring was Jane's favorite time of year as new life began bursting forth. She wondered if new hopes and dreams might come along with the spring flowers and warmer weather. She needed something to hold on to, something that would assure her that her current unhappiness would pass.

But something was wrong. She took a second glance at the dressmaker's shop and realized that the door was open. Mrs. Albert never worked on the weekends, not now she had three girls to help her, and neither of the apprentices had keys to the building. A knot tying itself tightly in her belly, she cautiously crossed the street and drew closer. As she did, she could see that there was a broken pane of glass in the door. She paused, wondering if she should go inside or call on Sheriff Hale and get him to do so.

She ran across the road and pounded on the door of the sheriff's office. He was probably at home. It was Sunday, after all. There was no answer. She wondered if she had time to run down the street to get him before the thief got away? She couldn't bear for Mrs. Albert to lose everything she had worked so hard for. Trying to muster some courage from the very depths of her being, she went back to the store and entered slowly. There was no evidence that anyone had been in the shop inside. The counters were as clear as they'd been when she'd closed up the night before, and the floor was clean and clear of clutter.

She picked up a large pair of scissors. They weren't much of a weapon but they would have to do. She made her way through the shop and into the workshop out the back. Again, there was no sign of anyone having been there since the night before. But when Jane pushed open the door of the fabric store, she could have cried. Every single one of the beautiful, expensive fabrics that she had brought back from New York was gone.

She must have just missed the thieves because there was nobody around. They must have taken advantage of the sleepy Sunday afternoon, when everyone was at home with their families, and just walked all those bolts of fabric out of the front door. She sank down on the floor and sobbed. Such a robbery seemed so unusual, so specific. She didn't doubt that whoever had done it had been in the store in the past weeks and she had taken them into the fabric store to pick one.

She picked herself up and wiped her eyes, then walked along the street, trying to remember every single face that had come into the shop in recent weeks. She stopped at the Hales' house and knocked on the door. Sheriff Hale opened the door, his shirt unbuttoned at the collar, his usually slicked-back hair a little disheveled. He looked a little sleepy. "Miss Brown, how may I help you?"

"There's been a robbery at the dressmaker's," Jane explained. Sheriff Hale grabbed his coat and closed the door.

"Tell me about it as we walk," he said.

She told him all she'd seen. "I'm stunned that such a thing could happen," she said.

"It is unusual, but it's well known that Mrs. Albert uses only the finest fabrics. And they'd be relatively easy to sell on at markets or even to other dressmakers."

"Do you think we will ever see them again?"

"I doubt it. But I'll do all I can."

Jane didn't doubt his word. She'd not had much to do with the good-looking sheriff since her arrival in town, but everyone in Eagle Creek spoke very highly of him. "What do we do? We've no material to make anything," she said, the reality sinking in. Some of the gowns they had on order had been cut and pinned, but not all of them. There would be many disappointed customers, and it would cost the shop a lot of money.

"Try not to panic," Sheriff Hale said calmly as he inspected every inch of the shop doors, and the roads outside the shop at front and back. He pointed to some cart tracks out the back. "They took it this way," he said. "I'll follow the tracks as far as I can, but I doubt I'll get far before I lose them among all the carts that would have attended services this morning."

"I'll tell Mrs. Albert," she said, nodding. "She'll be devastated."

Sheriff Hale nodded and went off, his eyes focused on the street. Jane patched up the front door with a small panel of wood and some nails, then locked up again. She dawdled to Mrs. Albert's house. How could she tell the kindly old woman that her entire life had gone? She rehearsed it in her head but decided in the end that the only way she could say it was to be to the point. She could only hope it wouldn't be too much of a shock. She couldn't bear the thought of such a thing robbing Mrs. Albert of her health.

CHAPTER 18

MARCH 14, 1893, EAGLE CREEK, MONTANA

Thankfully, Mrs. Albert had dealt with the robbery with stoic confidence. She'd decided that they would have to go to the market in Billings and buy whatever they could, and then Jane would go back to New York to buy more fabrics. Edwin Drayton had been called upon to fix the door and improve the locks on both the front and back doors. Mrs. Albert had also arranged to have a massive safe delivered. It would fill the entirety of the fabric store, and every bolt of fabric and every reel of lace would be stored inside it.

They had spent the past two days visiting every single customer to explain the situation in person, assuring them that their gowns were merely delayed. Everyone had been understanding, and only two people had withdrawn their orders as they needed their gowns for specific events. All in all, there was minimal damage.

Jane fetched the cart from the public stable at dawn. Mr. Gilpin gave her a sad smile as she went to pay him. "No, I'll not take your money for this," he insisted. "You've enough to worry about, and I can't do much else to help you."

"You are very kind."

"Mrs. Albert is just one of many ladies who ensured I was fed extremely well upon my arrival in Eagle Creek. I'd do anything to repay her. This is such a small thing I can do."

"I'll tell her of your kindness," Jane assured him. "Thank you."

She drove round to the shop. Mrs. Albert was giving the apprentices their instructions for while she and Jane were away. "Do not take any new orders," she said firmly. "But assure the ladies that we will be doing so upon our return."

"Come, or we'll not get to Billings in time," Jane said with a grin at the girls. "Mind your fingers on the Singer, be careful with the scissors, and don't do anything we've not told you to," she reminded them.

"We wouldn't dare," they said, grinning back. "Have a safe journey."

With Jane's assistance, Mrs. Albert struggled up onto the bench at the front of the cart. Once up, Jane wondered how they would get her back down, but that was a worry for later in the day. She climbed up herself, and they set off. Mrs. Albert pointed out all manner of birds as they traveled. Jane was surprised that she knew so much about them, and it helped to pass the time wonderfully.

When they reached the city, Jane struggled a little guiding the horse and wagon through the traffic. It seemed the entire world was in Billings this morning for the market. She found a hitching post near the marketplace, and they paid a young lad one dollar, to feed and rub down their horse while they shopped. Jane was a little cautious about leaving it with anyone they didn't know, but it was a busy place and there were plenty of other lads doing the same thing for others nearby.

They meandered through the busy stalls until they reached those selling fabric. The materials there were not as fine as that in New York, but they were deemed good enough by Mrs. Albert. She haggled with the stall owners for a good price and assurance that they would bring her purchases to the wagon. Jane had to stifle a chuckle as these burly men were so easily cowed by such a tiny old woman. Mrs. Albert drove a fierce bargain.

Their purchases made, Mrs. Albert bought some food from one of the many stalls selling pies and other simple foods. The two of them munched on their pies as they waited for their fabrics to be loaded into the back of the wagon. Mrs. Albert checked each order carefully, ensuring that every bolt was accounted for, and then they were on their way back home.

"Some people would struggle to recover from such a thing," Jane said as they drove along the leafy roads.

"I am blessed that I have my savings," Mrs. Albert said. "If I can give you any advice, dear Jane, it is this. Always ensure that you put away at least a quarter of all you earn. Life is long and hard, and there will be times when fate turns against you. You must have enough to weather every storm."

Jane nodded and took every word to heart. It was fine advice, and it was clearly helping Mrs. Albert now. She knew to the penny how much money had been paid for those fabrics. Replacing them would be beyond most dressmakers in such a situation. They would have spent every penny buying the fabric in the first place. They would have had little until every bolt had been made into something that could be sold.

"You don't mind returning to New York?" Mrs. Albert asked her. "After all that happened with your young man."

"I don't think that I can say that he was ever my young man – either of them," Jane said wryly. "New York is a grand and busy place. I think it is safe to say that I am unlikely to meet either of them during my brief stay. I shall choose and purchase the fabrics and then come home right away."

"I'd understand if you told me that you couldn't. I'd go, though it would be hard on me now."

"You don't need to worry. I'd not make you do that. The journey is so long, and arduous – even at my age."

"You are a good girl, and I'm sorry that things did not work out for you. But I must confess to being glad that nobody will be trying to steal you away from me."

"I can assure you that will never happen."

"You say that, but love is a powerful thing. I don't know many who wouldn't cross the entire world if they had truly found it."

"I doubt I will be that lucky. I'd be happy to accept fondness and affection."

"You are always making a bad deal for yourself, my dear Jane. You deserve so much more. You need to use your negotiation skills to get yourself the deal you deserve – not the one you're prepared to settle for." Jane smiled. She could not ever imagine doing such a thing, though she knew that Mrs. Albert was probably right.

Once back in Eagle Creek, they unloaded their purchases and locked them in the fabric store. It would take some time for the new safe to be delivered and installed, but Edwin had done all he could to keep things as safe as possible. Jane couldn't help feeling a little anxious as they locked up the store and went home, but she knew that they couldn't live in fear of the same thing happening again.

A somewhat sleepless night followed as she tried not to worry about whether she might bump into either of the Algoods in New York, whether she'd be able to make the types of deals she'd made before, and whether she would get up in time for her early train. She certainly hadn't needed to worry about the latter, she mused as she pulled on her clothes before the sun rose. It was actually good to be getting up and doing something. It stopped her brain from churning through the many worries and thoughts she could do little about.

APRIL 12, 1893, NEW YORK CITY, NEW YORK

Peter had to admit that he was glad to have his feet back on solid ground once more. His four months at sea had been much harder than he could have ever imagined, but it had also been so much more rewarding than he'd ever thought, too. He had seen and experienced new foods and places, and he'd worked alongside men who were now as close as family. He was surprised to find that he was looking forward to the next voyage. But now, he finally had to face his brother.

The house was empty when he arrived. He unpacked and had a bath. Such a simple thing, but such a delight after all the weeks of being lashed by the wind and salty water. He felt more like himself once he was dressed in clean clothes, but it felt strange to be wearing a tailored suit and cravat once more. As he looked at himself in the mirror, his skin tanned golden brown with just a hint of pink, he barely recognized himself. He heard a door slam downstairs and took a deep breath. "Peter?" Mark called out.

"Is that you at last? I've been worried sick."

"Yes, it's me," Peter confirmed as he made his way downstairs.

Mark was standing in the hallway. He looked thin and pale, and his eyes were ringed with dark circles. "Where have you been? I sent a telegram to Miss Brown, but she didn't reply."

"Perhaps because I wasn't with her. Once she found out what we'd done, she didn't want to have anything to do with either of us," Peter said with a shrug. "I can't say that I blame her. I'd not want anything to do with us either."

"So, where have you been?"

"On *The Madelaine*, in the West Indies, discovering new things and meeting new people."

"Your ship? You went on one of her voyages?"

"I did. I served as a deckhand. It was exhilarating," Peter said, holding out his heavily calloused hands for Mark to see how hard he'd been working.

"Whatever possessed you to do that?"

"I didn't want to come home," Peter said. "I was too angry with you for putting me and Miss Brown in that position. It was so wrong of you. You left me to tell her that the man she thought was you was in fact barely a copy."

"You are not barely a copy."

"Oh, I'm not. But I was trying to be you, remember? I wasn't that good at that. I kept slipping into being myself – and you don't care that I fell in love with her? You don't care that two lives were ruined because you were so rude, so selfish, and such a coward."

"You barely know her. How could you possibly be in love with her? Besides, I thought you'd sworn never to love again?"

"Oh, I know her. She is exactly as she seemed in her letters. She is sweet and clever and kind. And she is funny and pretty, and I fell in love with her despite my vow. You are a fool, Mark, because you don't even know what you've lost."

"You'll get over it. You got over Ellen."

"But what about her, Mark? Will she get over it? Being so betrayed, as she was? How will she ever trust enough again to keep looking for what she longs for? All she wants is a loving husband and a family of her own. It isn't much to ask for. And now, she'll probably never seek it out ever again."

"She'll get over it," Mark said, but he didn't sound too convinced.

"She might, she might not. But you will have to live with that."

Mark had the decency to look ashamed. "Are you staying?" he asked a little nervously.

"I'm here for three days."

"You're going back to sea?"

Peter nodded. "There's little to keep me here, and I enjoyed it. We're going to England. I'll be gone for a very long time. You'll need to look after yourself better than you did this time. You look dreadful."

"I can't cook," Mark said simply.

"I'll hire a housekeeper to take care of you," Peter said with an exasperated sigh. "You could have done that yourself."

"On my wages?" Mark said, trying not to whine, but he couldn't help it. He was such a child. It was strange how Peter had never noticed it before. Mark was used to having someone do everything for him, to ensure he was well fed and housed. He didn't need a wife because he had Peter. But when Peter wasn't there, he'd simply not known what to do to take care of himself. Even the idea of hiring someone to do it for him had passed him by. His only interest was his ledgers and making the numbers in them add up. And he was selfish. He only cared about how things affected him, never much thought about the feelings of anyone else.

Peter wondered how he'd not noticed it before. He wondered if it was his fault that Mark had become that way because he didn't remember him behaving like that when they'd been younger. Had Mark tried so hard not to care, as Peter had attempted to, in order to be like him? Mark had always copied him in almost everything. But had Mark truly closed off his heart? If he had, Peter would never forgive himself. Mark should not have had to become cold and unfeeling, as he so clearly had, to please him.

Peter cooked them a meal, and they sat down together. Mark looked a little revived from the hearty plateful.

"Mark, are you happy?" Peter asked as they pushed away their plates.

"I'm not sure what that really means," Mark admitted. "I like my work, and I enjoy my quiet life. I suppose that makes me happy."

"Why did you respond to a matrimonial advertisement if you didn't really want a wife?"

"Because having a wife is what is expected of a man, I suppose."

"But you don't want one?"

"Not particularly. It would be nice to have someone to clean the house and cook for me."

"But you don't want a woman's love? You don't want children." The face Mark pulled at the suggestion gave Peter his answer. He chuckled. "Mark, you do know that you don't have to be anything but yourself or do anything you don't want to for my sake, don't you? I just want you to be happy. I fear that you closed yourself off to everything when I did, after Ellen ran off."

"I never wanted those things, even then," Mark admitted. "I think that the longer I've been alone, the more I've realized who I am. I am a little grumpy, very self-absorbed, and I don't want anyone around when I get home from work."

"Not even me?"

"If there was someone else to feed me, I suppose I would manage without you," Mark said with a rueful smile. "But you're my brother. I love you, so I can bear you being there."

"You'll not lose me, even if I end up living on my ship," Peter said. "I hope you won't mind if I come home from time to time."

"You're welcome whenever you want to be here." He stood up and left the room. But he'd barely gotten halfway down the corridor before he turned and came back. "If you love her, you should fight for her."

He didn't say anything else before disappearing upstairs and leaving Peter to clean up after their meal. Peter shook his head. Mark was who he was. He had been as much of a fool as his brother for going along with his foolish plan. No wonder Mark had struggled to make himself meet Miss Brown if he didn't really want a wife in the first place. He'd been trying to make himself into something he wasn't, just as Peter had done in his stead.

CHAPTER 19

APRIL 13, 1893, NEW YORK CITY, NEW YORK

*J*ane had found the long journey even more tedious than usual. With nothing to look forward to other than finding fabrics and spending a little time with Mr. Albert and his family, she struggled to find any enthusiasm at all when she was asked by other passengers about her journey. She smiled as she listened to them talking with delight and excitement about friends and family they intended to see, but it did not rub off on her.

Each time they had to disembark and wait for a new train, she retired to a quiet place or to her boarding house room before anyone could suggest spending any time together. She was in no mood to be sociable. There was just too much weighing down her heart. She was exhausted and longed to sleep for a week by the time she finally reached New York, but she did not have time. Mrs. Albert had sent a telegram to her brother-in-law, and he was waiting at the station for her.

"You'll stay with us, Jane," he said, determined not to take no for an answer. "You need some home-cooked food and a comfortable bed."

"Thank you," Jane said weakly. It would make things easier, but the last thing she wanted was to be among the loving and loud Albert clan. The anonymity of a hotel would have been more welcome to her after all that had happened.

But she soon changed her mind. Enveloped in the warmth and comfort of the Albert home, surrounded by people who truly cared about her and what had happened to bring her back to them so suddenly was a balm to her injured soul. She let herself wallow in it a little. Sarah had a bath brought in and put in front of the fire for her. Jane sank into it gratefully, letting the hot water seep into her tight muscles. She almost fell asleep as she relaxed by the warmth of the fire.

A knock on the door woke her as she was about to sink beneath the water. "You're very quiet," Sarah said. "I thought it might be wise to check on you."

"I am glad you did, I was almost under the water completely," Jane said sleepily.

"Let's get you out and into bed, dear Jane," Sarah said, holding out a thick, soft bath sheet. Jane climbed out of the bath and took the sheet and wrapped it around her body. She followed Sarah into a small but prettily decorated room along the corridor. Jane's traveling bags had been unpacked, her two gowns hung up in the armoire, and her underthings folded neatly and placed into the chest at the end of the bed.

"You didn't need to unpack for me," she said. "But I am grateful."

"I laid out a nightgown on the bed," Sarah said, nodding at it. "Sleep well, my dear."

Jane did, and she awoke the next day feeling better than she had done in a long time. She smiled and stretched, washed and dressed, and went downstairs for some breakfast. Sarah handed her a plate of eggs and bacon, a cup of coffee, and a note from her husband. "He had to leave a little early, but he will meet you at his warehouse whenever you are ready," she told Jane.

"He is so kind to help me. You both are."

"You are family, Jane," Sarah said simply. "And when family needs you, you do all you can to help. I am going to return with you. Effie needs us, too."

"She does," Jane agreed. "She's been terribly brave, but I think it has been a terrible shock for her. I am sure she will be very glad to see you. She speaks very fondly of you and Alfred."

"That is good to know."

"I'll be glad of your company. It can be so lonely traveling so far without a companion."

Jane took a hansom to Alfred's warehouse, where he greeted her warmly and told her to look over his fabrics and to mark out any she wanted. When she asked him how much once she'd decided which she liked best, he refused payment. "You have a lot of fabric to replace. I owe Effie this, at least."

"She will be angry with me if I don't pay you something."

"She will, but that is partly why we're sending Sarah back with you," he said with a wink.

"I see," Jane said, amused by how well he knew his sister-in-law and how fond of her he clearly was.

They visited many other warehouses over the following days. It was exhilarating. The joy Jane found in fabrics continued to surprise her and those she was making deals with. She seemed to win them over easily and was happy with the prices she'd negotiated once more. Like the last time, Alfred arranged to ship all the fabrics together, and it was soon time for her to return home.

Alfred took her and Sarah to the station. They had to wait for a little while as their train had not yet arrived at the platform. Jane glanced around at the people rushing back and forth. She was so glad that life in Eagle Creek moved at a much slower pace. She wasn't sure if she would have been able to live in a city like New York, and that made her think of Mr. Algood for the first time since she'd arrived. She wondered if he'd have wanted her to live here if things had worked out differently. She had to admit that it would have been an insurmountable obstacle for her. Perhaps it was best that everything had fallen apart before such a decision needed to be made.

As the train pulled into the station, she was sure that she saw him. But when the smoke and steam cleared a little, there was no sign of him. It was just as well as she'd not have known if it was Mark or Peter, and having to talk to either of them would have been unutterably awkward. She would find a way to forgive him in time, but she wasn't ready, yet.

MARK'S ADVICE had been sensible enough, but Peter couldn't think of how he would even begin to get Miss Brown to forgive him. He'd gone to sea to distract himself from thoughts of her but had found her image dancing in his dreams as he lay in his hammock at night. He hated that he had caused her so much pain. What could he possibly do to even approach her now? Would she open a letter from him? Would she agree to meet him if he went to her beloved Eagle Creek?

And how could he do that, given the upcoming crossing to England? He could not leave her waiting if she wished to speak with him. But he might lose her entirely if he did not contact her at all. Would it be better for everyone if he simply left her alone so she could live her life? He wished he knew what to do. He'd not let himself care for anyone but his brother for such a long time, and now that he wanted to, he did not know what to do.

Impulsively, he grabbed his coat and hurried out of the door. He ran along the street, surprised to find that the effort of running three blocks was not as hard as it might have been before. His time at sea, hauling on ropes and climbing rigging, had clearly improved his health. He burst into the train station and waited in line at the ticket kiosk. He counted out the money for his ticket to Eagle Creek, then stood tapping his feet and sighing heavily every time a customer took too long to do something ahead of him.

When it was finally his turn, it was almost time for the train he wanted to get on to leave. He thrust his money at the clerk and barked his destination. The clerk seemed to take an age to write out the route and to calculate the fare.

"The money is there. I've done it before. I know the money is right. I had long enough in the line to count it out a hundred times," Peter said impatiently.

"There's no need to be hasty, Sir," the young man said calmly. "The train you need has been delayed and hasn't even arrived in the station, yet."

Peter knew he'd been rude. "I'm sorry, it is just very important that I get that train," he explained.

"I'm sure it is as important as it is for every person traveling today. And it is important that I ensure they have the right tickets. Some of them have rather complicated journeys ahead of them, as you yourself do." He handed Peter his ticket and itinerary.

"You are right, of course. Thank you. I am grateful, truly."

Peter hurried through the station and onto the platform. The train arrived just as he did. He went straight to his carriage, climbed on board, and settled himself into his compartment. Suddenly, he remembered that he had not sent word to Captain Jones that he would not be sailing with him. He glanced at his pocket watch and bit his lip. He did not know if the train would wait the usual amount of time given that it was already late. Quickly, he scribbled a note on a piece of paper and opened the window. He hailed one of the young porters, handed him the note, and pressed a dollar into his hand. "Have this taken to *The Madelaine*, in the docks, at once," he said. The boy nodded.

The train pulled out of the station, and Peter leaned back against the cushioned back panel of the seat. His folly struck him and made him laugh out loud. He'd come away with no luggage, nowhere to stay, and very little money. The latter was easily enough remedied – he'd send a telegram to his lawyer to arrange for him to draw money at his next stop – but he feared that he might not be too popular with his fellow travelers if he wasn't able to wash and change in all that time.

He checked the itinerary. He had to change in Pittsburgh for the train to Chicago and would need to stay overnight in the city. Thankfully, that wasn't too far away. He'd be able to purchase a change of clothes and arrange for funds to be sent on for him to draw on at the bank in Chicago. Reassured, he closed his eyes and dozed for a while.

He awoke to a grumbling stomach and guessed it was close to lunchtime. He made his way along the corridor to the dining car. It was already full when he arrived. The waiter gave him an apologetic look. "I'm sorry, Sir, could you come back in half an hour?"

"Of course," Peter said amenably. At the very end of the car, at a table alone, he saw a sight he'd not expected. Miss Brown was seated at a table with an elderly lady, eating soup. She looked up, saw him, and flushed red and muttered something to her companion.

He hurried over to her. "Miss Brown, how lovely to see you, I was on my way to Eagle Creek to do that, and here you are," he said in a rush, the words almost tumbling out of his mouth. He suddenly felt so nervous. She was just as lovely as she had ever been, but the look on her face told him just how much he'd hurt her. There were tears in her eyes as she tried to get up from her seat.

"Please, let me go," she said, her tone short and clipped. "We've said all we need to say."

"Please don't leave, because of me," Peter said. "I'll go. I understand. You should finish your meal." He turned to the lady opposite Jane. "My apologies for the intrusion."

Miss Brown sat back down with a sigh, but he couldn't bring himself to leave. He stood by the table, staring at her. "Mr. Algood," she said sternly.

"Yes, I'm sorry, of course." Peter backed away and made his way back through the other tables. He knew he'd just made everything so much worse – if that was even possible. Everyone on the train would be talking about them. He should not have confronted her in public that way, but he'd been so surprised to see her there. It had seemed like he had been given a sign that his choice to go to Eagle Creek was the right one, or why else would she have been there? But it was not a sign. It was just a coincidence. And she still did not wish to speak with him.

His appetite now gone, he went back to his compartment and sank down on the seat. What had possessed him to think that any encounter with Miss Brown could have gone any other way? Why should she have found a way to forgive him? He would not make her journey worse, fearing that she might have to see him again when she least wished to do so. He would get off at the very next stop, wherever it might be.

CHAPTER 20

APRIL 13, 1893, ON THE WAY TO PITTSBURGH

Jane took a few moments to calm herself, purposefully slowing her rapid breathing. She hated that she had reacted that way simply at the sight of him. Sarah fussed over her, but rather than it making things better, it only served to make Jane feel more disconcerted by what had just happened. But at least it had proven to her that she hadn't been seeing things at the station. He truly had been there. And if he was on a train to Eagle Creek, then surely that meant that he intended to come and see her – but why? What more could there possibly be to say? She thought she had made it quite clear that she could not trust him. And if she could not trust him, there was nothing more to be said.

But she could not risk bumping into him again that way. It had left her feeling most awkward, oddly ashamed, and as though everyone on the train was looking at her and talking about the two of them behind their backs. Should she perhaps hear him out? Was there a chance that anything might be salvaged from the chaos he and his brother had left in their wake?

She held her head high and finished her lunch, though she struggled to swallow every mouthful. "Sarah, would you excuse me for a few minutes?" she said. Sarah gave her an understanding look and nodded.

"I shall wait for you in our compartment, my dear."

Jane made her way through the dining car in the direction that Mr. Algood had gone. She peered into each compartment as she passed it. When she saw a guard up ahead, she called out to him. He turned and walked quickly back toward her.

"Ma'am?"

"Do you know which compartment Mr. Algood is in, please?"

The guard scratched his chin. "Algood, Algood. That's not a name I'm familiar with. Can you describe him for me?"

Jane gave him a rueful smile. "I only wish I could not,"

she said. "He is tall, with broad shoulders, dark hair, and vivid hazel eyes."

"I think I know the man you mean," he said with a smile. "He's in 16B."

Jane thanked him and made her way to the compartment. She paused for a moment, then knocked tentatively. The door slid back abruptly. When Mr. Algood saw her, his eyes lit up. "Miss Brown," he said. "I wasn't expecting to see you again. I will get off the train in Pittsburgh, I promise you."

"I didn't come to ask you to keep out of my way," she said quietly. "You said you wished to speak with me. You must have things to say. I cannot think what, but I am prepared to hear you out."

"Oh, Miss Brown, thank you," he exclaimed. He went to clasp her hands, but she pulled them away behind her back out of reach.

He nodded and beckoned that she should take a seat. She took the one opposite him, perching on the edge a little uncomfortably, folded her hands in her lap, and waited for him to speak. He sat down and ran his hands up and down his thighs nervously. He gave her a sheepish look. "I don't know where to start, now that you're here," he said.

"Wherever you wish," she said. "Mr. Algood, I don't hate you, if that in any way helps you. I was just so terribly disappointed when I found out the truth. I was angry, and I still am, I think. But I want to forgive you. I want that, very much."

It was true, and she'd thought of little else in the quiet moments alone at night ever since he'd left town. She did want to forgive him. If she did not, she might never be able to forget him – and that might mean that she might never be able to let herself trust any other man. Even if he did not deserve her forgiveness, she deserved the peace that it might bring her.

"I have rehearsed this moment so many times," Mr. Algood said. "I thought I knew exactly what I would say, and how you might respond. But I wasn't expecting to find you on the same train as me." He tried to smile.

"I must confess, it was a surprise for me, too."

"Miss Brown, I couldn't bear what our deceit had done to you. I couldn't consider even being in the same house as my brother for putting me in that position. I don't know if my brother told you much about what I do for a living, I know I did not. But I have a ship. I import raw cotton, sugar-cane, rum, and spices from places such as the West Indies, and export finished products, fabrics, guns, and so forth. I have a single ship, though my intention is to one day have my own fleet. Upon my return to New York, I could not face Mark. I was so angry with him for hurting you, for making me hurt you. I signed on aboard my own ship and went to sea."

"Oh my," Jane said with a gasp. "But wasn't that terribly dangerous?"

"It can be, but I have a fine captain and the crew are all

experienced men. It did me good. Made me strong and gave me time to think."

"And you have managed to forgive your brother?"

"I wouldn't say that, but it helped me to see him as he is. I think the time apart helped him to see himself more clearly, too. He has no desire to wed, not really, and he was just trying to do what was expected of him."

"That is all well and good, but it is a shame he did not think of the consequences of that before he replied to an advertisement to become a husband," Jane noted drily.

"I quite agree," Mr. Algood said. "But at least no other woman will go through what we put you through. He may never say sorry to you for what he did, but I am saying it for us both. I should never have agreed to take his place that first time you came to New York. I should certainly never have let him talk me into it a second time, but I liked you so much and wanted to see you again."

Jane wasn't sure how to respond to that. In her mind, if you truly cared for someone you simply did not lie to them. She kept quiet and waited for him to say more. He looked truly remorseful. Despite his tanned skin, he had dark circles under his eyes as though he'd not been sleeping well. Something had clearly been bothering him. She wasn't sure if she wanted to be responsible for his unhappiness as well as her own.

"Miss Brown, I know I have done nothing to deserve your trust, but I want you to know that I fell in love with you," he said eventually. "Truly and completely, despite myself."

"You're right, I do find it hard to believe that," she said softly. "After all, I barely even know who you are."

"Nevertheless, it is true. And though you are right that you do not know me as me, yet, I do know you – unless you were lying to me and my brother all along, too?"

"I most certainly was not."

"I did not think so," he said with a wry smile. "So, I am at an unfair advantage. I know who you are. I know how deeply I care for you, and I know how very, very sorry I am that we met the way that we did."

"We cannot change that now."

"No, we cannot. But I would be most honored if you might do me the honor of writing to me, so that I might tell you who I truly am, and so I might get to know you better. After all, you yourself said that you do not know who Peter Algood is. In truth, I think you rather know him better than you knew Mark. He was only ever himself in his letters."

She stared at him. What he was suggesting was preposterous. Or was it? He was right that she had not known anything about him, not even what he did to earn a living. But she had thought herself in love with the man she had met. Not the one she'd written to, but the person he'd been with her. Did she dare to let herself hope that the man she loved was perhaps real? That he cared as deeply for her as she did for him?

"You want to write to me?"

He nodded. "I intend to return to sea," he said. "But there are ways for mail to reach us, and it means more to the men on board than you could ever know to receive word from their loved ones. We cannot erase what happened, but please give me a chance to prove to you that I am not my brother. I am not even the man I thought myself to be before I met you. Meeting you has made me a better man, and I long for you to see that. To see *me* – not me being Mark."

"I shall think about it," she said, getting up. "I will send word to you before the train reaches Pittsburgh with my answer."

He did not try to stop her, and she was grateful for that. She let herself out of the compartment and walked slowly along the corridor, through the dining car, and back to her own compartment. Sarah waited until she had closed the door before embracing her. Jane knew that her friend would gladly listen to her troubles, but she was not ready to talk about it. She sank down onto her seat. Had what had just occurred truly happened? Was Mr. Peter Algood truly on this train to come and see her? Had he truly told her that he loved her? That he was sorry for everything and wanted another chance? Such things as this surely only happened in romantic novels, never to girls like her.

Could she let herself trust him? Or at least give him the chance to gain her trust? Could she bear how much it would hurt if he betrayed her again? All she had were questions, but this was a choice only she could make. She had to think about it most carefully. How she wished Marianne were with her so she could talk to her friend about what to do. Sarah was lovely, but it wasn't the same.

Jane tried to imagine what Marianne would say. She tried to imagine what she would say to anyone if they asked her advice about such an unusual situation. She simply did not know. Her heart longed to believe Peter Algood meant what he said, but her head knew all too well how much giving her heart to Mark Algood had hurt her when she'd found out about his betrayal. Could she be sure that Peter would not be just as duplicitous? After all, he had gone along with Mark's ruse, whatever his reasons.

But what could it hurt to write to him? She did not need to make him any promises. After all, he would be at sea for some time. He may not even receive her letters for months at a time, if they found him at all. It might be the only way that she would get the answers to her questions and the peace of mind of knowing whether she had fallen in love with a phantom or a real man.

She and Sarah dined early as Jane wished to avoid the other travelers' stares, and returned to their compartment to find that someone had been in and had made up their bed for the night. Jane wasn't quite ready to sleep, so she took a book from her bag and tried to read for a while, but her mind was elsewhere. With a heavy sigh, she got undressed and into bed. She doubted that sleep would come any more easily than following the words on a page had done, but at least she would be warm and comfortable.

After a night of tossing and turning in the narrow bunk, Jane rose early. Sarah was still sleeping soundly. Jane washed her face as quietly as she could and tried not to notice how haggard she looked. She didn't much want to eat, but it was easier for the train staff if she went to the dining car while they packed away her bunk, so she made her way to the dining car. She ordered strong coffee and eggs. She was picking at them listlessly when Mr. Algood appeared.

"May I sit with you?" he asked her politely. "There are no other tables."

"Of course," she said. "I'll not be here long, anyway."

"Did you think about what I said?" he asked once the waiter had taken his order and left them alone.

"I have, but I don't have an answer for you, yet," Jane said. "You must not pressure me. I have much to consider."

"I know," he said softly. "I am sorry for that. I'll not ask again."

Jane watched him eat as she finished her coffee. He seemed to have a heartier appetite than she remembered. He was wolfing down his eggs, bacon, and sausage, and even ordered more. "I didn't eat last night," he explained, seeing the look on her face. "I am so sorry. I usually have much better manners than this."

"You did not eat at all?"

"After you'd visited me, I had the most terrible knot in

my belly all night," he said shyly. "But I promised not to pressure you, so I will not weary you with my tales of woe."

She stood up. "You may write to me," she said in a whisper that only he could hear. "I shall look forward to it." She turned and hurried back to her cabin, not even daring to look back to see the delighted expression on his face.

CHAPTER 21

APRIL 20, 1893, NEW YORK CITY, NEW YORK

*P*eter had been buoyed by happiness as he traveled back to New York after Miss Brown had agreed to let him write to her. She had not promised she would write back, but it was more than he could have ever hoped for. He wrote his first letter to her on the train back to New York and mailed it as soon as he arrived. It should reach her not long before he reached port in Bristol, if they faced fair winds all the way.

There was much to do to ready *The Madelaine*. He also agreed to dine with Cable Poole, who wished to speak with him about something important, or so his messenger had said quite emphatically. After a day of checking the sails were seaworthy and raising them up onto their masts, being sociable was the last thing on his mind, but he owed Cable, who had done as Peter had asked and provided the church with everything it needed, and more, during the influenza outbreak.

He dressed carefully and took a hansom to Cable's house. He was welcomed warmly and shown to a large drawing room with bookshelves on one wall and a fine pianoforte at the other end. Cable shook his hand and handed him a glass of scotch whiskey. "Glad you could come," he said with a smile.

"I didn't feel I had much choice," Peter admitted.

"You always have a choice, my friend."

"I'm glad to hear it. But you wanted to speak to me about something in particular?"

"I did. I was impressed by your request. There aren't many men who'd humble themselves to ask for aid – especially when such aid was not required by themselves personally."

"If it had been for me, I'd have rather sold my ship than ask any man for help," Peter half-joked.

"Which is why you asking me means so much. I think we can do more, though."

"You do? The church is overjoyed by all they've been able to do, all the people they've been able to help."

"They might be, but they don't dare to think any bigger than surviving the next crisis." He paused, took a sip of his whiskey, and gave Peter's face a searching look. "Why did it matter so much to you?"

"People were dying," Peter said simply.

"People are dying all around us, every single day. What was it about the influenza outbreak that made you ask for help on their behalf?"

"My parents died of it," Peter admitted. "Seven years ago. There was nothing anyone could do. They were lucky, they got to die in their own beds, with the best medical care we could afford – but it wasn't enough. It so rarely is. I couldn't bear the thought of all those people suffering, in the crypt of a church of all places, surrounded by the dead they'd soon be joining."

Cable nodded solemnly. "I wish to pre-empt the next crisis. Every time something like this happens, I see the churches and hospitals overrun, unable to keep up with the demand. We need to improve people's living conditions now so they don't get so sick in the first instance."

"I absolutely agree, but what more can we do? I know you are a wealthy man, but you are already building new houses, schools, and clinics."

"We need to convince others to do so as well. And we need to build a hospital that will be completely free to anyone who needs care."

"I will gladly do all I can, but you know that I do not have the kind of wealth that you possess."

"No, but you do have a kind heart and a strong body. Please, Peter, think again about this voyage of yours. Stay here and help me to build a New York that its people deserve?"

"I don't know what to say," Peter said. He was flattered that Cable felt he had anything to offer and taken aback by the vision that had just been dangled in front of his eyes. Even for relatively comfortable New Yorkers, medical care was expensive. Peter had always known that Cable had big ideas of how things might change, but he'd never thought they would be this radical.

"Think about it, but quickly. I know your captain wishes to leave on the Saturday tide."

"I shall, I promise."

"Now, let us eat," Cable said, standing up and heading toward the door.

The rest of the evening was as convivial an evening as Peter had ever spent with Cable. The man had more stories than *The Madelaine*'s bosun, though, unlike the bosun's tall tales, Peter didn't doubt that every one of Cable's was true. The food was excellent, and there were fine wines and an excellent port to accompany a selection of some of the most delicious cheeses that Peter had ever tasted. He couldn't help thinking himself unspeakably blessed to have made Cable's acquaintance and to be able to enjoy such luxuries.

As Cable saw him to the door, Peter knew what he intended to do. "I'll stay," he said as he shook Cable's hand. "Let's make people's lives better."

Cable beamed. "Oh, my boy, I'm delighted to hear it."

"And now, I must face the wrath of my captain who will curse me for leaving him a man down at such short notice."

"He'll understand when you tell him why," Cable said. "We will be doing God's work."

"I'm not sure he'll be appeased by that," Peter said with a chuckle. "But I'll tell him you said so."

The men parted happily, and Peter walked down to the dock. A lamp was lit on board *The Madelaine*, up by the vast wheel on the bridge. He approached a little cautiously, not sure who he would find on board at such an hour. "Permission to board," he called out, as was customary.

He didn't expect an answer, and he didn't receive one. He walked the gangplank onto the deck and unhooked the lamp. He peered down into one of the hatches they used to load the cargo into the hold below the upper decks but couldn't see anyone. Perhaps the lamp had been left alight by accident. He climbed down onto the gundeck, where the men slept and four cannon were stored. As a merchant ship, *The Madelaine* was not heavily armed, but she needed to defend herself in the often-dangerous waters.

A single hammock was swinging as if its owner had just left it. Peter ran a hand over the thick canvas. It was still warm, and a blanket lay rumpled inside it. Whoever it was could not have gone far. He'd have seen them try to leave the ship, as there was only one gangplank – and a fact that always surprised him, few sailors were good swimmers. "Come out," he called. "It's me, Peter."

He walked the length of the deck, peering into the places he knew a man might be able to hide, but there was nobody. He climbed into the hold. It was full of barrels, trunks, and crates. It would be hard to find anyone among all the cargo. "Please, I'll not hurt you," he called into the darkness.

He heard a scuffling in the prow end. He moved closer, but it was just a rat. "Where's Mr. Mog?" he asked out loud. "That cat is the worst ratter a ship ever had."

"But he's a fine mouser," a rather high-pitched voice said behind him. Peter smiled. He recognized it well. He turned around and found himself facing the ship's boy, Aldwin.

"He is, but we need to convince Captain Jones that we need another for the rats," Peter said, putting a hand on the boy's shoulder. "What are you doing here, lad?"

"I've no home to go to," Aldwin explained. "Captain Jones said I could stay on board and keep an eye on things."

"Then I'll not say you can't, but wouldn't you like a real bed and a good hot meal?"

"I'd love one, but I've no family here in New York, Sir. I'm from Boston, not New York."

"You do have family," Peter told him firmly. "And you'll come home with me." Even as he'd said it, he knew he'd made a mistake. Telling the boy meant the rest of the crew would know soon enough that he wasn't who he claimed to be. But he'd not have the lad sleep here alone. All manner of men roamed the docks at night, and some of them would see a boy like Aldwin as fair game for their sport.

"Thank you, Sir," Aldwin said, beaming at him.

"Why are you calling me *sir*?" Peter asked. "You never normally do."

"Because you look all fancy, dressed up like that."

"I'm still me underneath," Peter assured him. "Though I must confess that there is something else I should probably tell you."

"That you own the ship?" Aldwin asked with a grin.

"You knew?"

"Every man on board knows," the lad said, laughing at Peter's surprise. "You've too soft manners to be one of us, Sir, and your hands were softer'n anything I've ever seen when you came aboard."

"Come on," Peter said, shaking his head and chuckling with the boy. "Let's get you warm and fed."

Mark barely seemed to notice that Peter had brought a young lad into their home for a few nights of comfort. He went about his days as he always did, largely unaware of anything anyone else was doing. After Peter had waved Aldwin and his ship off on her voyage, he went home and wrote to Miss Brown again. He felt it was only right that she should know that he had not gone back to sea. He started to tell her of Cable's ideas, then stopped himself. He did not wish to garner her approval for such acts. He was doing what he could because it was right, not to make her see that he was a better man than she believed him to be.

No, he would keep the news of the hospital and all that he and Cable planned to build a secret. At this stage, there was so much that might stand in their way. It would be wrong to brag about being a part of something that may never come to pass. But the thought of her being proud of him if it did spurred him on as he and Cable went about trying to raise the funds they would need and the goodwill among the wealthy and powerful men in the city they would need on their side.

As the days passed, he came to really enjoy his work. It wasn't easy, but it was worthwhile in a way that nothing he'd done before ever had been. He realized that he'd been searching for something more all his life and had misinterpreted that want as being a desire for more personal wealth and status. He knew now that he had longed for a purpose. Finally, he understood what Mark found in his work – there was a reason for it. And that reason brought him much joy as they inched closer to their goals.

Within three weeks, he and Cable had managed to raise almost half the money that Cable thought they would need to make a start on building the hospital. They had cajoled and convinced twenty wealthy shipowners and merchants to contribute regularly to a fund that would be used to care for the men who worked on the docks and their families. But they needed more money so they could raze the slums around the port to the ground and replace them with clean, safe houses. Peter had no idea how they would raise the sum required, but Cable was not prepared to give up.

CHAPTER 22

MAY 12, 1893, EAGLE CREEK, MONTANA

*a*ston Merryweather ran out of the postal office waving something at Jane. "Miss Brown, I have a letter for you," he called out. "From New York, I think."

"Thank you, Mr. Merryweather," Jane said, taking it from him. "I've been hoping this would come." She tucked it inside her coat to read later, away from the prying eyes of the postmaster. He was a very sweet and kind man, but also a terrible gossip. "How is Mrs. Merryweather? I heard that she has been a little unwell."

"She is doing much better now, thank you. She caught a nasty chill, but a few days in bed has done her good."

"She deserves a little rest," Jane said. "She looks after so many of us in town."

"That's my Helen," Mr. Merryweather said proudly. "She is like a mother hen."

It was an excellent description of the kindly lady, who often took newcomers under her wing and ensured they settled in the town well. "Please, do send her my very best wishes," Jane said politely.

"I shall. Thank you, Miss Brown."

The shop was busy when she arrived. Mrs. Albert, Hannah, and Kathy were showing customers a selection of fabrics and patterns. Mrs. Hale arrived just moments after Jane, the bell above the door jangling loudly to announce her arrival. With so many people in the small space, it was terribly crowded. Jane took off her coat and hat and hung them on a hook, then pulled a pinafore on over her gown before taking her place behind the counter.

"Good day," she said with a smile.

"And to you," Mrs. Hale replied. "I just need two yards of red ribbon, velvet if you have any."

Jane nodded and pulled out the tray of red ribbons. "Which would you like?"

"This one, please," Mrs. Hale said, pointing to a thick, wine-red velvet. "It's to trim my coat." She pointed at the worn areas along the seams and hems. "It does match, doesn't it?"

Jane held it up against the coat. "It does, perfectly, though you'd need to replace all the ribbon. It won't match what's already there." She turned to Mrs. Albert. "Did the shipment arrive yet?"

"It did, dear. It's all put away neatly," Mrs. Albert said with a smile.

"One moment," Jane said to Mrs. Hale. "I think I have just the thing."

She hurried into the workroom and opened up the safe. Inside were the new fabrics, all neatly stacked. Jane smiled to see them there and reached for one of the newer ribbons. She took it back into the shop and held it up against Mrs. Hale's coat. It matched the ribbon trim exactly. "There," she said happily. "That's the one you want."

"You are a marvel," Mrs. Hale said as Jane measured out two yards of the ribbon, rolled it, and wrapped it in paper. "Has Nate been to see you yet?"

"I only returned from New York yesterday," Jane said. "Do you know what he wanted to talk to us about?"

"I believe he's found the man who stole your fabrics."

"That would be wonderful, especially if he was able to recover any of them. If I have to go to New York again, it will be too soon."

Mrs. Albert laughed. "You hate it so very much?"

"I really do," Jane said. "Please tell me I'll not need to go back again for at least another year, preferably two, or five?"

"If he's recovered our other fabrics, I should think that might be possible," Mrs. Albert said.

"I'll tell him you're both here," Mrs. Hale said. She paid Jane for her ribbon and departed.

Jane went into the workshop and looked over the pieces on the girls' stations. Kathy had made a small error in her hemming, and Hannah had clearly rushed when attaching the seed pearls to an embroidered bodice. She'd have to get them both to unpick their work and start again. But mostly, it seemed that the little trio had managed well enough in her absence. She opened the large order ledger and ran a finger down it, looking at what had been finished while she was gone, what was in progress, and the new orders that had been taken. She was pleased to see that they had a steady amount of work.

Once she'd finished with her customers, Mrs. Albert joined her. "I am glad to have you back," she said. "I'm tired, and my bones ache," she grumbled as she sank into her armchair. "I may have to think about slowing down a little."

"We can manage," Jane assured her. "And you'd be just across the street if we needed you."

"I think I fear it, slowing down, I mean." She paused. "It is strange, isn't it? As a young person, all you want to do is earn your money, it doesn't matter much what you do. But as you get older, your work becomes more and more a reflection of who you are."

"I think I must have always been old, then," Jane said with a smile. "My work has always mattered so much to me. I've always wanted to do the best job I could."

"I know that, dear," Mrs. Albert said. "And I thank the heavens for it every day. I feel I could stop work altogether, knowing that the shop and the ladies of Eagle Creek are so well looked after in your capable hands."

"Then do it. Enjoy some time to yourself."

"I'm not sure I'd know how to fill my time."

Jane chuckled. She knew that feeling all too well. When she and Marianne had first come to Eagle Creek, she'd tried to do the work of the maids at every hotel they'd stayed in. She liked being busy and hated to see a task undone. "Then take the time you want and come to work when you want to do that," she suggested.

"We'll see."

The rest of the day passed quickly. She oversaw the girls as they redid their work, showing them little tricks to make the fiddly tasks easier, and started work on a christening gown for baby Elliot. She wanted it to be a surprise for Marianne when they finally set a date for his baptism. It was also a wonderful example of using lace to show the girls a skill they'd not yet learned. She showed the girls how to use the most delicate of fabrics to layer and create the long and flowing garment. Every single stitch needed to be done by hand while making sure not to snag or tear the lace.

She'd almost forgotten about her letter when she found it in her coat as she locked up for the night. She smiled and wondered what Mr. Algood would have to say to her. She hoped that he was safe, wherever he might be, and that the ship was making good time and enjoying fair weather. She dawdled a little on her way home, enjoying the spring air and the signs of new life all around her. She loved Eagle Creek more in the spring than at any other time of the year. It was so full of burgeoning hope and promise.

She stopped at the General Store to pick up some groceries, and at the baker to buy some bread. There was a fine-looking apple pie left, too. On an impulse, she bought it for herself. She didn't often indulge in sweets or desserts, at least not since she'd left dear Cook's wonderful creations behind in Texas. She really should write to her old friend, to see if things had improved much for her in recent months. She had sounded a little down about her new employers in her last letter.

Once home, she made herself a simple supper of bread and ham and cut herself a generous slice of pie, then smothered it in thick cream from Tom Greening's dairy. She wiped the container with her finger, then licked it. It was rich and decadent. She took her meal into her tiny parlor and sat down in her chair by the fire to eat it. The bread was fresh and soft, smothered in fresh butter, and the ham was salty and filling. But it was the pie that made her sigh with pleasure as she bit into the crisp crust, savored the tart apple filling, and luxuriated in the velvety cream.

Her meal completed, she pulled out her letter and opened it.

Dear Miss Brown,

Thank you for agreeing to let me write to you. I am still a little astonished that we were brought together on that train. I've never been much of a believer in fate or destiny, but it does seem strange that we should meet in such a way as we did that day. And before, too, I suppose. After all, I was not looking to meet anyone, and you were certainly not looking for a man like me.

Again, I am so dreadfully sorry for the pain that Mark and I put you through. I know it was never my intention, and I am sure that it was not Mark's either. He is not particularly good at understanding others' emotions, but he would never intentionally set out to hurt someone. But I will say no more on that, for we agreed to start afresh, to get to know one another as if we had not yet encountered one another. I look forward to learning more about you, so very much.

You said that Mark had told you almost nothing about me, so I will start with the simplest facts. I am a twin to a rather taciturn and bookish man. I own a ship and I trade in sugar, rum, raw cotton, fabrics, and more. I did not have a sailing background when I began this venture, but I knew that the only way that a man like me could make money was to risk it in shipping. There is no surer way to make a fortune – or to lose one!

I have been blessed with luck, so far. I do not take it for granted for when I started, I could not even get insurance for the journeys. Now that The Madelaine *has made a number of voyages, I have a business partner who insures every voyage. It has made matters considerably less stressful, and I no longer pace the slips every minute of the day for weeks when my ship is due into port. I still fret a little, but I am able to sit in the coffee shop now, at least, where I can enjoy the companionship of men who understand our strange and peculiar trade.*

But thanks in part to what happened between us, I have now learned that the easiest way to bear the wait is to actually be on board. Then I know where my ship is and how long it might take us to make port. I enjoyed my sojourn at sea. It was hard, back-breaking work at times, but the camaraderie between the crew is quite something. And it meant I finally left dry land and went somewhere few people can even imagine.

The West Indies are not really that far from New York when you think about the time it takes to reach them, but they could be a million miles away for the difference in the weather, the plants and animals, and the way of living that the locals enjoy. I loved the places we went to. I've rarely seen such beauty, but I did not much care for many of the men we traded with. They seemed hard and indifferent to the suffering of the poor men on the islands. They worked them too hard and paid them too little. I have given orders to my agent that he must seek out better men to trade with in the future. I'll not put money in the pockets of men who are little better than monsters.

We set sail again on Saturday, I am told, this time for

England. I am looking forward to this voyage as I long to see it. My grandfather came from a small town, not far from Bristol, and set out to sea to make his fortune in the New World. Without him, I'd not be here at all. My father always said that he escaped the most terrible poverty. It was hard for a man to make something of himself there. England does not welcome those who wish to change their stars, apparently.

But escape he did. And he did all he could to ensure that my father got a good education, and that in turn, so did Mark and myself. As a boy, my grandfather could not possibly have imagined where his determination would lead his family – to the fine townhouse in New York where Mark and I grew up and still live. I hope that he would be proud of us for continuing to improve our lot in life through hard work (in Mark's case) and a little risk (in mine).

Yes, I am admitting to you now, that I am a man who takes risks. I think it best to be honest with you about that. I know that when you placed your advertisement you wanted a decent and dependable man. You can most certainly rely on me, as Mark does, as my friends all do. I will always be there for you when you need me, and I will do all that is in my power to help you and give you my friendship and love quite freely. I do not ever risk that. But when it comes to my money, I am prepared to do whatever is needed to achieve my ends.

And those ends are to leave a legacy for my sons and

daughters, if I am so blessed to have any, so that they need never fear poverty and hardship, for I have seen what that means. I will do all I can to protect those I love from facing that.

I have spoken too much about myself, so I will stop there. I do hope that you will not be offended by my words here. I want you to know me – not the man you thought you met, who was not entirely me, nor entirely Mark. I hope that you like what you see, for I know that I like you, very much. Yet, I long to know more about you, so if you would be so kind as to write back, I would very much like to hear more about your childhood and how you came to be in Montana.

Yours, most eagerly

Peter Algood

It was a very heartfelt letter. Jane had not expected him to write so openly. He had bared his soul and shown himself to be a man of deep convictions who cares for his fellow men. It came as a surprise to her to learn that. This was a man she could truly come to admire, she was sure of it. Especially if his actions spoke even more loudly than his words. That was what she had hoped for from his brother – words that held meaning and truth, not just dull platitudes to try to curry favor. He talked of himself and of her, not just of books and nonsense that he thought she would wish to read. She had not been entirely sure whether she would write back to him until this moment, but now she was.

CHAPTER 23

MAY 18, 1893, EAGLE CREEK, MONTANA

*M*r. Merryweather was unlocking the door of the postal office as Jane walked past on her way to work. "Good morning," he greeted her cheerfully. "You've another letter, Miss Brown, if you'll just wait a moment. It came in on the last train, but it was so late, I thought it best to have Alfie deliver it today. But I may as well find it for you now."

"Thank you," Jane said, following him into the postal office. It was such a neat little store, and it had anything you could ever need to send a letter or a parcel. Mr. Merryweather went behind the counter and scanned the wall of small boxes for the one he wanted.

"Here it is," he said, taking a letter from the third row up. He handed it to her. "From New York again. Is it your young man? He seems keen, two letters in a week."

"He's not my young man," she told him. "A friend, nothing more."

She took the letter and bade him farewell. She opened it as she walked.

Dear Miss Brown

Please do not be alarmed by a letter sent so soon after my last one. I am not trying to hound you. Please take all the time you need to reply to me, if you intend to do so.

I simply thought it wise to tell you that I have not sailed to England as planned, so you may write to me in New York at the usual address.

My sincerest wishes for your health and happiness

Peter Algood

It was short, but it was most considerate of him to let her know. So many men wouldn't think to do such a thing. She wondered what had delayed his crossing or stopped him from sailing with it. She hoped that he was well and nothing had happened to him or to his twin. Even though Mark had treated her badly, she did not wish him any harm. She wondered why Peter hadn't explained his reasons, especially given the letter he'd sent just days earlier had been so open about so many things. Was he already regretting that? Would his letters become more taciturn, more like Mark's, as time went on? She truly hoped not.

She was glad that she had not managed to finish her response to him straight away. She'd struggled to know what to write. She wanted to be as open as he had been, but she'd never much spoken about, and certainly never written about, her childhood. In so many ways, her life had begun once she had left the orphanage and gone to work for Marianne. She tried not to think about the time before that. She wanted to tell him about it, but she simply hadn't yet found the words.

Perhaps he was right and some otherworldly force was bringing them together, marking their actions so that their lives would eventually collide. She preferred to think that God had a plan for her rather than thinking in terms of fate or destiny, but was Peter truly a part of that plan? She still hadn't truly found forgiveness for what had already passed between them, though she sought it desperately. She wanted to treat this as a clean slate, a new page in their story, but that story had come about because of some of the most painful pages that filled the book of her life.

Was that why she was struggling to reply? Was it why she had stared and stared at the page after she'd finished her supper and tried to sit down and write something, anything at all? No, she knew it wasn't that. It was that he had challenged her to be as honest about herself as he had been and she had realized that though she had felt that Mark's letters had been stilted and cold, hers had not been as forthcoming as she had thought, either. She had accused them of deceiving her because she didn't know who she had been writing to, but she was at least a little guilty of that herself.

She didn't want anything to go wrong this time. She felt as though she were walking on a cliff edge and might stumble and fall at any moment. She wondered if he felt the same way. She wanted him to like her because if even half of the man she had met in New York was Peter, she liked him more than she had ever imagined it possible to like anyone. He had such charisma, such charm, and there was just a little frisson of danger about him that made her feel reckless and wanted, and just a tiny bit daring herself.

She wanted to feel that. She didn't enjoy being dull and dependable, though she knew that she always would be. Peter's letter had made her realize that she could perhaps be both – dependable but also someone who took risks that might bring her happiness – and he was definitely a risk she wanted to take. She simply didn't know if she dared.

JUNE 15, 1893, NEW YORK CITY, NEW YORK

Peter had never been so busy. With the first portion of money, he and Cable had hired a man to draw up the plans for the hospital. They'd even chosen the man they wanted to run it once it was open and had insisted that he was consulted about what he and his team of doctors and nurses would need. It would be the most modern hospital in the country, with the very best equipment. And it would be free to anyone who needed it. That was Cable's most fervent wish.

Cable had taken on an assistant who had worked at one of the finest banks in New York for fifteen years. He knew all about how to protect their capital, and how to grow it so it would continue to provide for the hospital in the years to come. The three of them worked together closely, picking the perfect portfolio of investments. Cable had been managing his own investments for many years so there wasn't much Mr. Davidson could teach him, but Peter was an eager student. Such information was not available to the likes of him normally.

With the information he'd gleaned, he set up his own personal portfolio, ensuring a steady income that would take care of Mark whatever happened to Peter or *The Madelaine*. He did not know whether he would go back to sea one day or perhaps move to Montana if things progressed as he hoped with Miss Brown, but he didn't want Mark to struggle to keep the house or to look after himself as his own income was not really sufficient without Peter there.

When Peter stopped to think for a moment about how much his life had changed in the past year, he could hardly believe all that had happened. Being singled out by a man like Cable Poole had given him opportunities that he simply could not have dreamed of. Money was king in this busy city; without it, it was hard to make the connections needed to make more of it. Cable had opened the doors to the world of the wealthy and powerful to him, though he'd not needed to step far past the threshold as Cable's friendship had been more than enough.

"My friend, thank you for another delightful evening," Cable said as they retired to his study for brandy and cigars. "And for all of your help in my little venture."

"It is hardly little," Peter said grinning. "It will change the lives of hundreds, perhaps even thousands, of people."

"Oh, I do hope that it will be a good many more. I want our legacy to live on once we're gone, my boy," Cable said, handing him a cigar.

"I must confess that it would be wonderful to know that people are still being helped by our work even when we aren't here to see it."

Cable smiled. "But we must not neglect our own ambitions to make it so. It is perhaps time for you to consider adding to *The Madelaine.*"

"I would be delighted to, but I don't have the capital required to both buy and fit out another ship."

"Ah, but you do if you'll let me assist you," Cable said. "You are a good man. You deserve all the success I can send your way. How would you like to have a silent partner in a fleet of ships?"

"If that silent partner is you, I'd rather you weren't

entirely silent," Peter joked. But Cable looked deadly serious.

"Peter, I will gladly buy you three more ships. I will fit them out. After that, it is up to you to make them profitable, as you have your trusty *Madelaine*."

"It is too generous an offer. I cannot guarantee you any kind of return on your money, not for many years at least, if I ever manage to recoup enough to repay you."

"Shipping is not an investment I make to guarantee income," Cable said. "For that, as you have learned, there are much safer options than the sea. But the sea can bring such wealth that it would be foolish not to invest at least a small portion of my wealth in it. And when it comes to ship-ping, I can think of no man I would trust more to bring me a return on my money than you."

"Naturally, I am flattered, but there are better, more successful men out there than I."

"There are, but they don't need my help, and I don't trust them as I do you. Say yes, Peter. We are about to enter a brand-new century, and there will be such opportunities for us if we work together."

"What if I were to leave New York?" Peter asked, curious as to what Cable's reaction would be.

"Then we will ensure that we train a man to run the company in your stead, with your values and your vision. Your agent is a good man, and you already entrust much of the day-to-day running of your company to him. With telegrams and faster trains, there is so much that can be done that could not have been imagined even ten years ago."

"You are right, of course, but I am loath to commit to an enterprise that I would leave in a moment, if..." he tailed off.

"If your young lady says she wants you?" Cable finished for him. "I'm not a fool, Peter. I know that when a man suggests he might be leaving soon, it is because he is in love."

"I should know better than to try to keep a secret from you," Peter said with a rueful smile. "It may come to nothing. We did not have the most encouraging of starts, but I hope to convince her to take a chance on me."

"She'd be a fool not to," Cable said warmly. "And her gain will be my loss – but we cannot make plans based on maybes. Plan as if you will be here. We can adapt if it turns out differently. Do not live with the regret of not taking this chance, should things not go as you hope."

CHAPTER 24

*P*eter had spent much of the past few days thinking about Cable's offer. It was very generous indeed and would give him all that he had been working toward for so long. He would have his own fleet of ships, which would lessen his risk – for if one ship arrived late, another would be in soon. But every time he was sure that he would accept his friend's offer, thoughts of Miss Brown and the future he dreamed of with her would flood his thinking, clouding the issue. In that future, he did not see himself traveling back and forth between her and his work. He longed to be with her, every day of the rest of his life.

But he had not yet had a response to his letters, though a

reply could have easily reached him by now. He knew that there were often delays and that many letters and packages never found their destinations, but he was impatient. He longed to know more about her. He wondered if his letter had been too much, too soon. He had been very honest with her, but after all that had been before, he was sure that being completely open was the only way forward. He did not want her to think that he would ever keep something from her again.

He went about his work and tried not to dwell on either matter too often, but he knew that he had to make a decision about Cable's proposal. Cable could easily find twenty men as deserving as Peter to go into business with if that was truly what he wished to do. He was almost certain that it was a good idea, but to be sure he took out a sheet of paper and began to write a long list of the positive aspects of being Cable's partner and the negative ones. He included even the tiny niggling doubts and concerns he had and the small but often overlooked benefits of such an enterprise. When he was done, his list was heavily weighted to one side.

He left his office in the warehouse and crossed the dock to Cable's office. "Have your lawyers draw up a contract," he said. "I'll have mine look it over and we can begin negotiations."

"Oh, I am delighted, my boy," Cable said happily. "You must come to supper tonight so we may celebrate."

"Thank you, that would be lovely."

"Will you start looking for suitable ships immediately? I heard that Marston was looking to sell *The Splendide*."

"He is?" Peter was surprised. Marston was a successful man, and the ship was one of his finest.

"He bought every share available on William Jesson's voyage," Cable said with a wry smile. The entire port had been talking of little else but the tragic sinking of Jesson's only ship when a storm had struck while it had been leaving port in Jamaica. The captain had been warned of how bad the locals thought it would be, but he had still insisted on setting sail so as not to lose time. "I must admit, Peter, I've never much liked either man, so I'll not feel guilty for being glad that they've both suffered a fall."

Jesson was a harsh man who insisted that his sailors remain on board ship so they couldn't go ashore and decide not to return, leaving him short-handed. His captain was ordered to dole out harsh punishments for the tiniest of infractions, so few men wished to sail for him. And now, those who'd had no choice but to do so had lost their lives. It had been a terrible tragedy, but not surprisingly, Jesson was only worried about the cargo and gold in the hold that had gone down. He'd offered not one word of condolence to any of the families of the men who had died. But Peter had not heard that Marston had taken such a risk in being Jesson's only investor. He was a shrewd and canny man, so doing such a thing seemed out of character. It made Peter wonder if other troubles in Marston's life had led him to take such a dangerous gamble.

"They're talking about Jesson in the coffee shops in hushed voices," Peter said. "Offering him up as a cautionary tale to the smaller operators that risk all on just one ship, like me. I can't say that I've not had the fear that my ship won't return. It strikes me every voyage, and I'd not wish what happened to his crew on anyone. Every single one of those men deserved a better master. But Jesson has been a thorn in my side since I bought *The Madelaine.* He's done all he can to ruin me so he could prosper from the wreckage. I'll not weep for him now that he's lost everything."

"The best way to rub salt in his wounds is to succeed," Cable said sagely. "And remember that everything we are doing to ease the suffering in the slums will help the families of those he so cruelly treated. It is because of men like Marston and Jesson that they live as they do. If the masters would only pay enough for families to live, this world would be a better and happier place."

"I'll pay him a visit," Peter said. "*The Splendide* would be the ideal addition to our enterprise. But given all that has happened, are you not concerned that you are sinking so much money into one man?"

"One *man*, Peter," Cable stressed. "Not one ship run by the worst captain to ever achieve that rank and crewed by the most unhappy men in New York. I'll ensure that others buy a share in every voyage. I'm simply investing in the means to make those crossings happen."

The faith that Cable put in him meant a great deal to Peter. He still did not know what he had done to deserve it, but he was grateful for it. He wished his friend a good day and strode purposefully toward the other end of the port, where Marston had a large dock. Two ships lay in the slips, undergoing repairs. A third was in the dry dock, her impressive hull raised up precariously to be cleaned of the debris that attached itself over time, then re-caulked. It was *The Splendide*. Peter took the chance to look over every inch of her hull. She was well built, and there were only a few signs of wear and tear. He'd always admired her. She'd seemed vast when in the water. Out of it, she was immense.

He took the steps up to Marston's office two at a time and rapped smartly on the glass of the heavy oak door. "Enter," Marston called out, his voice terse and unwelcoming.

"Good day to you," Peter said cheerfully. Marston was poring over a thick ledger, and it wasn't doing much for his mood. He scowled at Peter but stood up and reached out his hand. Peter shook it a little grudgingly.

"I hear you are thinking of selling *The Splendide*. I wondered how much you were hoping to raise for her?"

"Someone you know interested?" Marston raised an eyebrow quizzically, a mocking smile on his thin lips.

"Me, actually," Peter confirmed, not letting the man's arrogance and thinly veiled contempt for him get to him.

"You've not got enough," Marston growled. "Don't waste my time."

"You are on excellent terms with my banker if you know how much I can or cannot afford," Peter said with a tight smile. "But I rather thought he was more trustworthy and a better judge of character if he's a friend of yours. I shall have to find a new one."

"Yet, you're here, trying to buy my ship," Marston said. "So, I'm good enough to do business with."

"You're quite right, of course. I'll leave you be," Peter said. "If you don't wish to sell her quickly to recoup some of your losses, then I do understand, but you hardly have a line outside your door asking after her."

He turned to leave. He'd barely opened the door before Marston called out. "No need to be so hasty."

Peter smiled as he turned back. "So, you're happy to give me a figure now?"

Marston scribbled a number on a piece of paper and handed it to him. "I'll not take a penny less."

Peter took it, gave it a cursory glance, and put it in his pocket. "I shall let you know," he said.

He walked briskly away from the dock and ducked into an alleyway so he could let out the laugh that had been bubbling up since Marston had called him back. He leaned back against the wall and shook his head. It was surprisingly enjoyable seeing the man so discomfited.

The figure he'd given Peter was a reasonable price for one of the finest ships that sailed out of New York City, but from what Peter had seen of *The Splendide* in the dry dock, she wasn't as seaworthy as she had once been. It wasn't a price he was willing to pay. He'd politely decline and suggest a more reasonable figure, but not until he'd left Marston to stew in his misery for a few days.

Feeling peculiarly cheerful, he made his way home. Mark was not yet in, but there was a letter waiting for him on the sideboard in the hallway. He smiled when he recognized Miss Brown's neat hand upon the envelope. This day was going surprisingly well.

Dear Mr. Algood,

I received your letter and read it with much surprise. I know you promised never to lie to me again, that you intended to be open and honest, but your frankness was a very pleasant surprise.

I envy you your enjoyment of your travels. I have learned that I am not one for gallivanting all over. I much prefer to be safe at home in the warm. That is not to say that I am not interested in hearing about other people's travels, though. I am happy to live vicariously through others, I just don't wish to go anywhere else ever again.

I've been thinking about that, as I tried to write this letter, for I feared that your delight in seeing new places might come to be a barrier between us. I think that I feel so strongly about staying in my place simply because I have finally found it. I am not sure how much your brother shared with you about me or how much of our conversations together that you remember, but as an orphan, I didn't really have a home until I came here, to Eagle Creek.

It is true that I went to work for Marianne when I was just a girl, and she and Cook made me feel welcome and wanted, but that big, fancy house was not my home. It was the place I worked, even if it did bring me a family of sorts. Eagle Creek is where I first had a home of my own. It is small and unimpressive, but it is cozy and warm. And I love it.

I find myself unwilling to leave it. I have Marianne and her family, just a few doors away, I have work I love, and I have many friends here who have welcomed me from the start. Even my trips to New York made me feel terribly home-sick, though I knew I would be returning as swiftly as it was possible to do. I pray every night that I will not have to ever go again. I am trying to convince Mrs. Albert that I could perhaps have the merchants send us samples of their cloth. I hope that we have sufficiently good relations with them all to do so.

But this then made me think of you. New York is your home, and your only family is there. Though I am still angry with him for what he did, I would not want him to lose you over me – and I fear you would miss him terribly should I demand that you come here. I cannot bring myself to do such a thing. I'll not ask of you something I would not be prepared to do for you – that seems most unfair and selfish of me.

Given our circumstances, I am still unsure as to where that leaves us. I struggle to see a way forward. For no matter how much I might come to like you, or how open we are with one another about anything and everything, this hurdle may eventually be too high for us to surmount.

But I have most certainly forgiven you, and Mark. And I wish you both well in your lives and pray that you both find the love and happiness that you wish for yourselves.

Yours, most sincerely, and most sadly

Jane Brown

Peter stared at it. Had she truly written to him to tell him that she feared everything was impossible? He read the letter again. There was no mistaking her intentions. But how could he convince her that her concerns were ill-founded? He did not wish her to leave Eagle Creek. In truth, he could hardly wait to join her there. But was she actually saying that she didn't want him there, in her allusions to his life of travel and adventure? Was she saying she still wished to write to him, to hear of his travels? He was confused. He needed to see her and ask her what she had meant by this strange and rather pessimistic letter.

CHAPTER 25

JULY 19, 1893, NEAR LAFAYETTE, INDIANA

The room Peter woke up in was dark. The window was shrouded by a ragged, dirty, red curtain. He seemed to be lying on a bed but the linens upon it, if they could be called that, were dirty, smelled foul, and were filled with rips and tears. He gagged at the stench. Even the dank water-filled hold of *The Madelaine* had not smelled so bad.

Where was he? How had he ended up here? He ached from head to toe and felt a weariness he'd never felt before. There was a throbbing sensation coming from the back of his head. He rubbed at it cautiously. There was a large lump on the back of his skull, and when he brought his fingers back in front of his eyes, he could see dark stains on his fingertips. At least that explained why he could not remember anything since getting on the train in Indianapolis. Someone had hit him hard enough to knock him out, but not to kill him. But why him?

He tried to pull himself up, but his body felt so weary he couldn't even push his own weight up with his arms. He sank back against the revolting bed, trying not to breathe too deeply. His mouth was dry, but he couldn't see if his captors had left him any water or food. He was glad that they hadn't bound him, at least, though that seemed a rather strange omission.

He lay listening to the sounds of the building and the heavy rain pounding on the windows. He was sure that there was nobody there as he'd heard not so much as a footstep on the floorboards. He tried to get up again and managed to get to his feet this time. His head spun wildly, and his legs felt soft, as though there were no bones inside them anymore. He staggered to the door and tried the handle. Not surprisingly, it didn't budge. He was locked in.

He used the wall to support him as he tried to reach the window, falling a couple of times, but hauling himself up after each one. He pushed the ragged curtain back and was dismayed to see that the window itself was boarded up from the outside, so only the slightest cracks of light spilled through into the room. At least it offered him a little light and would help him know how much time was passing, though he wasn't entirely sure how much he wanted to know that.

The air by the window was less fetid, so he sank down onto the floor, pulled his knees up before him, and clasped his arms around them. He was shaking a little from the exertion of getting here and any thoughts he might have had that he could somehow fight his way free of his captors had vanished. But where were they? Would they even return for him?

Two days passed before anyone returned for him. When Peter heard a door slam outside his room, his heart rate quickened. He tried to stand up. He didn't want them to think him weak, though he'd never felt more so in his life. He braced his weight against the wall as they turned the key in the door and slid back three bolts. Glorious sunlight spilled into Peter's room, making him blink as his eyes adjusted slowly. A tall man with an unshaven chin and a dark tan stood in the doorway. He was wearing a black Stetson and had a gun holstered at each hip. Peter didn't doubt he knew how to use them and that one move from him would have the barrel of at least one of them pointed at his head.

"Awake," the man said with a wry smile and a nod. "That's good, Mr. Algood. You're not much use to me unconscious." He pointed to Peter's head. "My man may have struck you a little harder than he intended, so I must convey my employer's apologies for the inconvenience."

"And who might your employer be?" Peter asked boldly, though his belly was filled with a mass of writhing worms. "I'll see him ruined for this."

"Ah, you see, he'd not like that, and if our negotiations end that way, I doubt he'll be happy with me. I don't like to disappoint him, so we'll be working on the proviso that you're going to cooperate," the man said. He cracked his knuckles loudly, then formed his large hand into a fist.

Peter knew exactly what manner of negotiations he had in mind, and there was only one man he could think of that might wish to see him beaten and bloodied in order to get his own way, and that was Heinrich Marston. But surely even he wouldn't have dealings with a man like this? He wasn't even sure why Marston would go to such lengths as this as he had only enquired about buying a ship he had openly placed on the market.

"So, what does your employer want from me?" he asked. "I'm sure we could have come to some reasonable agreement without all this." He gestured at the dirty room.

"He wants everything you have," the man said simply. "Your ship, your partner, your opportunities. Your luck."

"Then he should do what I did, and make them happen," Peter said tartly. He now realized precisely who was behind this kidnapping. It was a surprise. He'd not have thought that William Jesson could command the services of a man such as this, who no doubt charged highly for his services. Jesson had lost everything. He must look at Peter and think how different his life might have been had he thrown in his lot with Cable Poole rather than Heinrich Marston. "One cannot just expect such things to land in one's lap."

"Oh, he has worked for them, but he hasn't had the blessings you have had. So, he's going to do it the old-fashioned way and take what he wants."

Peter shook his head and chuckled softly. "He can't just take it all at the barrel of a gun and expect others to accept that. He can't just take my place and expect my partner to work with him."

"Oh, he knows that. But there are ways of breaking a man like Poole to his ends."

Peter did not doubt that Jesson thought that, but Cable was stronger than many would give him credit for. He was not just a wealthy man who had lived an easy life. Like Peter, he'd worked hard for everything he had. He'd admitted to Peter one night over dinner that he'd started his life in one of the slums he was so determined to eradicate. It had made Poole's resolve much more understandable.

"So, I'm not to let you go until you agree to sign over *The Madelaine* and your warehouse to him."

Peter laughed out loud. He could easily do that. It didn't mean that Cable would let him set foot on his dockyard. Jesson would never be able to gain access to his boat because Captain Jones would bring her into dock there and nowhere else. Jesson thought that taking his ship would ruin Peter, that it would leave him back at the start all over again.

He didn't understand, as Peter did now, that his ship had only been a single tool among many that were available to him. He probably never would.

"Tell your employer to come and face me to make his negotiations himself," Peter said with a confidence he did not feel. "I'll give him a reasonable price for my ship and my warehouse if that is truly what he wants."

"I don't think you understand," the man said with an evil smile. "He doesn't intend to pay for anything. You will be doing that."

"I don't understand."

"I'm to take payment from your flesh," the man said, looking unnaturally delighted by the idea of it. "Until you agree to give him everything."

Peter shuddered and shrank back against the wall. How could things have come to this? Surely someone was looking for him by now? But Miss Brown wasn't expecting him, and Mark couldn't be expected to know how long the journey to Eagle Creek took, even though he'd undertaken it himself. Nobody would even think to look for him here, wherever *here* might be.

"And will I be free to go once I sign over my property?" Peter asked.

"Of course. I'll even give you five dollars for your journey to wherever you wish to go."

"Then, if you have the documents for me to sign, let's not waste each other's time," Peter said. "I'll sign."

The man looked disappointed. "Well, I must confess I hadn't expected it to be that easy. My employer was sure you wouldn't give up so easily."

He pulled out some documents from his vest and handed them to Peter, who skimmed through them quickly. The contracts were rudimentary, not containing the kinds of clauses that Cable Poole's did. Peter was sure that he'd be able to contest them easily enough once he returned to New York. The man handed him a pen and ink, and he signed.

"So, what happens now?"

"Now, I lock you in again," the man said. He grinned when he saw Peter's reaction to his words. "Yes, I'd rather not be within a hundred miles of this place when you are set free, my friend. I'll arrange for someone to come and let you out in a week or two. He'll give you your five dollars, too."

"So, I'm to take your word that you'll actually do that?" Peter said, kicking himself that he'd not clarified more details before he'd signed. Such a man was going to look after himself. Peter wasn't sure he could bear the idea of a whole week, trapped in the darkness.

"You don't have much choice, do you?" the man said. He took the contracts from Peter and closed the door behind him.

"I suppose not," Peter muttered under his breath as the key turned in the lock and the bolts were slid back into place. "What about food? Water?" he yelled.

"I'll make arrangements," the man called back.

Peter wasn't sure if he would. Whenever he escaped from this place, he vowed to take vengeance on Jesson. It was ridiculous that the violent man he'd employed hadn't given his name. As soon as Peter returned to New York, it would be obvious who had been responsible for his imprisonment and this foul extortion.

He went to the window and tried to break it, but his arm was too weak to punch it hard enough. He glanced around for anything hard he could use, but there was nothing. He let out a savage scream of infuriation. How could everything have gone so horribly wrong? First, Miss Brown's letter implying she did not wish to write to him any longer, and now this. But though he'd never been robbed before he'd been rejected, at least. He thought back to the day that Ellen had left him at the altar and realized that he'd not been even half as upset by her betrayal as he had been by Miss Brown's quiet refusal of his suit.

He wondered for a moment how Ellen and Harry were now. The last news he'd had of them was that their marriage had not been a happy one. He prayed that they had been able to heal their love. Even though he had been hurt by them both, he no longer wished them ill. He smiled to himself as he thought how much knowing Miss Brown had changed him, all of it for the better. She may never know how much of an impact she had made on him, how much she had healed his heart and mind, but he had every intention of telling her and begging her to reconsider. He would go to her first. His business matters could wait. After he had won her heart, he would visit Ellen and Harry. He wanted them to know that he forgave them and that he simply wanted them to be happy in the lives they had chosen for themselves.

For a moment, he let himself think about how much he missed them both. Harry had been his friend from when they were just small boys, and they had gotten into all manner of mischief together – much of it frowned upon by Mark, who hadn't much been one for fun even then. But Mark had been there for him when Harry and Ellen had broken his heart. He wasn't as cold or as self-absorbed as Peter sometimes felt him to be. Inside the very focused and often taciturn man was a warm heart. Peter had to remember that. And whatever happened in Eagle Creek, he had to make sure that Mark knew Peter still needed him to be a part of his life. If anyone did actually come and let him go, that was.

He was relieved when he heard the sound of the door outside his opening some hours later. A small hatch at the bottom of the door opened, letting in a shaft of lamplight, a plate of watery stew, and a glass of milk. The hatch closed again. "Thank you," Peter called out, but there was no answer. "You have to let me out." He waited for a moment. "Please, speak to me?" he begged, but all he heard was the sound of the front door closing again, and then there was silence.

CHAPTER 26

JULY 30, 1893, EAGLE CREEK, MONTANA

"*M*iss Jane, there's a telegram for you," Hannah called excitedly, running into the workshop. "Who is it from?"

Jane took it from her and opened it. She was surprised to find that it was from Mark Algood.

Tell Peter I need him to come home immediately.

It was short and had very little detail, but it sounded important. But why was he telling her to send his brother home? Peter wasn't here, and after the letter she'd written to him, she was sure that she would never see him again, even though that thought filled her heart with sadness. She had hated writing every word of that letter. She'd longed to tell him that she shared his hopes for the future, that she thought as he did, that they could forget the past and begin again. But too much had happened between them. Though she could forgive, it was hard to forget. And she would not ask anyone to give up a life that so clearly suited them, as Peter's did. She feared he would one day come to regret that, and then hate her for making him choose.

She hoped that he hadn't decided to come to try to change her mind. It had been hard enough to make her decision when he was not there to influence her with his handsome face and kind smile. He would be a hard man to say no to in person, especially as she didn't want to say no. She wanted him to insist that he did not mind that she wanted what she wanted, that it was all he longed for, too. But his was an adventurous spirit. It would be wrong to try to tame him.

That Mark, of all people, had sent her this telegram told her that something terrible must have happened. She hurried to the postal office to send him a reply. She hoped he would keep her updated on what was happening for she would worry terribly until she had news that Peter was safe and well. She knew that all manner of dangers lurked when one was traveling. One of the ladies who had been on the train from Long Point who had befriended her and Marianne, had told them of her sister, who had been kidnapped by bandits. It had scared Jane half to death. It was probably one of the reasons she hated to travel so much, as she had a tendency to fear the worst in all situations, rather than hoping for the best.

Unable to be alone with her worries, she knocked on Marianne's door urgently. Her friend opened it within moments, took one look at her face, and embraced her tightly. "What has happened?" she asked, as she took Jane into the parlor, where she sat her by the fire, in the chair Mr. Delaney usually sat in. "You are pale as milk."

"It is Peter. Well, it is Mark," Jane said confusingly. "Mark sent me a telegram telling me that Peter was to come home immediately, but he's not here. Why would Peter tell his brother he would be here if he had no intention of coming here?"

"Perhaps he is still on his way?"

"Surely he would have told me he was coming?"

"Not if he meant to surprise you," Marianne countered. "Is there a reason he might wish to come and see you?"

"I wrote to him and told him that I would not be writing again."

"Ah," Marianne said. "Then he is probably still on his way. Do you know when he set out?"

"No, Mark didn't say. I'm not sure it's the sort of detail he'd think to include. He can be rather brusque, Peter told me, and his letters never said much at all."

"Then until we know more, there is little reason to fret. He will arrive in a few days, perhaps a week, and he can contact his brother then."

She disappeared into the kitchen and returned with two large slices of homemade cake. "Cook's recipe?" Jane asked, recognizing the frosting.

"Of course. There is no other in the world like it, though it isn't as good as hers, of course."

"I do so miss her."

"I do, too. But I have news. She has decided that she is not happy with her new employers, and has finally accepted my offer to come here and be our cook again."

"She'll be here, in Eagle Creek? I can hardly believe it," Jane cried happily. "How wonderful. When does she arrive?"

"Next week," Marianne said. She pulled a telegram out of a drawer and showed it to Jane. "She sent me this, just yesterday."

The telegram explained that Cook had missed her connection in Chicago and gone to the boarding house Marianne had told her of there and had managed to get a seat on a train leaving three days later. "I wonder what she makes of Chicago," Jane mused.

"I am sure she will tell us all about her adventures when she gets here," Marianne said with a smile. "I hope she hasn't been too uncomfortable. Though I sent her enough money to travel first class, I doubt many would have been happy to have her there."

"I fear for anyone who tried to tell her she shouldn't be anywhere she didn't want to be," Jane said, thinking of

Cook's withering stares and her way of getting her way, whoever she was talking to.

"She'll have all the bored, wealthy women eating out of her hands with all her tales," Marianne said. "They'll all try to poach her."

"She'd not be swayed. She's coming to family."

"Yes, she is."

They ate their cake and lost themselves in memories of Long Point. Though it hadn't been the life any of them would have chosen, they'd made it a good life. Talking helped to keep Jane's mind from wandering to all the terrible things that might have happened to Peter. But when they stopped reminiscing, her worries resurfaced.

"You truly care for him, don't you?" Marianne asked, looking at her furrowed brow.

"I didn't mean to," Jane said. "I thought myself in love with the man I thought was Mark. It was so hard to accept that he hadn't existed at all, but I think there was more of him in Peter than he thinks. His letter to me was just as he is in person. He talks so freely about the things that interest him and the things that concern him. And he doesn't seem to mind that I am just a seamstress."

"That is what you do, not who you are," Marianne reminded her. "You are the kindest and sweetest woman I know. Any man with any sense would fall in love with you for that alone. Yet you are witty and clever, talented and fun. And you cook almost as well as Cook."

Jane laughed. "I cannot hold a candle to her, but it is sweet of you to say so."

"Jane, I know you think yourself to be plain, dull, and quiet, but I see a strong and beautiful woman. I believe that your Peter does, too. Perhaps you should try getting to know him. Let him decide whether he loves you enough to come here, whether he loves it here enough to do so. He seemed utterly enchanted with the place, and with you, when he visited."

"If he is even coming here," Jane said. "What if he told Mark that but has gone back to sea? Mark would worry less about him if he'd said he was coming here – and we know he's not averse to a little deception."

"Jane, you have to stop that. He did not intend to deceive you. He was just trying to help his brother. He didn't mean to hurt you. Unless James, my father, and I are all wrong, we would swear that he has deep feelings for you. He told you the truth, face to face. He did not do it the easy way or trust that his brother would confess. He came to you and told you. That took a lot of courage."

"Courage would have had him standing up to his brother," Jane countered a little petulantly.

"It is hard to say no to the people we love," Marianne said. "And sometimes, it can work out well for us when we do as they wish."

"Obeying your father is a little different," Jane pointed out.

"In some ways, but in others, it is for the same reason. I loved my father and did not wish to let him down. Peter did not know he loved you when he agreed to the switch, but he did know he loved his brother. As soon as he realized he loved you, he could not live with the lie any longer."

"It is a pretty fiction," Jane said. "But one we can only assume. He may have wished to tell me to spite his brother for making him play a part in it all."

"And why would that be problematic for him here, in Eagle Creek, but not when you met in New York? Why would he be angry with his brother then?"

Jane shook her head. Marianne was far more worldly than she was, far better versed in the ways of love. But Jane couldn't bring herself to believe it. The hope of Peter's love was too painful to bear because she wanted it so very desperately. She would not let herself believe, then he could not disappoint her.

In the nursery upstairs, Elliot cried out for his mama. "I should go," Jane said. "Thank you for letting me talk, for distracting me a little."

"You are welcome here whenever you wish to come. I know you have your cottage, but this is your home, too. I hope that you know that," Marianne said, giving her a concerned look.

"I do," Jane assured her.

She let herself out as Marianne went to soothe her son. She couldn't ever admit, not even to Marianne, that the reason she liked her cottage was because she could shut out everyone around her who had everything she longed for – including Marianne and James. There were so many happy couples in Eagle Creek, so many loving families. It was hard sometimes to watch them living as she wished to do.

But tonight, the world outside knocked loudly on her door, in the person of a dripping wet Nate Hale. "I'm sorry to disturb you so late, Miss Brown, but I've had a rather strange telegram."

"If there is anything I can do to help, I'll be glad to," Jane said, ushering him inside out of the heavy rain. "I had a rather strange one myself."

"You did?"

"Yes, from an acquaintance of mine in New York?"

"Mr. Mark Algood, by any chance? The gentleman you were writing to?"

"Yes, but how did you know that?"

"Because he's the man who contacted me, too."

"Whatever is going on?" Jane asked him. "What did he tell you?"

"Did you know that Mr. Algood, Mr. Peter Algood, was on his way to Eagle Creek?"

"I did not. I sent him a letter, more than two months ago now, saying that I did not wish to write to him."

"Mark Algood seems to think that letter upset his brother and he set out to come and see you immediately after receiving it. He's not heard from him since."

"You're saying that Mark thinks that Peter is missing?" Jane asked, aghast. "He's probably still on his way if that was his intention. It is a very long trip."

"I know, I've been to New York, too," Sheriff Hale said kindly. "But no, he didn't imply that Peter was missing. He seemed sure that he was and that someone was responsible for his disappearance."

"Your telegram said a lot more than mine," Jane said, trying weakly to make a joke as her heart plummeted into her boots. She handed her telegram to him.

Sheriff Hale read it and handed it back to her. "I think that we may need to start a search for him," he said solemnly. "I presume that you would like me to keep you informed?"

"I would, very much," Jane said. "He can't be hurt. He has to be alright. I couldn't bear it if he isn't."

"Shall I send for Marianne, to come and comfort you?"

"No, I was just there. I'd rather not worry her, too. Not tonight. I'll tell her tomorrow," Jane said.

"I don't want to leave you here alone."

"If we don't find him, I'll always be alone," she said sadly. "What more is one night?"

With a concerned look in his eye, the town sheriff bade her goodnight. She closed the door behind him and leaned her forehead against it. How could this be happening? Where was Peter? Why had he been so foolish? She had been quite clear. They were too different. His impulsive rush across the country only proved that to her even more clearly. She would never think of just up and leaving everything, not even for him. She would have sat, fretted, cried, and just gone on with her life, alone.

What could have happened to him? Had he even made it onto the train that would take him to Chicago, or had he gone missing much earlier on his journey? Had he even left New York at all? There were so many miles between here and there, how could Nate possibly hope to find him? How could anyone think they could?

She sank down onto the floor, tears pouring down her cheeks silently as she remembered the meal they had shared in New York and the time he'd taken her to see the waterfall that she'd known nothing about. She wondered how much more vivid and full of adventures her life could be if she was brave enough to let him into her life. But even if she opened her heart now, would it make a difference? What if he was never found? She would die, never having told him how much she loved him.

She should have said that in her letter, not that she did not think there was any hope for them. Love could have found a way. If she'd not told him it was over, he'd never have set out so impulsively to try to change her mind. If he did not wish to continue writing to her, getting to know her, why would he have bothered? Marianne was right about that. A man who did not mind made little effort to do anything, whereas a man in love would move mountains.

Could she let herself believe that he loved her enough to travel the entire country to be with her? Even if it was true? She had never hoped for so much in her life, it seemed greedy to even want such a thing, but his actions spoke so loudly that it was hard to ignore them. And now he was gone, missing, and she might never see him again.

CHAPTER 27

AUGUST 7, 1893, NEAR LAFAYETTE, INDIANA

*T*he door opened slowly. A rather gangly looking boy stood there, hunching his shoulders as if he wished to hide his height and make himself smaller, somehow. He didn't say a word, just looked down at the floor. He stood back as Peter slowly made his way through the doorway.

"Thank you for bringing me food," Peter said as he walked past, but the boy still did not say a word. He didn't react at all to Peter's voice.

"Can you hear me?" Peter asked. He moved in front of the boy and tilted his face up. "Can you hear me?" he asked again loudly, enunciating each word carefully. The boy looked petrified, his eyes wide, but he shook his head and pointed to his mouth. "You're mute, too?" The boy nodded and then pointed to Peter's lips indicating that he could lipread. "Do you have a family? Who looks after you?"

The boy looked frustrated, and Peter realized he'd asked the wrong kind of question. "Do you have anyone to look after you?" he asked. The boy shook his head. "You're alone?" A nod. The poor lad. It must be hard for him to survive. The boy didn't seem to be the criminal kind, but Peter could understand that he might have felt he had no other choice. There wasn't much work for those with such impediments as his.

"Do you like living that way?" Peter asked him. Another shake. "Would you like to come with me?" A stunned expression followed by a slow nod and then the tiniest of smiles. "You can, if you want to," Peter assured him. "I'll give you a job, an honest job, and you'll live well." The boy nodded more eagerly, his grubby face lighting up as a smile spread all across it.

"Let's get away from this place and make a better life for us both. Where are we, by the way?" The boy looked pained. "Can you write?" He nodded. Peter still had the pen and ink in his room he'd used to sign the contracts. He fetched them and pointed to a broken table. The boy carefully formed his letters, spelling out the words *Twenty miles from Lafayette.*

Peter still had a long journey ahead of him to get to Eagle Creek, and it would take almost the same length of time to get back to New York. He looked at the boy, thought about the mess awaiting him at home, and realized that he had to go there first. He needed to deal with everything that had just happened, even though it meant he could not be with Miss Brown or tell her how he felt. He only hoped that he wouldn't be too late when he finally did get back to Eagle Creek. He would write to her and beg her to wait for him. It had to be enough, for now at least.

"Do you have a name?" Peter asked the boy. *Wilbur,* he wrote. "That's a good strong name. Well, Wilbur. Do you have a horse or a wagon? We need to get to Lafayette and onto a train back east."

East?

"Yes, I live in New York," Peter explained. "The man who employed you has taken everything from me, well almost everything. I need to get it back."

Wilbur nodded and gestured that they should go outside, where there was a small buggy with a rather ragged pony in the shafts. Peter beamed at him. It wasn't the finest vehicle he'd ever traveled in, but it was definitely the most welcome one he'd ever seen.

Wilbur was an excellent driver. He guided the buggy along a rutted path through thick woodland and out onto a rough road. The going was slow, and they stopped to camp overnight by a stream, where Wilbur made them coffee and handed Peter a chunk of hard rye bread to dunk into it. He threw a threadbare blanket to Peter from the back of the buggy, and they lay down by the fire. As the sun rose, they rolled up their blankets, had another cup of coffee, doused the fire, and then got back onto the road. They reached Lafayette in the early afternoon.

Peter had never been so happy to see anywhere. His first telegram was to his lawyer to arrange for him to be able to draw sufficient funds for their return to New York from the local bank. His second was to his brother. Even though Mark had probably not even noticed he was gone, he felt that it would be for the best. His third was to Cable, asking for his assistance.

He and Wilbur had barely gotten settled in the boarding house by the station when their landlady knocked on their door. "Mr. Algood, there's a sheriff here, looking for you," Mrs. Knightley said nervously. "You're not in any trouble, are you? I run a respectable house here."

"I'm not, at least not anymore," Peter said to her with an understanding smile. She didn't look entirely mollified but stood back so he could go past her and head down the stairs.

A tall man in a dark shirt and denim pants was standing in the hallway. He was holding a beige Stetson in his hand and had heavy silver spurs on his boots. He turned when he heard Peter's tread on the stairs, and Peter saw the gold badge on his chest. "Mr. Algood?" he asked.

"Yes. How may I help you, Sheriff?"

"Well, I rather hope that I might be able to help you," the sheriff said. "Is there somewhere we can sit and talk?"

Peter turned to Mrs. Knightley, who had followed him down the stairs. She nodded toward a door beside the sheriff.

"Thank you, Ma'am," the sheriff said politely. He opened the door to a small but pretty parlor.

Peter followed him inside, and they sat down by the fireplace, facing each other. The sheriff had closed the door behind them, but Peter knew there would be no privacy. Mrs. Knightley would be listening at the door. She was that type.

"We had a report that you were missing," the sheriff said. "And then word that you'd sent word to your brother that you were here. Might I ask where you've been?"

"You might," Peter said with a wry smile. "I'm a little fuzzy on all the details, but I can tell you all I know." He quickly outlined what he knew of his abduction and how he had come to be free, leaving out the details of Wilbur's involvement in that. He did not want the boy to have to pay for other men's misdeeds.

The sheriff shook his head. "I am sorry that happened to you, but I am glad that you were wise enough to do as he asked. Too many men are stubborn in such situations, and it only ever ends badly for them. You have been very lucky that he kept his word. Can you describe the man who imprisoned you? I can have a warrant for his arrest sent throughout the country. We'll get him, though it may take time. I assume that you will be taking legal advice about your property upon your return to New York. I hope that whoever tried to take everything from you meets his comeuppance."

"Oh, I can assure you that they will," Peter said. He gave the sheriff as much detail as he could about the man, and they shook hands at the door. "Thank you for coming. I'm glad to know that my telegram reached my brother."

"He has been very worried," the sheriff said. "We received word of your disappearance from the sheriff of Eagle Creek, in Montana. He must have contacted someone there."

"Eagle Creek?" Peter said, aghast. If Nathaniel Hale had been the one to raise the alarm, it meant that Miss Brown must have heard. Mark must have contacted her and scared her with his concerns. His intention to return to New York to deal with the ramifications for his business faded into the distance. The idea that Miss Brown had been in any way inconvenienced by any of this made him shake with rage.

"Where may I contact you if we have any news of this man?" the sheriff asked him.

"Send word via my lawyer in New York," Peter said. "I think I need to go to Eagle Creek first, after all." He pulled out a small notebook from his pocket and quickly wrote down the details, ripped out the sheet and handed it to the sheriff.

Peter was impatient to get away, but it took his lawyer a couple of days to arrange for him to draw enough funds for his journey. He hoped that Miss Brown had at least been told that he had been found, but he couldn't bring himself to send her a telegram. It seemed terribly presumptuous that she would be concerned about him, but he had to know if she had been. If she had, it meant she cared for him, and that meant that there was a chance she might change her mind.

Wilbur seemed unbothered by the change to their plans. Peter had bought him a small, leather-bound notebook so they could converse more easily. Wilbur had been deaf and mute from birth and orphaned when he was just thirteen. He'd been doing all he could to look after himself since then as nobody had wanted to take him in. He had been seen as too much trouble due to his difficulties communicating. Peter was angry with the boy's family, who had let him down when they should have done all they could to help him.

Wilbur was very clever, and like Mark, he had a real head for figures. Peter wondered if his brother would be able to get him a job in his office as a clerk. He could see him fitting in well in the quiet and studious environment, but he enjoyed his company and wondered if it was time for him to take on a bookkeeper himself rather than relying on Mark to help him out when making up his accounts. Whatever happened, Wilbur could live with them and would have a better life in the future.

When the funds finally arrived, Peter purchased them both tickets to Eagle Creek. Cable was furious with him. His telegrams kept insisting that Peter return to New York immediately, but Peter knew that he had to do this. He had to be sure that Miss Brown was well and had not been too afraid for him. Her happiness meant more to him than *The Madelaine* ever would.

CHAPTER 28

AUGUST 14, 1893, EAGLE CREEK, MONTANA

*W*ilbur was delighted by the train. He enjoyed watching the world rush by his window, and Peter enjoyed watching his rapt expression. It was like traveling for the first time again. Not that long ago, travel like this had been a distant possibility for men such as himself, Peter reflected. And that word could be sent from one side of the country to the other in the blink of an eye was something to be marveled at. Peter didn't doubt that progress would continue and that the new century ahead of them would bring remarkable leaps in technology, making life easier for men of all ranks of society.

Thankfully, Wilbur's delight lasted the long days and nights it took to get from Lafayette to Eagle Creek. The boy was also enchanted by the mountains of Montana and didn't stop smiling as they traveled in the carriage from the station up to The Eyrie. Peter settled him in, then borrowed a horse from the stable to go back into town, where he went straight to Mrs. Albert's store.

The bell over the door clanged loudly at the force of his entrance, but there was nobody in the shop. He waited for someone to appear, biting his lip. A young woman appeared, but it wasn't Miss Brown. "Good day," she said brightly. "How may I help you, Sir?"

"I, er, is Miss Brown not here today?" he asked nervously.

"She's just gone to lunch," the girl said. "I can tell her you called, if you like? She'll be back in about half an hour."

"No, I'll call on her at home," he said.

He left the shop and crossed the street, then ran to her tiny cottage. He knocked on the door and waited. "One moment," a voice called from behind the door. Just hearing her lovely voice again made Peter smile. He had missed her very much.

"I'll wait," he said. He'd wait through all eternity for her.

The door opened abruptly. "What are you doing here?" Miss Brown asked, her eyes wide. Her hair was in disarray, and there was a soot mark on her cheek. She started to smooth her hair back a little self-consciously, then glanced at her ash-covered hands and gave him a rueful look. "I've just made it all so much worse, haven't I?"

"You look quite lovely to me, but what have you been doing?"

"A bird was nesting in my chimney, I was trying to dislodge its nest," she explained. "I thought I'd have time to remedy it as I took my lunch, but I now think I should have waited for a day when I had more time to do so."

"May I help at all?"

"I would be most grateful. And may I say that I am so glad to see you," she paused and shook her head. "To see that you are well and safe, I mean."

"I'm just glad to see you," he said fervently. "You may say whatever you like."

"It was quite a shock receiving that telegram from your brother," she said as he took off his jacket and laid it over the back of a kitchen chair, removed his cravat and then rolled up his sleeves. "Whatever happened to you? If you were coming here, you should have been here weeks and weeks ago."

He told her as he picked up the long chimney brush and began to feed it slowly upwards. She gasped, her hands flying to cover her mouth as he spoke, her skin pale. "Oh my!" she exclaimed. "I thought you were looking a little thin and wan, but I could not have imagined such an ordeal."

"I can assure you that I am quite well. If I am honest, it was harder receiving your letter. I hated the thought that I might never get to speak with you or see your lovely face again. It broke my heart to think that you'd given up on even the hope of us finding a future together."

The brush met with some resistance, so he gave it a little shove and a twist, and suddenly twigs rained down into the fireplace. He gave the chimney a thorough sweep while he was there, and then brought the brush back down and packed it away carefully.

"There you go, that should take care of that," he said softly. His hand brushed hers as they both went to pick up the same twig. A frisson of energy coursed through him, sensitizing every inch of his body. She flushed prettily and snatched her hand away, but he knew in that moment that she felt as strongly for him as he did for her. She'd felt the surge between them, too.

She turned away and swept up the last of the soot, then hurried outside to throw the ashes on her vegetables. When she returned, she looked thoughtful. "Why would Mark send the telegram he did? Nate said that he seemed to know you were missing, but he didn't mention a word of that in mine. It just sounded like he was being petulant and needed you to go home."

"I don't know," Peter admitted. "But that is not what concerns me now. You are all I care about, Miss Brown – Jane. I need to know how you truly feel about me."

JANE STARED AT HIM. She didn't know how to respond. She was still a little taken aback that he was here at all and had gone through so much to get there, let alone that he had deemed it important enough to come to her before dealing with everything he needed to following his abduction. She could hardly believe that he had been through such an ordeal, especially as he seemed to be unbothered by any of it, even losing his ship – and she knew how much *The Madelaine* meant to him.

"Miss Brown, please tell me that you did not mean to tell me that there was no hope for us?" he begged.

"I, I didn't mean to say that exactly," she said awkwardly. "But I find it hard to see a way for us to be together. Your life is in New York. If this incident shows us anything, it is that your world is a dangerous one – and I have no desire to live in constant fear for your life. You are a most gregarious man, and I am a most shy woman. You wish for adventure and travel, and I long to stay here, where it is quiet and safe. We are just too different. You must see that?"

"I see only you," he said. It was a romantic reply, but she needed him to be realistic, not to try to woo her. She would give in to him all too easily, and one of them had to remain aware of the realities they faced.

"Mr. Algood, I am flattered, truly I am, but though it seems to be enough now, that cannot tide us through the hard times a life split between two places would be bound to bring."

"I am not a fool, Miss Brown," he said, looking deeply into her eyes, searching for something. Jane wondered if he found it. "I would give it all up for you, don't you know that?"

"I could not ask that of you," she said firmly. "I will not ask that of you."

"You don't have to. I'd do it willingly." He paused. "You know, when he asked me to sign over everything, I didn't flinch. I just did it. Do you know why? Because I knew that there was only one thing in my life that mattered to me, and as long as he did not want that he could have everything else. That thing is you. Please, Miss Brown, dearest Jane, don't turn me away. Give me at least a tiny sliver of hope that I might be able to win your heart? That you'll let me prove to you that I don't need New York, I don't need to travel anywhere. I just need to be here, with you."

Jane wanted to believe him, but she simply couldn't. She hadn't lived a particularly exciting life herself, but she knew that those who did struggled to settle anywhere. She did not want to be responsible for making this wonderful, carefree, and daring man less than he was. She wanted him to fly and experience the world as he longed to do, not be trapped in a small town surrounded only by mountains that would one day come to feel like a prison of sorts for him.

"What can I do to prove this to you?" he asked her.

"I don't know," she said simply. "I just don't think you can change your nature simply because you wish to, just as I cannot change mine."

"Please, at least let me continue to write to you while I take care of matters in New York?"

She paused before answering. It would only make matters worse if they drew any closer before the end inevitably came, but she couldn't say no to him. He looked so sad, his handsome face pale and more chiseled than ever thanks to the weight he had lost during his captivity. He was so much more of a man than she could have ever dreamed of, and she did love him, no matter how foolish that was. "You may write to me," she said softly. "But I will not change my mind."

"Then I will have to change it for you, and I will, Jane. I will. I love you and I intend to make you my wife. I'll not give up on that hope, though I would gladly give up everything else in my life."

Reluctantly, he left her alone to think about all he'd come so far to say to her. She didn't doubt the depth of his feelings for her, but she couldn't get past her fears that someday that wouldn't be enough. She washed her face and hands, then glanced in the mirror. Her hair was still full of soot. She could not return to work as she wouldn't risk dirtying the fabrics, but she needed to be busy. She had much to think about.

She headed to Mrs. Albert's house. "Would you mind

watching the shop this afternoon?" she asked when her mentor opened the door.

"Not at all," Mrs. Albert said. "And I can see why." She grinned and put a hand out toward Jane's hair, though she didn't touch it. "There's something else, though, isn't there? Is it your young man? Didn't you say he had been found and that all was well?"

"He is here, in Eagle Creek," Jane said. "He came to talk to me before he returned to New York. He says none of that matters."

"Oh my!"

"Indeed."

"Take all the time you need to think about what to do, my dear. Walk in the mountains, swim in the creek. I find that nature can be very healing."

"Thank you, I may do just that," Jane said.

She went home and packed a basket with some clean undergarments, a bath sheet, some soap, and a comb, then made her way down to the creek. She walked along it until she reached the creek. There was nobody there, which was unusual for the time of year. She sat down on the shore and unpinned her hair, tucking the pins away in her basket carefully so she wouldn't lose them, then stripped off her gown and eased herself into the cold water. It made her gasp, and it took her a few minutes to get her shoulders fully under the water. It took her another few minutes longer before she felt brave enough to dunk her head as well.

She floated on her back for a short while, then made her way back to the shallows and began to lather her hair. She took her time, focusing on the repetitive motions and listening for the quiet squeak that would tell her that her hair was fully clean. She swam out and dove under the water to rinse out her long tresses. When she swam back to the shore, a couple of children had arrived and were stripping off their clothes ready to run into the water. She smiled at them, recognizing them as two of Aidan and Meredith O'Shaunessy's children.

"Good day, Miss Jane," they called out. "How is the water?"

"A little chilly, but delicious," she told them. "You're late here today, aren't you?"

"Dad wanted us to do chores on the farm," the older of the two called back. "Mom didn't bring us into town until just now. I think she hoped to see you. She was going to call by the store."

"I'll stop in on my way home," Jane said, wondering if Meredith wanted a new gown. Thanks to her ever-growing family, it was rare that she had the money to buy new dresses for herself and she tended to alter those she already had.

She pulled the bath sheet she'd brought with her out of the basket and wrapped it around herself tightly. She sat down and watched the children splash and play for a moment, then carefully removed her undergarments underneath the sheet creating a sort of tent around her to do so, and put on the clean ones she'd brought with her. She pulled on her dress and then packed everything up and went back to town.

CHAPTER 29

AUGUST 14, 1893, EAGLE CREEK, MONTANA

ane's head felt clearer after her swim, but she felt no closer to an answer for Mr. Algood. She stopped by the store and was glad to find that Meredith was still there. "I bumped into your two at the creek," she explained. "They said you hoped to speak with me."

"I did. I wondered if you wanted to join me for lunch on Sunday. I know you normally go to Marianne's, but I understand that she and James are visiting Marla somewhere in Minnesota while the school is closed for the summer."

"I would be delighted," Jane said. She liked Meredith, and her family was as full of life and love as Marianne's.

As she made her way home, she realized that she'd not thought for a moment about Mr. Algood and his intentions towards her. The afternoon had been just what she had needed to clear her head, but she had to give him a definite answer before he left town again. She had to make a decision, and stick to it for both of their sakes. And she wished that Marianne was there to talk it through with.

Back home, Jane took a seat on her porch, looking out over her tiny rear garden, where she grew vegetables and herbs for the kitchen. She spotted a few weeds, so she fetched some tools and a bucket and began to dig them out as she tried to work out what to say to Peter and how she would get him to actually hear what she was saying. He had a terrible tendency of ignoring what he didn't want to hear.

Peter was impossibly handsome. He was funny and warm, and she liked him more than she should. Her heart longed to run to him and beg him to take her with him, but she knew that she would be miserable in New York. She had not enjoyed any of her visits there, except for her time with him. She thought about how much he had said he liked Eagle Creek, which was wonderful, but there was a great deal of difference between visiting a place for a few days and living there for the rest of one's life. She knew that he might say the same to her about New York, of course, but she was a quiet person, she loved her life here. She did not have the nature to thrive in a place as busy and hard as New

York. And she truly feared that he would come to see Eagle Creek as a jail and her as the keeper of the keys. He was used to the hustle and bustle of New York, and he fitted in there. She simply couldn't imagine how he would entertain himself here.

It was somewhat strange that she had once hoped that his twin might come to love it here, as he had seemed so unbothered about his surroundings or anything else in his letters. Yet, from what Peter had told her, Mark had hated it here while he had fallen in love with the mountains, the meadows, and the eagles overhead. But was it just a passing fancy? Could she take the chance that he might truly be happy here and thrive?

Would he get bored? There was no sea to lure him away, and there were few distractions to amuse him. They relied on traveling troupes for theater and musical performances, and though they were some of the most wonderful nights Jane had experienced here, they would probably seem paltry and provincial to a man like Peter. Would he end up in the saloon most nights? Or would he seek out other ways to excite himself? She knew of men who had taken to climbing the hardest mountains, swimming in the most dangerous waters, and clambering into tiny caves behind and under the waterfalls. Many had been injured, and some had even died, all because they needed to seek out experience and thrills that small-town life simply could not provide. Others turned to gambling and drinking. She could not bear the thought of Peter as a drunken sot, the entire town laughing at him and pitying her.

She began weeding the bed where her fruit bushes grew and remembered that they had once been up by the house. They had wilted and been unhappy, not getting enough sunlight. It was hard to grow fruit in Montana – the winters were long and the summers short – but if you chose the right spot and gave them the right care, most plants could thrive. She wondered if her love would be enough to ensure Peter could continue to grow, to be happy and healthy. She so longed to believe it could be true, and she knew that she had to at least give them the chance to find out. She dropped her tools and ran out of the garden.

THE VIEWS from the deck of The Eyrie were some of the most spectacular that Peter had ever seen. There were often eagles circling in the skies above it, and he could stare at the vast sky for hours and never grow bored. But today, he barely noticed the beauty around him. Wilbur watched as Peter paced up and down on the deck. He waved at Peter and scribbled something rapidly in his notebook. *What is wrong? We've barely been here five minutes and now we're going to go again?*

"It must seem so strange to you. I'm sorry, I should have explained everything to you."

Then tell me now.

"There is a woman I love, and she doesn't want me." It sounded so harsh as he said it out loud.

Are you sure?

"As I am of anything. I think she loves me, or at least cares for me. But I betrayed her once, and she simply can't forgive me."

Is she short, with a kind face?

"I suppose you might describe her that way," Peter said, giving him a quizzical look. "How did you know?"

Because she's ten steps behind you, on the path.

Wilbur grinned and quietly left as Peter turned and saw Jane approaching him. "Miss Brown, why are you here? You said what you needed to. I'll be leaving town tomorrow."

"And I want you to write to me to let me know that you are home safely. In fact, I'd rather you sent me a telegram to let me know that so I don't have to wait to know you are safe."

"I'll send one at every stop we make along the route if it will ease your mind?" She nodded, then ducked her head away shyly. "Jane, I never meant to lie to you, you do know that, don't you?"

"Mr. Algood, Peter, I do, and I forgave you some time ago. I do care for you, more than I would perhaps like to admit, and I am sure that you care for me, but I do have concerns that we are not compatible. I doubt that those concerns will ever go away, but we will never know unless we try."

"You are still worried that I will not like living here?" Peter asked.

"Yes, you are not the kind of man to stay still, Peter Algood," she said with a wry smile. "And I am the kind of girl who never wants to go anywhere again. I fear that may come between us someday in the future, when you can bear being here no longer."

"But, darling Jane, I do not have to remain here all the time, though you may do just that. And after my adventures recently, I am disinclined to travel anywhere ever again. If I could stay here now, I would do so, but I must return to New York and deal with my affairs. I have a partner who has been most kind to me, and I would prefer to tell him my plans to his face, and hopefully receive his blessings. And I must tell Mark and reassure him that all he'll ever need to do is to send for me and I will come."

"I understand that, and I know it will not be a short stay," Jane said. "So, we will write and continue to get to know each other. And then we will see."

She had not agreed to become his wife, but she had not closed the door on him forever. He was overjoyed to have at least that much. He would do all he could to prove to her in the coming months that things would work out, that he could be constant to both her and the idea of a life here in the mountains. In truth, he would have lived in that filthy hovel he'd been locked up in as long as she was by his side. He knew now that she truly was all that he needed.

But he also knew that she was serious about her concerns and he would need to be gentle with her. He could not rush her or force her into anything. He did not want to. She was worth waiting for, so he would be patient and understanding and show her that he was the man she wanted with his every word and action. All he wished to do was spend the rest of his life loving her.

By the time he returned to their rooms, Wilbur had packed their bags and was ready to leave. Peter couldn't help but be impressed by the young man who had suffered so much during his young life. He was perceptive and smart. One day, he would make a fine man of business if he received the right education and had a good mentor. He wondered if Cable would consider taking him on, because Peter could think of nobody better.

Their journey back to New York was long. Peter took the chance to begin Wilbur's education in business matters. As he'd predicted, the boy learned quickly and seemed interested in the work. He was quicker than Peter at reading and making sense of the accounts, but he also had a way of reading things into the numbers that Mark did not. He saw patterns in what was selling well and when, how prices changed according to the time of year, and what they might do to improve their profits. He saw opportunities, but he also spied hazards that could lose money – and both were essential to Peter.

CHAPTER 30

SEPTEMBER 14, 1893, NEW YORK CITY,
NEW YORK

*B*y the time they arrived in New York, Peter had become convinced that Wilbur could run his business better than he ever had. The boy was naturally gifted, and he had a raw intelligence that came out of his need to survive. The question was whether he would want to run the business. Even if he did, he and Cable needed to get along. Cable was a good partner to have. He offered guidance and advice, and he was happy to invest his wealth – but that was because he trusted Peter and valued his character. Peter needed him, and so would Wilbur.

Their first stop was Peter's home. Mark was in the snug

and he and Wilbur became friends immediately. Mark actually seemed pleased that Peter had brought someone to live with them, something Peter had been concerned about as Mark wasn't always an easy man to share a home with. He and Wilbur bonded over their love of mathematical puzzles and Wilbur's ability to make a tasty stew. Peter felt glad as they fell into a silent but nonetheless expressive companionship as the days passed. One of his concerns had been easily managed.

Peter needed to speak with his brother about Jane and his intention to move to Eagle Creek as soon as possible, but he was strangely nervous about doing so. Mark seemed happy that Peter was back at home, and they seemed to be healing the rift that Mark's treatment of Jane had caused. But Peter feared that raising her name and telling Mark his intentions toward her might reignite the bitterness that had sprung up between them. And so, he kept putting it off.

Telling Cable had also been hard, but his mentor and friend had been happy that things seemed to have worked out well with Jane. Of course, he had known how deeply Peter felt about her, and he was happy for him, but it had led to some rather strained conversations about what would happen to their partnership in the future.

"I just don't see how you can run such an enterprise as this from so far away," Cable said thoughtfully as they sat in the coffee shop.

"I don't intend to run it," Peter said, taking the opportunity to broach the idea that had only grown stronger with every day he had worked alongside Wilbur. "I intend to hand it over to my protégé."

"Your protégé? When have you had the time to find one of those?" Cable looked intrigued, if a little wary.

Peter quickly told him about how Wilbur had come into his life and the aptitude he showed for the work. Cable gasped when Peter spoke of his abduction. "Why did you not tell me before? Why didn't your brother tell me he had his concerns?"

"I think he simply didn't think to," Peter said. "He isn't always good at thinking of anyone but himself. He worried Jane half to death."

"Then it is as well you went to her first, though you have been sorely missed here."

"I hope that I've reassured her. She made me promise to send her regular telegrams to continue to do so."

"Then she does love you," Cable said, nodding sagely. "She'd not be concerned if she did not."

"I do hope so, but I have to convince her that I mean what I say. She thinks that I will grow restless and want to leave her and Eagle Creek."

"And you think you won't?"

"Honestly, I simply don't know. I can't guarantee that won't happen, but I do not want to be anywhere else right now."

"There is so much that may happen in the future,

nobody can really promise anyone that they won't want more one day," Cable agreed. "But you are different from the man you were when I met you. He was determined to beat the world, to change his stars, but you're happy where you are in the constellation now, aren't you?"

"I am," Peter admitted. "I never thought I would have all that I do or that my life would be at risk because my success was something others envied. I'm happy to pass the reins to a man who needs to change his life."

"Your Wilbur?"

Peter nodded. "He'll need help, probably for some time," he said. "I will stay as long as he needs, but I can think of nobody better."

"When will I meet this paragon?"

Peter chuckled. "He's certainly not that, but he's a good lad and he's eager to succeed. He and my brother get along well, so I doubt Mark will have any concerns about him continuing to stay in the house when I'm gone, and I do hope that you will continue to mentor and care for Wilbur as you have me, my dear friend."

"You know that I am fussy about that," Cable said with a wry smile. "I do hope you've chosen as well as you think you have, my boy."

"You'll see when you meet him."

"Which will be when?"

"Next week. I wanted to give him time to adapt to his

new life in New York first. He's been through a lot, and I didn't want to overwhelm him with everything at once."

"I understand. But now I must tell you what has happened in your absence," Cable said, rubbing his hands together. "Marston is ruined. He's lost everything. Every man in New York he owed money to called him on his debts, and he couldn't sell everything fast enough. Jesson disappeared for a short while and returned saying you'd sold him *The Madelaine* and your warehouse, and that was when I knew something was awry. You don't own your warehouse – I do. You'd not be able to sign away anything more than your lease. Hearing your story, it now makes perfect sense."

"I knew you'd know straight away if I signed away the warehouse."

"It was quick thinking in a difficult situation, and it made me cautious dealing with him. I held my tongue and took my concerns to your brother, and we called at the sheriff's office together."

Suddenly, Peter recalled a question that Jane had asked him. Mark had known all along that something had stopped Peter from reaching Eagle Creek, yet he had sent a telegram that even he must have realized would cause her concern.

"What is it?" Cable asked him. "You look shocked."

"I'm trying to think of a reason why my brother would contact Jane as he did, knowing that I could not possibly have reached her?" Cable gave him a puzzled look. "He simply demanded that she tell me to come home."

Cable shrugged and shook his head. "I don't know, Peter. Only Mark can answer that question. Perhaps he's not as comfortable with the idea of you courting her as he has told you?"

"Excuse me, my friend. I know we have much to talk about, but I think I need to speak with my brother."

He got up and threw a few dollars onto the table to pay for their meal. Cable tried to refuse him, but Peter shook his head. "Let me do this, just for once."

He hurried across town to the bureau where his brother worked. Mark's behavior made so little sense. He had known that Peter had signed over his belongings and that Cable had believed there to be something untoward occurring, but he'd rather spitefully sent a telegram that had never needed to be sent.

He found Mark poring over a large ledger at his desk. "Mark, why did you send that telegram?" he demanded. "To Miss Brown? What possible use could it have served?"

Mark looked up at him once he'd finished entering the figures he needed to. "I wasn't thinking," he said simply. "I was worried about you."

"No, Mark. I don't accept that. You knew that it was unlikely that I had made it to Eagle Creek. You knew that Miss Brown knew nothing about my visit to her. You sent it to worry her intentionally. Why?"

Mark frowned, his brow furrowing. "It is all so easy for you, isn't it? You always get everything you want."

"I'm sorry, I don't understand?" Peter said.

"Did you know that I loved Ellen?" Mark asked completely unexpectedly. "I thought for a short while that she might come to love me, but then she met you. And you are so much better at being with people than me and she forgot all about me."

"Are you forgetting that she didn't choose me, either?" Peter pointed out. "And you never said anything. If you'd told me you liked her, I would have moved heaven and earth to bring you together and would never have courted her myself."

"I thought you knew me well enough to know."

"How can I know what you keep in your head? You can be so secretive, Mark. I know you well, probably better than anyone does, but I often feel that you are a stranger to me."

"Oh," Mark said. He picked up his pen and started to write again. It was as if he thought the discussion was already over.

"Mark, you can't just say that and ignore my question," Peter said. "This is what you do. You give me half of what I need, at most, and then blame me for not understanding you."

Mark placed his pen down with pointed precision. "Peter. You were supposed to be making her care for me. You made her care only for you. Even when writing to me, she only spoke about the time she'd spent with you and wanted me to be like you."

"She thought you were me," Peter said, frustrated at him being so ridiculous, so petty. "You punished her for a situation that you put her in? Is that truly what you're telling me?"

"She liked you better and she never even met me, but she was supposed to be mine." He said it as though he thought it the most reasonable thing in the world.

"Mark, I am going to say this slowly and simply," Peter said clearly. "You wrote to a lady with a view of making her your wife. You refused to meet with her. You insisted I see her in your place. You cannot blame either of us for a situation caused by your choices and actions. And you never even wished to marry anyone, so you spitefully punished Miss Brown for something she could not have helped. You will write to her and apologize, or I will never forgive you."

"I have nothing to apologize for. The two of you should be saying sorry to me," Mark said petulantly.

"I know that you believe that to be true, but you are a man of logic, not passion. How can you not see the truth of this matter?"

He shook his head sadly and walked away. Mark would never see what he had done. He would never understand that you cannot manipulate others and expect them to be grateful. Why was he like that? Peter thought back to how understanding and compassionate he'd been when Ellen had left him at the altar. It was hard to reconcile that caring man with the hard and implacable one he'd just left. Had it simply been that he had understood then because he felt that Ellen had left him, too? Did Mark even know what love truly was, or did he just feel that he somehow owned both Ellen and Jane?

The question now was whether Peter could continue to make excuses for him. Could he forgive him for this if he continued to show no remorse for the situation that he had caused by throwing them together as he had, and then for causing Jane so much unnecessary anguish while Peter had been missing? He wasn't entirely sure he could, but could he truly turn his back entirely upon his own twin? He didn't know, but he did know that their relationship would never be the same again.

CHAPTER 31

SEPTEMBER 17, 1893, EAGLE CREEK, MONTANA

*J*ane had to decline Marianne's invitation to dine with them after church and had instead taken a walk up into the mountains. The nights were already drawing in earlier and she wished to make the most of the fine weather before it disappeared entirely. She strode purposefully, enjoying the feeling of her legs working hard and being just a little out of breath. The colors on the trees were changing, greens fading to gold and russet before the leaves fell into a rustling carpet underfoot.

As she climbed further upward, her boots pinched her toes and rubbed her heels just a little, but she ignored the discomfort. She reached a rocky outcrop and tucked her skirts up as she clambered up and over it and looked up at the inhospitable peak. There was no path, just some rocky scree and the snow-capped peak that would need skills and equipment she did not possess.

She stood up and looked down at Eagle Creek. She knew that if she took the path down the other side of the mountain, she'd eventually reach the Crow Village. She had never visited it, but she was friendly with several Crow who worked and traded in the town. It was probably too far to walk there and back in a day, but she might be able to prevail upon Many Birds or Walks With The Sun to drive her back to the town.

The path downward wound its way down the steeper side of the mountain in a series of sharp turns. It was barely wide enough for a wagon and would need a very skilled driver to negotiate it. Her admiration for The Crow's skills with horses grew even more. They were known throughout the land for the quality of their animals.

As she walked, she heard a rustling in the trees to her right. She turned and saw a deer in the distance, staring at her intently. She stared back, marveling at the animal's delicate beauty. She didn't move a muscle, just watched and waited. Eventually, the deer moved on, but it was not alone. A fawn followed her closely, and a large stag emerged a moment or two later. Jane could hardly believe her luck in seeing such regal creatures. They truly were magnificent, and it was a memory she would cherish forever.

By the time she reached the valley floor, she was tired. She sat down on a fallen tree, took off her boots and stockings, and checked her heels and toes for blisters. Not surprisingly, there were some forming. She put her stockings back on and tried to pull them as tightly as she could before putting her boots on. She rather wished she'd not been so intent on reaching the Crow Village and had been sensible enough to return home when she'd reached the outcrop.

She'd always imagined the Crow Village to be close to the path, but she was dismayed to find that it was still quite some way away. It was almost dark when she reached it. Strikes The Iron, the wife of Chief Plenty Coups, saw her entering the village and hurried to greet her. "Miss Jane, whatever are you doing here?" she asked.

"I think I misjudged how far away you are from us," Jane said with a weary smile. "I wanted to see the village for myself. I rather hoped that I might be able to convince someone to drive me home as I have blisters now."

"Well, you are most welcome, and I am sure we will find someone to take you home. Come inside, I'll fetch us some tea and you will eat with us tonight. Plenty Coups is making his famous venison stew."

"He cooks?"

"He does. Many Crow men can cook well."

"I'm impressed. Most men of my acquaintance barely know where the kitchen is."

Strikes The Iron smiled and took her into a home that wasn't very different from Jane's own. It was small and cozy with a large fireplace that had a heavy iron pot hanging from a hook over the fire. The stew inside it made the house smell wonderful.

"Sit, warm yourself," her hostess said, indicating the pile of skins and furs by the fire.

Jane sank down into them and was immediately enveloped in the warmth and luxuriant softness. "I should get one of these for my armchair," she said.

"I can fetch some for you. I'll gladly swap some for one of your gowns," Strikes The Iron said.

"I only need one, but would be glad to make you a gown for that."

"Do you have a fur coat for winter?"

"No, but I do have a good, thick woolen one."

"Then I'll find one you can make into a coat. You'll notice the difference and be glad of it."

Jane was touched by the woman's generosity. They had met in the marketplace on a couple of occasions, but such kindness was what one might expect of a close friend, not a mere acquaintance. But it seemed that Strikes The Iron thought she had by far the better part of their bargain. Jane was flattered that her work was so well thought of, even here.

Chief Plenty Coups arrived just as the two women had finished their raspberry leaf tea. He smiled warmly at Jane, but she was always a little in awe of the famous chief. He was an impressive-looking man with a leathery face and sharp, hawklike eyes.

"Miss Jane, I do hope you are hungry," he said as he took the lid off the cooking pot and stirred the stew. A waft of the rich, meaty scent filled the room and made Jane's mouth water and her stomach growl. He laughed. "I think that gives me my answer."

She flushed. "I apologize, but it really does smell wonderful."

"I only hope it tastes as good as it smells," Plenty Coups said as he began to ladle it into wooden bowls. Jane tried to get up and help him, but he insisted she stay seated. "You are our guest, Miss Jane."

He handed her a bowl and a wooden spoon, gave another to his wife, and finally sat down with his own. They ate in companionable silence. Jane savored every mouthful of the delicious stew. The meat was tender, the vegetables soft, and the broth rich with marrowfat and flavor from the bones. A slight hint of juniper berries and other herbs brought the dish to a level she'd not thought possible. "I'll have to ask you for lessons," she said when she'd finished the bowl.

"It helps that Strikes The Iron has the best collection of dried herbs in the land," he said, looking fondly at his wife.

"Though she uses them for medicines and teas, not to cook with."

There was a loud noise outside. Plenty Coups jumped to his feet and looked outside. He frowned and cursed under his breath. "Stay inside," he said before running out into the darkness. The door slammed loudly behind him.

Jane and Strikes The Iron both got to their feet. Jane peered out of the window as Strikes The Iron opened the door and gasped. "Oh my," she cried. Flames were flickering in the night.

"What is it?" Jane asked, not sure what she was seeing.

"Many Birds' skin lodge," Strikes The Iron explained. "It is on fire. And there are many teepees and lodges nearby that could catch quickly if the wind changes."

"Oh," Jane said. "I know the chief said to stay here, but is there anything we can do?"

"The men seem to have it under control, but I think it may be an idea for us to get the women together to create a chain from the river in case they need more water than we have."

Jane nodded. She followed Strikes The Iron outside, and they soon had a group of women strung out in a line from the village to the river, passing buckets back and forth to the men as they tried to fight the flames. She was impressed by how calm everyone was, how easily they took their places and did what was required, even as the fire began to spread. Her heart was beating so hard and so fast that she feared it might leap out of her chest.

The rhythmic task of passing water and empty buckets helped to calm her nerves, even though the air they were breathing was growing harsher from the acrid smoke. She focused on the task at hand. They may have spent hours passing the buckets, it may have been just a few minutes, but it seemed endless. Finally, Chief Plenty Coups called out that the fires were out, and everyone cheered.

They reveled in their success for a short while, then began to take stock of the damage. Jane felt useless as those whose homes had burned tried to see what had survived the fire while others made offers to take them in. The entire tribe rallied around those whose lives had been upended. Many Birds and his son, Walks With The Sun, came back to Plenty Coups' home with them. Many Birds looked exhausted, and his family had lost everything they owned.

"I am so sorry," Jane said to him.

"We can rebuild," Many Birds said, "but there were things that my wife, and her mother and grandmother, made that we'll not be able to replace. But everyone is safe, and that is all that matters."

Jane wasn't so sure that she would be so calm if her home had burned to the ground. She supposed that there were differences in how The Crow lived and the way her own kind did. Many of The Crow still moved around with the seasons, following the herds and living in easily movable structures like Many Birds' skin lodge and the teepees close to it.

"We'll build new homes for you all in the morning," Plenty Coups assured him. "I've plenty of skins in storage, and we have more than enough bowls, plates, and spoons to give you."

Strikes The Iron brought out some brightly colored blankets. Jane had never seen anything like them. She reached out impulsively, wondering if they were as soft as they looked. They were as smooth to the touch as the furs she'd been sitting on earlier.

"You will definitely have to show me how to make these," she said, shaking her head in disbelief at how pretty they were.

Strikes The Iron smiled. "I fear you will need to spend the night with us, Miss Jane. I'll not ask anyone to go out again tonight. You shall share the bed with me. The men can bunk out here by the fire."

"I'll take you home in the morning," Walks With The Sun said. "I have to go to work early, though."

"I understand, and am honored to be invited to stay," Jane said. "Thank you. Thank you all."

In the room where she would be sleeping, there were several pretty beaded necklaces and other jewelry. They were like nothing she'd ever seen before, and they made her wonder when The Crow wore them and if they had any special significance. She asked Strikes The Iron when she came in after settling the men in the other room. The older woman smiled. "Indeed, but it would take me too long to explain everything now, and I think we all need rest."

The women climbed into bed. Jane pulled a blanket tightly around her body and was surprised to find that she was indeed very tired. She yawned, closed her eyes, and was fast asleep in moments. She woke before dawn, feeling refreshed. Strikes The Iron was still sleeping, so she climbed out of the bed as carefully and quietly as she could and crept into the other room. Walks With The Sun was drinking coffee by the fire while his father and Plenty Coups continued to snore loudly. He grinned at her and handed her a cup.

They went outside, where Walks With The Sun whistled to the horses in a small enclosure at the edge of the village. A painted horse trotted toward them, and Walks With The Sun quickly harnessed it to a small cart, then offered Jane his hand so she could climb up. She tried not to panic while he took the tricky path back up the mountain and down into Eagle Creek, but she needn't have worried. The boy was an excellent driver.

She'd never been gladder to let herself into her little cottage. She didn't want to imagine how distraught she would feel if it burned to the ground before her eyes. It still amazed her that The Crow had been so calm about their losses. But her home was her anchor, the place she felt she belonged after so many years of not belonging anywhere.

She supposed that The Crow could feel that way anywhere because their anchors were one another – not the homes they laid their heads in. She wondered if she would feel differently if she had someone who loved her and needed her as The Crow loved and needed one another.

CHAPTER 32

OCTOBER 6, 1893, NEW YORK CITY, NEW YORK

*D*ear Peter,

I must confess, it still feels strange to address a letter this way, but I do like it.

I do hope you are well and that your business in New York is progressing as you'd hoped. I must confess that I miss you and hope you will be able to visit again soon.

I experienced the most wonderful, frightening, and enlightening night of my life. I took a long walk and went to visit the Crow Village. It is the most peculiar mixture of buildings, from little cottages like mine to a large lodge where they can all gather together, all built among many of their traditional skin lodges and teepees. I don't know if you've ever seen such things. From the outside, they look as if they will be small and difficult to live in, but I must confess that having seen them, that they are no smaller inside in many ways than my cottage.

While I was there, one of the skin lodges caught on fire. The flames spread with the wind, razing many teepees and lodges to the ground. The people who lived in them lost everything – and yet they seemed unfazed by it. It made me see that they regard their belongings in a very different way to the way that we do. We hope to guard and keep things, to hand them down to our children, to maintain a line of ownership that proves our place in the world. They seem to care little for that and more for the impact they leave on the land that is their home and the people in their lives.

I wonder if they maybe have better priorities than us? I am, as you know, very attached to my home here in Eagle Creek, but I found myself asking if it was because it is mine or if it is because of where it is and who is around me. I am ever more convinced that it is the latter, for everyone I think of as family (except for you, of course) is here.

I'm not sure if I told you before, but our dear Cook has moved here to be with us too. Marianne and I are delighted to be reunited with her, and she is settling into her new life remarkably well. She is such a doting nanny to baby Elliot and is already teaching Flora-Rose to cook. I knew I had missed her but until she was here I don't think I had allowed myself to acknowledge just how much.

And so, with these lessons I am learning, I want to tell you how much I long for you to be here, too. I know that the people I love are my home now, not my house – though I do love that, and am most fortunate to have it. As long as I have people I love, I will always have a home – wherever I may be. So, if you cannot make arrangements for your business and cannot leave New York, know that I will happily travel to you. I will not say that I won't miss my family here, but I believe that you are my family, too.

Yours, most thoughtfully

Jane

It was an unexpected letter, which had initially made Peter fearful. He was so glad that she seemed to have escaped her adventure unscathed – and perhaps even enlightened. She sounded so happy and had, in a rather peculiar way, admitted that she loved him, and that made his heart sing. He missed her terribly, and with each passing day he was growing more certain that leaving his enterprise in Wilbur's capable hands would be the best thing for all of them. Wilbur continued to shine in every challenge that he and Cable put his way. But there was the matter of ensuring that Jesson received the justice he deserved. And Mark.

Relations with his twin had not improved. Their home was now witness to their war, with poor Wilbur caught awkwardly in the middle of the silence between them. Mark had completely withdrawn, despite Peter's attempts to reason with him. He knew that Mark felt betrayed, and he could understand how much that hurt, but he did not need to feel that way. If only Mark could accept that it was his own actions that had led them to this juncture, everything would still be well between them.

But he did not have time to try to change his brother's mind. Nor did he have any idea as to how he might do so. Mark was stubborn. He had to come to things on his own terms. Perhaps Peter had always tried too hard to protect him from himself, to save Mark from hurt. He knew that he was in part responsible for Mark's nature, having indulged Mark's peculiarities more than he should have done. But Mark was a man grown, and he had to learn at some point that his actions and words had consequences. It might as well be now.

Wilbur entered Peter's office and handed the manifest for *The Splendide* to Peter, who looked it over. It still amused him that Marston had not known who had purchased his favorite ship until Peter had returned to New York and taken a tour of it with its new captain. Marston had watched them from one of the nearby coffee shops. When Mr. Kingshott had informed him that the gentleman who had anonymously bought most of his fleet was in fact Peter, Marston had stormed out of the shop and hadn't been seen since.

"A lot of sugar," Peter said with a frown. "There's not much of a market for it here at the moment."

But there is in Bristol, Wilbur pointed out.

Peter nodded. "Is she seaworthy?"

Yes, her sails are all mended and her hull is sound.

"What of her masts? It's a long trip through treacherous waters, I'd not want her to founder in a storm because of a crack."

She's sound, Wilbur scribbled quickly. *Captain Jones checked her over for me as I know you aren't yet sure of Captain Hackett.*

"He seems a good man, and Kingshott values him, but I have to get used to his ways," Peter admitted.

Shall I tell him to make ready for a voyage?

"Yes, unload the tobacco and replace it with cigars and rum. The English will gladly buy the cotton and sugar."

Wilbur nodded and hurried out again. He didn't waste a moment, and he was efficient and amiable. Cable had struggled with him initially, unsure how to deal with Wilbur's hurriedly written notes, but he'd soon gotten used to them, and the two could often be found huddled together as Cable taught him all about how to run a shipping enterprise, the rules of the dock, and involved him in their efforts to care for the local people.

It was thanks to the additional pair of hands that they had now raised enough money to run the hospital for its first five years, and Cable hoped that the building would be ready for staff and patients before Christmas, or possibly early in the New Year. Peter hoped it would be sooner because he wanted to see it opened and helping people but he longed to spend his first Christmas with Jane in Eagle Creek. He wondered if she would come to the grand opening if he asked her. He didn't want to crow about his good deeds, but he wanted her to be by his side for such an important moment.

As he thought about that, he realized that he'd never really spoken to her about their charitable endeavors. He would need to remedy that, so he quickly penned a response to her letter. As he wrote about the new houses that had been built and the progress of the hospital, he felt as though he was trying too hard to impress her and tried to change the words to make it seem less important – but it was impossible to do so. He knew that Jane, of all people, would understand the need to provide poor children with good homes and healthcare.

He prayed that she wouldn't think that it was another thing that he hadn't told her the truth about. There were so many things he'd not told her yet, but they had shared so few letters and so little time. She had to understand that there would be things that they would continue to learn about each other. He was sure that there were many things that she had not yet told him about her life, too, and tried to reassure himself that she would be impressed and not hurt by his news.

Not entirely happy with what he had written but unable to find another way to say it all, he finished the letter with a request that she join him in New York for the grand opening and a tentative hope that he might be able to spend Christmas with her in Montana. He put it to one side and finished his work. He and Wilbur closed up the office and walked the couple of blocks to Cable's house.

They were welcomed warmly and fed with thick steaks and crisply roasted potatoes, then they retired to Cable's study with a decanter of port and a box of cigars. Wilbur sat quietly by the window, puffing happily on his cigar. Even now, he still looked surprised to have found himself in such company, enjoying such luxuries. He truly seemed content in his new world, which made Peter very happy.

"There's a problem," Cable said as he took the plans for the hospital from his desk and pointed to one of the buildings. "I don't think we'll be opening until the spring, possibly not even until next summer."

"That isn't good news. What is the delay? I thought we were hoping to be ready in a couple of months at most."

"I'd put off work on that wing until everything else was built as I didn't have the land yet. I was hoping we'd be able to start on it by now, but I can't convince Beddington to sell the land. I'm sorry, Peter. I know you don't want to leave New York until we're done."

"Ah, I didn't realize it was his," Peter said. Albert

Beddington didn't much like either of them. "How do we convince him?"

"I simply don't know. I've tried everything, including offering him far more money than it is worth."

"Can we not move that wing?"

"I've been trying to get my man to find a way to use the land we do have. He says it isn't possible, not as we've already started building the rest of it."

Wilbur got up from his seat and peered over Peter's shoulder at the plans. For a moment they were all quiet, then Wilbur took the plans from Peter and went to the desk. He picked up a pencil and took a clean sheet of paper and began to make a sketch. He frowned, screwed up the sketch, then started again. And again. And again. He was soon surrounded by screwed-up pieces of paper. Peter picked some of them up and unscrewed them. The drawings were just as good as anything that Cable's man had drawn, the lines as straight and clean as if Wilbur had been designing and planning buildings since he was a boy.

It took him almost twenty attempts before he handed a sketch to Cable, who looked it over, then shook his head as he chuckled a little. "You, my boy, are full of hidden talents, aren't you?"

Wilbur grinned at the praise as Cable handed the sketch to Peter. Somehow, he'd managed to solve the problem using the land they already had. It would save them a small fortune

– and it would mean that there would be no delay in construction. Peter clapped him on the back.

"You're a genius," he said, admiring the sketch. "How have you learned all the things you have? When I think about how I found you, struggling to make ends meet and having to take whatever work you could get." He shook his head, bemused.

I watch and learn more than most, I suppose. I can't rely on my ears to learn or tell people that I'm not the idiot they take me to be, so they do all manner of things in front of me.

"Well, I am glad that I never thought you a fool," Peter said. "And I am glad that you were taking work from bandits so that I could meet you."

"I think we can start to plan our opening now," Cable said happily. "How would you feel about Christmas Eve?"

Peter frowned. "I'd hoped that I would be able to visit Jane for Christmas," he said. "I always knew I'd probably need to return again, but I miss her and want to propose to her."

Cable smiled. "I think we can delay until you return. Perhaps you can convince her to return with you so I may meet her?"

"I will certainly ask her," Peter said.

She's very pretty.

"Is she, Wilbur?" Cable asked. "More importantly, how does she feel about our Peter?"

I am sure she loves him as much as he loves her.

"I am glad to hear that," Cable said with a smile. "How did you feel about Eagle Creek? You're not going to up and leave me, too, are you?"

No, Sir! I'm happier here, though I did like it there. I'll be happy to visit Peter from time to time, but you're stuck with me.

"I'm even more glad to hear that," Cable said, chuckling.

CHAPTER 33

"*W*ilbur, this has to be finished before I go," Peter said, handing back the guest list for the grand opening of the hospital that they had finally decided would be taking place on Saturday, January 27. "I can't expect Cable to take this on as well. We have to get these invitations out, or there'll be nobody there anyway."

Who is missing?

"Beddington, Marston, to name just a couple."

You're inviting Beddington and Marston? Wilbur raised a quizzical eyebrow.

"Yes. If we don't, they'll never let us forget it, and we want to set an example to all the men who employ the sailors and stevedores who live in the slums – and all of them can hold a grudge. How many invitations have been sent?"

About half. But I wouldn't say no to some assistance writing out the rest. My wrist is killing me!

"Bring them all in here. We can do them together."

Wilbur beamed, went into his office next door, and fetched the boxes of freshly printed invitations and his list of attendees. The two men began to carefully write them out and slip them into the heavy parchment envelopes. They would land on the doormats of the great and the good of New York in the coming days. Peter hoped that most of them would come. So many people went away for Christmas and New Year's Eve, and many didn't return until February or even March.

It was dark by the time they had finished. "Come, I'll take you out for some supper," Peter said, clapping Wilbur on the back affectionately. "I'll miss you while I'm gone."

It will be strange.

"Anything you need, go to Cable, not to Mark. Mark is useless in a crisis. He won't even know where anything is in the house."

I know that. I asked him where the coal was to light the fire. He didn't know he needed to order it, or where it went when it arrived.

Peter sighed. "I'm sorry lad, but I'm glad that you're still there with him. He's not an easy man, and he has no idea how to take care of himself. He needs someone to keep an eye on him."

What will you do when you come back? Will you stay in the hotel? You can't live on the floor of your office if you bring Miss Brown back with you.

Peter gave a rueful smile. "I keep hoping that Mark will see sense so I can go home. But he's not going to. I'll have to look into finding something near the docks. Perhaps Cable will let me have one of the apartments in his block?"

They walked out of the dockyard side by side and went into their favorite coffee shop. Mrs. Wilmslow made a fine steak pie in the evenings. They both ordered and sat down at a table by the window. A ship was coming into harbor, her sails neatly tied as the tug brought her into the dock. The tiny boat was dwarfed by the ship she dragged through the harbor to her mooring. As soon as she drew close, the crew jumped down, ropes flew, and she had been tied fast in no time at all.

Peter still loved watching the efficiency of the sailing crews and stevedores as they unloaded a ship. There were no delays, as time mattered. The merchants wanted their goods to sell, and the ships needed new cargoes. Everything moved smoothly and quickly, keeping the ship owners as prosperous as possible.

Their food arrived, and he and Wilbur ate hungrily. Peter listened to the talk around them. Many were talking about William Jesson's trial. He'd been sentenced to hang for what he'd done to Peter. Though he could understand the man's desperation, Peter wished he'd not felt compelled to take such drastic action. Every man deserved a second chance, even if they had as bad a reputation as Jesson.

But it looked as though no evidence could pin Marston to the crimes. The news hadn't surprised Peter and Cable when the sheriff had delivered it a few weeks earlier, Marston was as slippery as they came, and both men were keeping a close eye on him as they knew all too well that a cornered rat was the most dangerous one. Marston had only one ship left and was trying desperately to make his fortune back, but Peter knew how hard it was to do so and wouldn't be surprised if Marston tried to take a shortcut somewhere.

But for now, things seemed quiet enough. Peter could ignore men talking about him, he'd been doing it for years. He just got on with his work. But he was glad that Wilbur couldn't hear everything that was said sometimes. The lad was very fond of him, and of Cable. It was for the best if he didn't know that many men looked on them as being somehow unusual and unmanly for their rather peculiar interest in helping men below them on the slippery ladder of life.

Peter didn't care what these men said. Once, he had longed to be accepted by them, to be a part of their gossipy circles. He'd hoped they would agree to insure his voyages, to buy a share in them, but he'd bypassed them — and they did not like him for it. That he'd thrown in his lot with the eccentric Cable Poole made them snigger behind his back.

There was no doubt that Cable's ideas were unusual. He enjoyed his wealth but was not as attached to it as they were. Most of them simply didn't understand him, so they cast him out, making him a loner. But Peter knew that Cable was more likely to be remembered when he was gone than any of them. He was building things that would help so many people. Peter was proud to be his friend and to have been infected with his radical ideas about improving living and working conditions for everyone.

After they'd eaten, Peter walked Wilbur back to the townhouse he'd once shared with his brother. He paused outside for a moment, wondering if he should go in and try to talk to Mark again, but what else was there to say? He simply couldn't think of anything until Mark could see that he held as much responsibility for his own woes as anyone else did. Peter refused to keep taking all the blame for things that Mark had brought about. It did neither of them any good.

He was about to walk away when Wilbur burst out of the door waving a small envelope at him. His beam told Peter that it was from Jane. He smiled at the lad and took the letter from him. "Thank you." Wilbur gave him a little salute and went back inside.

Peter didn't wait to get back to his office to open it. He wanted to read her words. He opened it carefully and sat down on a low wall just a few doors down from the town-house. He hoped she hadn't minded that he'd only sent her a short letter following her rather lovely one following her visit to the Crow Village, but he'd just been so busy and there had been little to share with her, other than all the work that was happening on the hospital – and he wanted to tell her about that in person.

Dear Peter

I was so happy to receive your letter. Of course, I under-stand how busy you are and that you won't have the time to write endless letters to me.

I do hope your work is progressing so that you can still come and spend Christmas here in Eagle Creek. It is such a special time here, with the snow everywhere, and the villagers hang homemade decorations from every surface. On Christmas Eve, there is a candlelit walk to the church for mass. Father Timothy always makes the Christmas services so special. And, of course, there is the Christmas meal at Marianne's, which will this year be cooked by Cook – who has insisted that she will tolerate nobody else in her kitchen that day.

I cannot tell you how wonderful it is to have her here, at last. I missed her terribly, and even though I knew that it only came truly clear once she was here and she hugged me. I had missed that so much. I am sure I will feel the same way about your absence, for I know I miss you – but when I see you, it will remind me that I didn't know just how much.

Have matters improved between yourself and Mark? I do hope so. I hate the idea that I have in some way come between you. To have a sibling is such an important bond. To have a twin is one I can barely imagine. Whether he tells you it or not, I am certain that he must miss you. Have you tried to talk to him again? I know you said you intended to, but you did not write and tell me how it went.

Will you write and tell me when you'll be here? I so want to be able to be at the station to meet you, but Mrs. Albert rarely comes into the store now. Her knees are so bad that she can barely stand. Her sister-in-law came back when I did, to stay with her for a while, but she had to return to New York, though they hope to return for Christmas, too. I do hope that they will, for I am not sure how many more Christmases Mrs. Albert has left in her. She is so sad and feels lonesome, though we try to ensure she has visitors all the time. I think she believes herself to be a burden to us all, and she is not the type of woman to want to rely on others.

I can hardly wait to see you again.

Yours, most excitedly

Jane

She sounded so eager, it brought a smile to his lips. He stood up and glanced at the townhouse. He caught a glimpse of a shadowy figure standing in the upstairs room, looking down at him. He waved to his brother, but Mark did not wave back. Peter waited for a few moments, his heart full of hope that Mark would come down and speak to him, but he did not. And so, he made his way back toward the dockyard and let himself into the quiet warehouse.

He hated sleeping here, but he was used to it as he'd done it so often when waiting for a ship to come into port. He had a comfortable enough chaise longue and warm blankets, but he'd rather be anywhere than here in the depths of winter. The fire was still burning, though it was barely embers now. He stoked the tiny stove and added more wood, then huddled around it, leaving his coat and gloves on. When the room was warm, he took off his gloves and sat at his desk to write a reply to Jane.

Once he was happy with it, he sealed it ready to mail the next day, then banked the fire so it would burn all night, curled up under his blankets, and tried to sleep. His dreams were filled with memories of the time he'd kissed Jane by the waterfall interspersed with Mark's angry face at the window that very evening. He tossed and turned all night, fretting about how to make things better between himself and his twin, but he was no closer to an answer when he rose before dawn.

CHAPTER 34

DECEMBER 20, 1893, EAGLE CREEK, MONTANA

*P*eter would be arriving today. It was strange, but Jane felt as nervous as she had the first night when she'd met him, thinking he was Mark. It was as if they were meeting properly for the first time despite everything that had passed between them since. She glanced at her reflection in the cheval glass and frowned. The dress she'd chosen because she thought it flattered her, looked rumpled and dowdy. She took it off and tried on another. She didn't feel right in that one either. Glad that, as a dressmaker, she had an unusually large choice of gowns for a girl like her, she stood in front of the armoire in her room, took them all out, and laid them on her bed.

Having tried on five dresses, she finally returned to the one she'd discarded in the first place and decided to pin her hair differently instead. She fidgeted with it, stabbing her head and fingers with the pins hard enough to draw blood a number of times. She shook her head and looked at her flushed face in the mirror. Peter knew what she looked like, and he liked her. No, he'd said he loved her. He knew that she wasn't some fashion plate from New York. He just wanted to see her, not a facsimile of her.

She fixed her hair as she always did, splashed her overly hot face with cold water and took a few deep breaths. She had nothing to fear. Peter was coming for Christmas, and they were going to have the most wonderful time. She pulled on her fur coat, made from the gift that Strikes The Iron had given her, and went out into the icy cold.

There had been fresh snowfall overnight, and it lay thick and glistening white on the ground everywhere but Main Street and around the station. It made Eagle Creek look like something out of a dream, and it seemed so quiet and calm. She couldn't quite describe it, but when the world was covered in snow, it seemed so much more still and the quietest of whispers sounded like a shout. Whatever it was, she loved it, and it was just one of the many things she loved about living here, despite the cold.

Her heart felt like it was trying to leap out of her chest as she stood on the platform and heard the whistle of the train in the distance. She had never been so excited, or so afraid, to see anyone in her life. As the train rounded the bend and pulled into the station, she could barely breathe. She coughed a little as a fug of smoke and steam filled the platform and tried to peer through it. She could barely see her hand in front of her, much less who might be climbing out of the carriages as the doors opened and slammed against the sides.

When the smoke finally cleared, Peter was standing in front of her, smiling. She had thought she remembered every tiny detail of his handsome face, but she realized how much she had forgotten. He was so impossibly handsome. She had to pinch herself to think that he was here to see her, plain Jane. She smiled back at him as he took her hand and turned it over to press a kiss into her palm, then close her fingers over the top of it. "Good day, dearest Jane," he said.

"You are well?" she asked, looking closer and seeing that there were bags under his eyes.

"I am now I am here. I've not been sleeping too well recently, but I'm sure that will ease soon enough with some rest in the luxurious beds at The Eyrie and some good home cooking."

"Mark is still not talking to you then?"

"No," he said with a slight grimace. "Wilbur tells me how he is but says he doesn't talk to him."

"How is dear Wilbur? Such a bright boy."

"He is well," Peter said. "I still find it strange that I

should have found such a fine man under such peculiar circumstances."

"I am glad that something good came out of such a dreadful situation," Jane said. "Now, the sled will be here for you shortly. I thought you might prefer a quiet night after the long journey, but I could come up and dine with you there if you want me to?"

"Of course I want you to," Peter said firmly as she slipped her arm through his. "I came all this way to see you, not to be separated from you."

"I am so happy to hear that," she said, beaming up at him like a giddy girl.

He grinned and pulled her closer so he could whisper in her ear. "If we weren't in public, I would kiss you as I did at the waterfall."

She felt a flush creep up her chest and throat into her cheeks as she giggled. "You should not be so naughty," she scolded him. "But I must confess that I wish that, too."

Peter reluctantly left her to get into the vast sleigh that would take him and his belongings to The Eyrie, and she returned to her work. There was much to do to make the last-minute alterations to dresses that were to be gifts, those that were to be worn to Christmas events, and even to the curtains and tablecloths, ready for family and friends to visit. She could not leave Kathy and Hannah to deal with things alone, though both were showing great aptitude now for all aspects of their work.

The time passed terribly slowly as she waited for the clock to tick past six o'clock so she could hurry home and dress for dinner. Jonas had the gig waiting for her and gave her a cheeky wink as he sent her on her way without charging her. "Just ensure we are invited to your wedding," he teased. She assured him she would if that were what were to happen, but she had no expectations at this stage.

She tried not to think too far ahead, but as she drove up the mountain, she couldn't help thinking how wonderful it would be to be Peter's wife. She wanted that, more than anything.

~

DECEMBER 24, 1893, EAGLE CREEK, MONTANA

Peter had found it hard to fill his days while Jane had been working. He'd taken walks, but the thick snow made going too far alone very dangerous, so he stayed close to the hotel, or to the town. He met Jane for lunch every day, and they dined in the hotel together every evening. He felt terrible that Jane had to drive herself back and forth alone at night. He knew that she was a better driver than he was and knew the roads well, but that didn't stop him from fretting until he saw her again the next day.

Tonight, there was to be a party along Main Street. He'd offered his help to hang lanterns and decorations from every surface that could hold them and to build a dance floor and a huge bonfire with dry wood. Everyone involved prayed that there would be no rain or snow, and it seemed that the good Lord had listened to them as the night had brought clear skies and twinkling stars above.

Once he was dressed, he pulled a small velvet box from his trunk and tucked it into his pocket. He looked in the mirror and smoothed an unruly curl away from his collar before running down the stairs to take his place in the convoy of sleds that would take all the guests at the hotel down to the town for the party. He chatted amicably with his fellow guests on the drive down. Everyone was wrapped up in thick fur coats, hats, and mittens, their knees covered with sheepskin rugs. With pink cheeks and bright eyes, everyone was excited for the festivities ahead.

Peter helped his fellow travelers out of the sleigh when it came to a halt outside the brightly lit saloon, then hurried to Jane's house. He knocked loudly on the door three times. She opened it before he'd even finished the third knock. She grinned at him. "I thought you might never get here."

"I was rather held up by everyone else," he said. He kissed her cheek and offered her his arm. "But now, I intend to dance with you all night on the dance floor I helped to build."

"Who knew you were so handy?" she teased.

"I am a very useful man to know. I can caulk a ship, darn a sail, mend a stay, and climb the rigging."

They laughed. "Very useful skills on land, I'm sure," Jane said, her eyes sparkling with mischief.

"Very useful indeed for climbing up to strange places to hang lanterns." Peter pointed out some of the lights that were in particularly tricky-to-reach places.

"Very useful," she agreed as they were approached by Nate Hale and his wife.

"Good evening, Mr. Algood," Sheriff Hale said. "I am glad that we are meeting under better circumstances, this time."

"Me too," Peter said, shaking his hand.

"This is my wife, Clara."

Peter greeted her politely. She was a very pretty lady, and the tall sheriff was clearly besotted with her. As they walked onward, Jane leaned into him. "They met because of an advertisement, too."

"Really?" Peter asked, taken aback.

"As did Marianne and James, in a way, though they'd known each other since they were children. And Elise and Tom – over there with the boy with the performing dog."

"That dog is a genius," Peter remarked. He'd seen Bailey and Quinto practicing their show earlier.

"He is, but he's getting older now. He can't do all the tricks he used to. Elise fears that he might not be with them much longer, and poor Meredith lost her Fliss this year, who was part of their act for a while."

"That is sad," Peter said. "Bailey will take it very hard."

"He will," Jane agreed. "But not tonight. Tonight, he will perform his tricks for everyone."

"Well, I look forward to that later, but right now there is a band playing, so shall we dance?" Peter asked.

Jane nodded, and he led her to the dance floor. He took her in his arms and began to whirl her around the floor. She fitted so beautifully in his arms, and she danced well, keeping up with him on light feet, not treading on his toes once. The waltz became a quadrille, and they took their places in a square, then a slow and stately mazurka began. Peter did not know the steps, but Jane soon taught him. Some local dances followed, and Jane showed him them all.

"How do you know all these?" he asked her breathlessly as they pranced together in line.

"One of the things Marianne and I were involved with when we first came here was a ball for the children as they finished school. We taught them all the dances Marianne had learned as a young girl in New York Society, and they taught us the local dances. It was so much fun."

"I'm sure it was, but may we have a rest soon? My feet are sore, and I desperately need a drink," Peter joked.

She grinned at him and took pity, leading him off the floor and toward the trestles near the fireplace where large kettles full of mulled cider and wine were warming over the fire.

As they drank their sweet and spicy wine, Jane pointed out some of the couples still dancing. "Meredith and Aidan met via the newspaper as well. In truth, I think most of the town found love on the matrimonials page."

Peter shook his head. It was quite something to hear that so many people had been brought together that way in one small town. "Well, let's hope a little of their luck rubs off on us – though it wasn't me who actually replied to your letter."

"But you are the man I met because of it," she pointed out.

"I am. Jane, I've loved you from that very first day, though I tried so hard not to for my brother's sake. I can't live my life trying not to hurt him, trying to protect him – especially as he has pushed me away. I want to live my life making you happy, loving you, caring for you, and raising a family with you, here in Eagle Creek. Though I never thought that small-town life would be for me, I find that as long as you are with me, I want to be nowhere else." He paused and pulled the jewelry box from his pocket. He opened it up as he got on one knee. "Will you marry me, Jane Brown, and make me the happiest man alive?"

She gasped and clasped her flushing cheeks, her eyes wide as saucers. "Oh, I will." She sighed happily.

He stood up, placed the ring on her finger, and embraced her tightly. "I am so glad you said yes. I feared you might tell me we don't really suit again."

"Perhaps in our case, opposites do attract," she said with a smile as he kissed her in full sight of the entire town, not caring one jot who saw.

CHAPTER 35

DECEMBER 25, 1893, EAGLE CREEK, MONTANA

*P*eter was a little nervous about attending lunch with the Dennys. Marianne and James had given him a warm enough welcome and had seemed to be delighted when Jane had shown them her ring, but Peter could barely remember a Christmas spent with a loving family. It had been just him and Mark for such a long time. And he had not yet told Jane that he had to leave the next day in order to be back in time for the hospital's grand opening.

It was strange that he found it so hard to tell her about it. He had no trouble telling her the worst aspects of his character, but he found it very hard to tell her about the better side of his nature. It felt like he was bragging, claiming praise he had done little to deserve. He had simply done what was needed and what he could. He did not want accolades from her, or from anyone.

As they walked to the Denny house after church that morning, he knew he had to tell her. As the cheery family went inside, he held Jane's arm and pulled her to a gentle stop. "May I speak with you for just a moment?"

"Of course," she said, her eyes searching his face, looking a little concerned. "You aren't having second thoughts already, are you?" she joked weakly as the door closed, leaving them alone on the porch.

"Not at all, though I fear you may do, for I've been keeping things from you again," he admitted with a rueful look.

She stood back and folded her arms across her chest. "What is it this time? Surely it cannot be anything as bad as you not being your brother?"

"Nothing so bad," he reassured her. "In truth, I hope you will think it is good."

"So, tell me," she said patiently.

"Part of the reason I had to return to New York last time rather than stay here with you as I longed to do was because I have been busy working on a project with Cable."

"You told me he had funded the expansion of your fleet," Jane said, looking a little confused.

"Not that. I could have happily left that in Wilbur's hands, or Cable's. But there was something else, and I wanted to see it through. I'm not sure if Mark or I ever told you, but our parents died due to an outbreak of influenza. We were luckier than many. We had a house to live in and enough money to stay in school until we were old enough to go out and work. An uncle stopped by often to make sure we were well, but nobody seemed to mind that there was no adult looking after us."

"Though I am sad for your loss," Jane said gently, "I can't help being a little envious. When my parents died, or left me, or whatever they did, there was nowhere for me but the orphanage."

"I know, we had it easy. But so many do not, and there was another terrible outbreak last winter. I asked Cable to do what he could when I went to sea. When I returned, we decided to build a hospital that would be free to everyone in need."

"Oh, my, but that is wonderful," Jane said, clapping her hands with delight.

"I am so glad you think so because I need to leave you again, only temporarily this time, to go to New York for the grand opening. I would love you to accompany me, but I understand that you might find it hard to leave at short notice."

"How short is the notice?"

"Tomorrow," Peter said with a pained look. "I know I

should have said something earlier, but I didn't tell you for so long that it just became impossible to do so. It felt like I would be telling you to try to win your favor, and I did not want to do that."

"So you waited until I'd already said yes," Jane said with a gentle smile. "The shop will be quiet through most of January. If Mrs. Albert feels well enough to manage while I'm gone, I am sure we can arrange something. Now, we should go in, or everyone will think we are arguing already."

The meal was wonderful, one of the finest meals Peter had ever had, and he was delighted to be introduced to Cook, who enveloped him in her thick arms, burying his face in her copious bosom, then beamed at his slight embarrassment all day.

"I'm so glad my Jane has finally found love," she said happily as he helped her to do the dishes after the meal. "And one who is happy to help around the house."

"I've been taking care of my brother for most of my life," Peter said. "I cook, too, though not even close to the way you do."

"It's a skill you learn, Peter," she drawled, her thick Southern twang as warm and soothing as hot caramel. "I'll teach you. My girl works too hard, she'll need someone to look after her."

"I'd be glad to learn from you."

"I'll look forward to it," Cook said. She waggled a large,

sharp knife at him a little ominously. "But you hurt that chile again, and you'll see the back of my hand."

"Understood," Peter said solemnly. "I am certainly going to try my best to make her happy."

He had a similar talk with Marianne, then another with James. He was fully expecting young Flora-Rose and baby Elliot to give him a lecture too, especially when Mr. Delaney took him out on the deck for a cigar.

"I have some documents I need to go to New York, would I be able to entrust them to you?" he asked. "I don't want to mail them in case they go missing."

"Might I ask what they are?"

"You may, and I may reserve the right not to tell you," Mr. Delaney said a little curtly.

"Then I also have the right to refuse. I'll not take anything illegal," Peter said simply.

"I'm a lawyer," he protested.

"In my experience, they're often the most likely to try to bend the law," Peter said with a wry smile.

"Touché. I don't want Marianne to know about it, but I have decided that it is time to sell the New York house. I have no intention of ever returning, and there are things I'd like to be able to do here."

Peter nodded. "Then I'll be glad to take your documents. Do you want me to check on the house while I am there?"

"If you have the time."

"In truth, I'd be grateful if you'd let me and Miss Brown stay there. I don't know if you've heard of my troubles with my brother, but I've been sleeping in my office and I'm not sure my back can take it for much longer."

Mr. Delaney chuckled. "I'd be happy for you to, though I must insist that you take a chaperone for dear Jane. I'll not have you impugning her reputation before she's wed."

"I'd not wish to do anything to harm her. I rather hoped that we would be able to convince you and Marianne to come to New York with us."

"I'm not young enough for all the back and forth, I'm happy here – though I'll gladly donate to your hospital – but Marianne might be happy to go to a party, and she'd know her little ones are safe in Cook's hands, now she's here."

"I'll ask her very nicely," Peter joked.

JANUARY 27, 1894, NEW YORK CITY, NEW YORK

"My goodness," Peter exclaimed as they entered the hospital gates.

"I was about to say the same thing," Jane said with a giggle. "But surely you knew what it would look like?"

"I had an idea, of course, but when I left in November, there were still builders and carpenters everywhere. You couldn't really get the full impression. It is quite something to see it all."

"I see there are markings in the grounds. Are they planning a grand garden?" Marianne asked, noting all the bits of string tied to sticks, marking out where lawns and flowerbeds would go.

"Yes, Cable is insistent that trees and flowers are good for the soul, and he has his own gardener planning glorious gardens for invalids to spend time in."

"I know they are for me, so I agree with him. I'm looking forward to meeting him. I'm rather surprised that I don't already know him," Marianne said.

"He doesn't spend much time in Society," Peter said with a grin as his eccentric mentor walked out of the grand front doors of the hospital, his arms open wide. Peter greeted him and found himself embraced in Cable's arms.

"I missed you too much, my boy," Cable said quietly so only Peter would hear. "I may have to visit you in Eagle Creek often. I'll go half-mad without you, I fear."

"You will always be most welcome," Peter said. "Jane, this is my mentor, partner, and dearest friend, Cable Poole. Cable, this is Jane and her dearest friend, Marianne Denny."

"Denny as in Denny, Delaney, and Wilson?" Cable asked, his eyes widening.

"The very same," Marianne said with a grin. "Born a Delaney, married and widowed a Wilson, and now married a Denny."

"Well, that all sounds quite confusing, but Peter, you did not tell me that you were acquainted with New York royalty."

"We're not so high in Society as that," Marianne insisted. "And we live in Eagle Creek now. My husband is the schoolmaster."

Jane watched their interaction shyly, not sure if she should be embarrassed that Mr. Poole had completely ignored her and was only talking to Marianne or glad that he wasn't scrutinizing her. But he soon remembered his manners.

"Miss Brown, forgive me," he said, taking her hand and kissing the air above it. "But anyone who has spent any time in New York knows that this young lady comes from a very fine pedigree. Forgive me for being distracted by it."

"Of course," Jane said quietly. "Marianne is far more interesting than me."

"Now, I doubt that," Mr. Poole said with a twinkly eyed smile. "You have won the heart of my protégé, so I am sure there is much to interest me about you."

"And Cable cares little for Society," Peter reminded them all. "He shuns it."

"It doesn't mean I am not interested and intrigued by it when it walks into my world," Mr. Poole said. "And given what we are here for today, having such an esteemed guest will do wonders for helping us to raise funds for the hospital in the future."

Peter laughed. "Always looking for the angle. That's the Cable Poole I know. Which reminds me, Marianne's father said he would arrange a generous donation, and I am sure that where he leads, others will follow."

"Oh, my boy, you do always bring me the best things," Cable said happily.

"Speaking of good things, where is Wilbur?" Peter asked.

"Running a few last-minute errands. He'll be here shortly. He's as keen to see you all as I am."

Mr. Poole took Jane's arm and tucked it through his own. She glanced nervously at Peter, who nodded encouragingly. "Now, I shall give your lovely fiancée and her friend a tour before our guests arrive," Cable said.

Peter grinned. "Do you mind if I skip it so I can wait for Wilbur?" he asked Jane.

"Not at all. You have much to discuss with him, I know," she said. "I think we are in safe hands."

Mr. Poole walked swiftly and talked even faster. He explained the thinking behind every aspect of the hospital. It was quite remarkable how much they had achieved in such a short time. Everything was brand new, and the most up-to-date methods and equipment would be used – no matter how poor the patient was. Everyone would receive the same care. It was quite a revolutionary idea, one Jane wasn't sure would ever catch on, but one that would be most welcome to those who didn't have the money to call out a doctor even for the gravest of illnesses.

Marianne asked him lots of questions, and he had the answers, no matter how difficult a question it was. She was obviously impressed by him, but Jane felt that there was something he was leaving unsaid.

"Mr. Poole, I am sorry that Peter will be moving away from you," she said tentatively as they looked at the gleaming operating theater. "I know you will miss him."

"I shall, but now I have met you I can understand why," he said gallantly. "And I shall simply have to become a regular guest in your little Montana town if you will not mind that?"

"We will always be happy to see you, though I doubt that my little house would be quite what you are used to."

"Peter will build you a new one. You'll need a bigger one for your family. You are intending to have children, aren't you? I long to be a godfather."

"We are, and I am sure your name will be at the top of the list," Jane assured him. "I don't wish to take Peter away from you. I am more than willing to share."

"And I am more than willing to give you both my blessing. I simply want Peter to be happy. He has brought so much happiness to my life. I am glad you bring joy to his."

"You do, too," Jane said. "He is very fond of you, very fond indeed."

When they returned to the foyer, it had begun to fill with people. It was a diverse mixture of those who were wealthy enough to become patrons and those who needed the services the most. They did not mix much with one another. The wealthy huddled together, happy to take tours to see the facilities – and to get away from the poor, as if they were afraid to breathe the same air as them. The poorer men and women gazed around in wonder at the beautiful building, eyes wide and mouths agape, occasionally asking questions of the doctors and nurses who were showing them around.

Jane watched as Peter, Marianne, and Mr. Poole moved effortlessly between the different groups, making small talk and garnering pledges of donations from the wealthy, and offering warm encouragement to the poor, reassuring them that this grand place was all for them and that they should come and see the doctors and nurses here whenever they or their families were sick. Marianne was particularly adept at introducing people, and because she was who she was, the wealthy were happy to follow her example. Her presence seemed to give them permission to do what they would not normally even consider.

"She is a marvel," Peter said as she introduced an elderly judge to a stevedore and his wife. Before long, they were all talking as if they were old friends. "She's made the evening, and our coffers are filled for years to come."

"I'm sorry I am not so adept in such company," Jane said

sadly. She'd felt a little on the edge of everything tonight, not really feeling like she belonged.

"So, ignore the Society types and talk to the people you can," Peter said with a simple shrug. "I know you are good at putting people at ease, I've seen you do it."

"My own kind, yes," Jane said. "Hard-working people."

"And most of the guests here are just that," he reminded her. "They need to know that we are like them and that we understand their needs. Who better than you to encourage them to use this place?"

Buoyed by his faith in her, Jane began to talk with some of the stevedores, sailors, and their wives. She loved hearing their stories of the docks and giggled when they forgot themselves and used language they shouldn't in polite company. Some of them had been orphans like her, with similar stories of neglect and punishment from nuns and monks. They all seemed relieved that there would be somewhere to bring their children, but few believed that there would truly be no cost. Jane was glad to assure them that Peter and Mr. Poole could be trusted to keep their word, and it seemed that her word was enough.

As the evening wore on and the groups began to mix a little more, people began to dance. Mr. Poole had hired a wonderful orchestra, and they switched from elegant waltzes and other dances that might be seen in the ballrooms of the wealthy to seaside shanties and rowdy reels that would be recognized by the working men and women. Jane and Marianne started teaching everyone the steps of the dances, and soon everyone was laughing together as they all tried to keep up with one another. It was a wonderful night, and Jane was glad that she had played her part in its success. She wanted to be a good wife to Peter. She was so very proud of him for all he had achieved.

CHAPTER 36

MARCH 6, 1894, EAGLE CREEK, MONTANA

"He's returned it," Peter said, angrily bursting into Jane's house. He was waving an invitation.

"Mark?" she asked.

He nodded. "He could have just ignored it, but to send it back? I know things are strained between us, but I have tried to hold out the proverbial olive branch. Why will he not take it?"

"I don't know, my love, but I am so sorry that he won't."

Peter looked close to tears, but Jane simply didn't know what to tell him. He had given up so much for her and she'd never wanted him to end up estranged from his brother. "Stop that," Peter said, looking at her with a slight smile.

"What?"

"Thinking it is your fault again. It isn't. It is Mark's. Never forget that. He pushed us together. He has no right to be angry about it now."

"How do you read my mind that way?" she marveled.

"I know you," he said with a shrug. "When you feel guilty, your eyes narrow and you frown just a little. It is a very sweet face, but I'd rather not see it so often. You have nothing to feel guilty about."

"I just wish there was a way to get Mark to come, to forgive us both."

"I do, too. I keep trying to convince myself that it doesn't matter and I will eventually come to accept it, but I'm not sure that I ever will. He is my twin. We've been two halves of the same whole our entire lives."

"What will you do?"

"I shall send it back, with another letter begging him to come, of course," Peter said.

He hugged her tightly and kissed her forehead. "Now, tell me of happier things. How is your wedding dress coming along?"

"I will not tell you a word," she said with a smile. "You'll have to wait and see it on the day. But it is looking lovely, that is all I will say."

"Keep your secrets, my love. Just be there on April 21, that is all I ask."

"I'll not leave you waiting, I promise you," she said fervently. She knew how afraid he was that she would do what Ellen had done all those years ago. She didn't mind it when his anxieties came out, though he tried to hide them from her most of the time. It was understandable that he was concerned after what had happened then. "But I must leave you now, I have to get to work."

He kissed her tenderly, then took her coat from the rack and helped her to put it on. "Have a good day. I shall see you tomorrow."

She looked at him blankly for a second, then remembered why he would not be dining with her. "You will be with The Crow tonight, I had forgotten that you would be joining Many Birds to choose a horse. I am so glad that you have a chance to enjoy their hospitality. They are such kind people. Please send them my very best regards."

She kissed his cheek and made her way to work. Kathy was out in the store, using the Singer machine to hem the tablecloths she had embroidered with Jane and Peter's initials for the wedding breakfast. Jane greeted her warmly and hurried into the workshop, where her dress was hanging on the dressmaker's dummy. She couldn't help smiling to herself when she saw it. Even though there were still pins sticking out of it, she could see the dress it would become – and it would be the most perfect thing she had ever made.

Carefully, she took it down, laid it on the workbench, and began to finish the seams of the bodice. Hannah watched her carefully, fascinated by how delicate the ivory fabric was and how easy it was to damage, learning how to work with it for the future. "How do you keep the seam from running?" she asked. "I practiced on some of the scraps, and I can't do it."

"Patience, and very tiny stitches," Jane said. "It cannot be done on the machine as it would snag and ruin the fabric in a moment. Having a delicate hand and being prepared to take your time is the only way to work with fabric like this."

"I hope I will be able to one day," Hannah said.

"You will. Just keep practicing. It comes. When I started here, I could do all the things that you and Kathy have learned so far, but Mrs. Albert taught me how to work with the more delicate fabrics. I made just as many errors as you, I can assure you. And you are far better at beadwork than I am already."

"Thank you," Hannah said proudly. "I shall keep working on it. Will you let me do the beadwork for this?"

"I am insisting that you do it. I just said you are better than me, didn't I?" Jane teased.

Hannah flushed with pride. "I drew a design. I know you had one in mind, but I changed it a little and thought I would offer to do it as a wedding gift, in my own time." She pulled out one of the large drawing pads and showed Jane her ideas.

"Oh, Hannah, these are quite lovely." Jane sighed. "I

would love you to do this one." She pointed at one on the second page. "Thank you for this, this is a lovely gift to offer, and one I will gladly accept. I'll have the bodice finished by the end of the day so you can take it home. In the meantime, use the scraps to practice attaching the beads so you are confident before you begin."

APRIL 21, 1894, EAGLE CREEK, MONTANA

Peter hauled himself out of the bath and dried himself with a clean bath sheet. He pulled on a shirt and pants and went into the parlor of his hotel suite. Cable grinned at him from his seat on the sofa. He was already dressed in a bright blue velvet suit with satin lapels, and a buttonhole of spring flowers was pinned to one of them. His cravat was tied particularly extravagantly, and a large diamond pin was holding it in place.

"At least you will be a clean bridegroom, even if you are a badly dressed one," Cable teased, taking a sip of brandy from his glass.

"I won't be wearing this," Peter said, shaking his head.

"Quite right you won't," Cable said firmly. He reached behind the sofa and pulled out a tailor's bag and opened it to reveal a very well-cut suit and a new linen shirt. "My gift to you."

"Cable, you did not need to," Peter said. "You already sent us plans for a new house and money to put toward building it."

"But I wanted to. You are a fine-looking man, Peter Algood, and you are wealthy now, yet you dress like a poor man still. I didn't want our lovely girl to have to walk down the aisle toward a beggar. Especially as, with her skills, she'll no doubt be very finely dressed indeed."

"She won't tell me anything about her gown. I've tried every way I could to get her to give something away, but not a word."

"A bride's prerogative."

"So I am told."

Wilbur came through from his bedchamber, dressed in a suit similar to the one Cable had just presented Peter with. He looked very smart, like a completely different lad to the one Peter had first met.

"You look handsome," Peter said.

Thank you. I feel silly.

Cable and Peter laughed.

It's all well and good for you two to dress like a couple of swells, but I'm just not that kind.

"You should be," Peter said. "It suits you even better than it suits Cable, and I've never seen a man dress as well as him before."

"I don't have Wilbur's broad shoulders and slim hips,"

Cable said sadly. "Though I did in my youth. I had a fine pair of calves, too. I looked wonderful in breeches."

"You still look wonderful for your age," Peter assured him. "And I am sure your calves would still turn heads."

Cable basked in the compliment, then gasped when the clock struck eleven. "You need to dress, now," he said. "I will not let you be late to the church."

Peter took the suit into his bedchamber and laid it beside the one he'd intended to wear. Cable was right. Even though his suit was new, it wasn't as fine as the one Cable had bought him, and Jane definitely deserved him to look his best. He dressed quickly, then looked at himself in the cheval glass. The cut of the suit was perfect, and he did look much better. He emerged, still trying to tie his cravat. Cable stood up, took it from him, tied it simply, and fixed it with a small pearl pin. "Not everyone is made to carry something so extravagant," he said with a grin, briefly touching his own pin.

Wilbur pinned Peter's buttonhole to his lapel and beamed. *The carriage is ready downstairs.*

The three men descended the grand staircase. People in the foyer below looked up at them and stared, making Peter feel a little uncomfortable. Then they suddenly began to clap, and he felt very uncomfortable. Cable just bowed, and Wilbur grinned. Mr. Hemsley, the hotel owner, and Mr. King, the maître d', greeted them warmly and walked out with them to the carriage. The weather was fine, so they'd brought out one of the open carriages. It was luxurious, with cream velvet upholstery over thickly padded seats.

"We will see you shortly. You'll be pleased to know that everything is ready for the party," Mr. King said.

"We are honored you chose to hold your celebrations here," Mr. Hemsley added.

Peter shook both their hands and accepted their wishes of good luck, and then the carriage was on its way. This time, he had no concerns, no fears. He knew that Jane loved him. She would be there, as she had promised she would. And they would be happy together. But as the three men entered the church, Peter wished his brother were by his side. Having Cable and Wilbur here was wonderful, but it wasn't the same. Mark should be the one carrying the ring. Mark should be the one trying to keep him calm.

Marianne entered the church first, holding Flora-Rose's hand as she scattered petals along the aisle. Peter grinned at her and bent down to the little girl when she reached him at the altar. "Thank you, little one," he said. He handed her a gift Jane had given him to give to her at this moment. Flora-Rose gasped and flung her arms around his neck.

"Thank you," she said happily.

Marianne gave his arm a reassuring squeeze. "She's outside and can hardly wait to come in," she said softly. Peter smiled and thanked her for the message. Obviously, Jane had told her about what had happened with Ellen. He remembered again how Mark had been there to calm him that day, how he had, for once, stepped up and taken control of matters when Ellen had not arrived and Peter had been unable to face anyone. He felt a pang of loss. Mark could be a selfish man, but he'd always been there when it truly mattered before. That he was not here today made Peter feel rotten.

But as soon as Jane began walking down the aisle on Mr. Delaney's arm, he forgot about anyone else but her. She was the loveliest thing he had ever seen, and not because of her dress, though it was spectacular. The fitted bodice accentuated her figure beautifully and the full skirt billowed behind her as she walked. The dress even seemed to glisten. When she drew close, he could see it was because there were thousands of tiny beads sewn in intricate patterns over the bodice and hem of the gown. It must have taken them many weeks to make, and he knew that Jane had poured every ounce of her love for him into it.

He took her hand and kissed it, then waited impatiently for Father Timothy to get through the ceremony to the part where he made his vows to her. He looked into her eyes and spoke them directly to her, and she did the same to him. As the priest declared them husband and wife the congregation behind cheered loudly. Peter was shocked. He'd almost forgotten that anyone was there but himself and Jane. He grinned at Jane, and she smiled back.

"Mrs. Peter Algood," he said softly as they walked down the aisle.

"It sounds wonderful, doesn't it?" she whispered back. "I'm so sorry Mark didn't come."

"I am too, but there is little I can do about that. Today is about us. About our love. And I won't let him spoil it for us because he is too petulant to forgive or take responsibility for his own part in this mess."

"It's hard though, isn't it?" she said, squeezing his hand.

"It is," he admitted. "It definitely is."

CHAPTER 37

MAY 30, 1894, EAGLE CREEK, MONTANA

"Telegram for you, Sir," Alfie Pinchin said as Peter opened the door, rubbing his eyes. It was barely past dawn, and he'd still been in bed.

"Thank you," Peter said, taking it. "Do you want to come in for coffee?"

"Can't stop, Sir, too much to do."

Peter watched as he jumped onto his bicycle and rode away at speed, marveling that anyone could be so bright and cheerful so early in the day. He put the kettle on the stove for coffee, then opened the telegram.

Mark is very sick. Brought into the hospital. Come at once.

Cable.

Peter's eyes opened wide. The coffee was no longer needed. "Jane, pack our bags. We have to go to New York," he yelled up the stairs.

"What's happened?"

"It's Mark. He's sick. Cable sent word that we should come at once."

Jane came down the stairs, still clad in her nightgown. "I can't just up and leave," she said.

"Well, I have to," he said. "I can't leave him to be ill alone."

"Will he even see you if you go?" she asked. "I don't wish to sound harsh, but what if you get all that way and he won't speak with you, even then?"

"It doesn't matter," Peter insisted. "I still have to go, and I have to hope that if it were the other way around that he would do the same for me."

Jane nodded. "I understand," she said softly. "I'll go and see Mrs. Albert and ask for more time away."

"You don't have to come. I know it will be hard for you."

"You are my husband, and he is your brother. It is right that I come," she said firmly. "I'll not leave you to bear this alone."

She went upstairs and dressed quickly, then left to speak with her employer. Peter went to the postal office to send a telegram to Cable asking for more information, then returned to begin packing while Jane was gone. He wondered what had made Mark so ill that Cable thought it necessary to travel with no notice, but he knew that his friend would not have raised the alarm for no reason. He couldn't help fearing it was influenza. Once his own trunk was full, he went downstairs and began to make some breakfast.

Jane returned as the eggs and bacon were ready. "Sarah and Arthur are here," she said with a smile, "so Mrs. Albert is happy to let me go. They've said they'll help out in the shop and that we should take all the time we need."

"I'm glad," Peter said, taking her hand across the table. "I don't think I'd be able to bear it without you."

"I checked at the station, and there is a train at eleven. We can be on it if we hurry," she said. "I'll go and pack now. Have you any preferences for what you'll take?"

"I packed already," he said. "I wasn't sure what you wanted, or I would have packed your things, too."

"I still forget that I married a most capable man," Jane said. She kissed the top of his head as she passed him on the way upstairs. "I am a very lucky woman."

Peter paced up and down on the porch while he waited for her, then took the stairs two at a time when she called him to come and help her bring the trunks downstairs. He loaded them onto a small cart, and they trundled along Main Street toward the station. Aston Merryweather hurried out of the postal office to greet them.

"Alfie told me of your news. I am so sorry. I hope you

will find your brother well when you arrive," he said, shaking Peter's hand and giving Jane a sad look.

"So do we," she said. "Thank you, Mr. Merryweather."

"I know we will be far away from you, but if there is anything we can do, just send word."

"We will. Thank you. If you wouldn't mind keeping an eye on the house and perhaps watering my garden if it needs it, that would be most helpful," Jane said.

"Oh, I'd be honored," the portly postmaster said. He said goodbye and wished them a safe journey, and they continued on their way.

"He means well, but he is such a gossip," Peter said. "You handled him very well."

"He just wants to be helpful to everyone. He cares about us."

"I know, but you are definitely more patient than I am. I'd not have thought to ask him to do something to make him feel better about matters."

"I know I'd want to be able to do something for those I care about. It's a little thing, but I will be grateful for it when I return and don't have to start all over again – or we have no vegetables at all this summer."

Peter smiled at her and put his arm around her shoulders. "You are a wonderful wife."

"And you are a wonderful husband. Now, go and be useful and purchase our tickets," she teased. "I'll find a boy to take our things."

He purchased their tickets but was unable to get them a compartment to themselves until they reached Billings. Jane acted unfazed by this, but he would have rather had a little privacy. "It barely takes a blink of an eye to go that far," she reminded him. "We'll have a sleeping compartment to ourselves when we change trains. It will be quite alright."

"There is little choice, I suppose."

They got themselves settled in the public carriage, and Peter glanced around at their fellow travelers. Most were probably only making local journeys as they had small bags with them. An elderly man had a couple of chickens in a rudimentary cage tucked under his seat. A young couple with children were sitting on the seats on the other side of the carriage, the children swinging their legs, laughing, and occasionally breaking into song. The windows were all open, letting in a cool breeze that was welcome in the otherwise stuffy carriage. Peter couldn't help thinking that Mark would have hated it. It was noisy and a little chaotic, but he was surprised to find that the normality of it all was actually quite soothing to him. When they changed trains at Billings, he actually missed the noise and the activity of the public carriage, so he made his way along the train so he could see into the next carriage, leaving Jane alone to read quietly.

Watching other people became fascinating to him. He enjoyed making up stories in his head about what they were all doing and where they were going. It helped to pass the time on the long journey. Each time they stopped along the way, he sent a telegram, asking Cable for news, letting him know where they would be changing trains next. At each stop, Cable made sure there was a telegram waiting for him with news.

Mark had indeed caught influenza, but it had gone down into his chest, and he had suffered from pneumonia for weeks. His doctors feared for his life as he had grown very weak and was not able to eat due to swelling in his throat. With each update, Peter feared they might arrive in New York too late, and he couldn't bear the thought that he might lose his brother before they were reconciled. He wanted Mark to know he was loved, and that he was not and never would be alone.

JUNE 23, 1894, NEW YORK CITY, NEW YORK

Cable sent word that he would meet them at a coffee shop near the townhouse that Peter had once shared with Mark. Jane had never been to this part of New York before and was a little surprised that the area was not as well-to-do as she had expected it to be. She knew, of course, that Peter had not grown up among the wealthy, but she had thought that his family had been comfortable. The houses nearby all looked a little shabby and neglected, with dirty windows and fading paint on the trim.

"It was quite nice when we were young," Peter said, seeing the look on her face and reading her mind as he so often did, "but places change and fade. As people did better for themselves, they moved to nicer areas and new people moved in. Not all of them were good neighbors. Mark didn't want to move. He was comfortable here. I didn't care where I lived, and it's not too far from the docks, so it suited me well enough. But he's let the house decay, even in the short time since I left."

"I'm sorry, Peter," Jane said. "This must be so hard for you."

Cable burst into the coffee shop and marched straight to their table, his face black as thunder. "He's discharged himself," he said, shaking his head in disbelief. "Refused further treatment and took himself home. The man can barely speak, can hardly walk, and has eaten little in weeks, but he thinks he can take care of himself. He's an utter fool, and there's no talking to him."

Peter gave a wry chuckle. "He's the most stubborn man alive. But if he's gone home, he'll never let me in the door, though Wilbur might sneak me in."

"Wilbur isn't living with him any longer," Cable said. "He's moved in with me. Mark was acting oddly, even before he got sick. Kept picking fights with Wilbur after he got back from your wedding."

Peter shook his head. "I hate to say it, but that doesn't

surprise me. He doesn't like it when he doesn't get his way. He probably wanted Wilbur to take his side."

Jane frowned. "He's still unwell?" she asked.

"Very unwell indeed," Cable confirmed.

"Then he will need help. Do you think we'd be able to at least convince him to have a nurse? To live in, or even just to check on him daily."

"We could try. He does at least talk to me through the door when I call on him," Cable said. "But I doubt he'll consider it."

"Then we need to present it as something he cannot refuse," Peter said. "The nurse will have to insist she was sent by his doctors. If people are firm with him, he will give in."

"We can't involve a nurse in such deviousness," Jane pointed out. "It wouldn't be fair."

"But what choice do we have? He won't let any of us inside."

"Not if he knows it is us, no, I doubt it," she agreed. "But he's never actually met me, has he? Has he even seen a picture of me?"

"Not as far as I know," Peter said, giving her a curious look. For once, he wasn't able to read her mind. She smiled at that.

"Well, we met because of the deception that Mark and you played upon me. Why do we not use similar tactics to ensure he gets the care that he needs? What if I pretend to be a nurse sent by the hospital?"

Cable laughed out loud. "It is ingenious," he declared. "I knew I liked your wife, Peter. She's quite wonderful."

"Are you sure you could bear it? He's not an easy man, even when he is perfectly well," Peter asked her.

"I grew up caring for the little ones at the orphanage, I helped Marianne nurse her first husband, and I take care of Mrs. Albert now. I can do the work. My only concern is that he won't let me in. But at least we can try."

They finished their coffee and went to the hospital, where Cable asked one of the nurses to fetch Jane a uniform and a bag with everything she would need to care for Mark at home. The girl looked a little taken aback by his request, but the matron nodded that she should do as she was told.

"The most important thing you can do is to keep him drinking," she told Jane. "He'll not survive long without fluid. If you can entice him with his favorite foods, that will build him up more quickly, and don't hesitate to send for us if there is blood in his stool or in what he coughs up."

"I'll do my best," Jane said.

The young nurse returned with everything they had asked for. Matron helped Jane to dress, showing her how to fix the rather tricky headdress, then checked that Jane knew how to check her patient's pulse and listen to his heart and lungs.

Around the corner from the house, Peter held Jane

tightly and kissed her fervently. "Good luck," he said. "I shall miss you, but I will be in the coffee shop every day at eleven."

Jane hugged him one last time, exhaled sharply, then walked slowly around the corner and along the street to the townhouse. She climbed the steps to the front door and knocked loudly. She heard a loud coughing behind the door somewhere. It sounded terrible, which made her resolve grow. Mark needed them, even if he didn't know it. She would not let him turn her away.

CHAPTER 38

JULY 17, 1894, NEW YORK CITY, NEW YORK

"Nurse, I need more soup," Mark called out loudly.

Jane shook her head. He was strong enough now to come down the stairs and eat in the dining room or the kitchen, but over the past weeks, he had gradually shifted from his stubborn refusal of her assistance to a grumpy acceptance of it, and he was now malingering, making much of the tiniest symptoms that he had left. She was close to the end of her tether with him, but she was glad that he had made an almost full recovery under her care.

"Then you should come downstairs and fetch it," she called up the stairs, trying to keep her voice calm. "The doctor said that you need to move more to strengthen your legs again after so long in bed."

"Silly old quack, he doesn't know anything," Mark said, reluctantly coming down the stairs. He took them slowly, clinging tightly to the banister, one foot onto the step and then the other, taking a break before attempting the next step. She watched him carefully and encouraged him to try taking a few steps at a time. "It's never enough for you, is it?" he said angrily. "Do you have somewhere else you'd rather be?"

She was determined not to let him win such snide exchanges, but he really did try her patience at times. "I'm sure you'd understand if I said that I do," she said. "I do not enjoy your being unwell any more than you do, Mr. Algood. I just want you to regain your health. Don't you think that you will be happier once you can return to work and have something to fill your days again?"

He thought about that, but he did not answer her. Jane was glad she'd made him think about the work he loved. His employers were kindly holding his place, but they wouldn't do so forever. If he could not find a reason to make improvements, he would continue to play the invalid. "Now, I've fixed you some eggs for your lunch today, but there is soup on the stove if they're too much. I know that your throat can sometimes still be sore."

"Thank you," he said grudgingly as he took a seat in the dining room. It was the coldest room in the house, but it was clear that he wanted her to wait on him rather than join her in the warmth of the kitchen, where she could just hand him things across the old pine table.

"I'll fetch some blankets if you wish to eat in here. But it's warmer in the kitchen," she reminded him.

"Light a fire in here."

"It won't warm the room until you've finished eating, even if I do," she said. He truly was oblivious to the simplest things in life, utterly unaware of how things worked. Peter had sheltered him from things, and he'd not bothered to learn anything in his brother's absence.

With a heavy sigh, he followed her into the kitchen, leaning heavily against the walls rather than letting her help him or even using a cane to support his still-weak legs, and sat down at the head of the table. Jane handed him a plate of eggs and watched him pick at them ungratefully. She ladled some soup into a bowl and pushed that across the table to him. He picked up a spoon and began to eat it without complaint, slurping loudly.

"I have to run some errands. We've run out of your medicine, and I need to fetch some clean uniforms," she told him. "I'll be no longer than a couple of hours."

"I suppose I'll have to manage."

"Perhaps you could read something. Didn't you tell me once that you like to read?"

"Not anymore," he said, a tinge of sadness in his voice. "I don't enjoy it anymore."

"Why not? Have you tried?"

"I liked reading the stories about Huckleberry Finn and Tom Sawyer," he said, confiding in her more than he'd done in the weeks she'd been caring for him. "They reminded me of my brother and me."

"Your brother?" Jane asked, feigning ignorance.

"I have a twin. But he left me. Everyone leaves. My parents left. He left. Wilbur left."

"I thought your parents passed away?"

"They did, but they still left, didn't they?"

"I'm sure your brother misses you, too."

"Didn't say I missed him, did I?" he said, glaring at her. "Don't meddle in things that are not your business."

"Sorry, I just wanted to help."

"Then help him to understand he can't just take the things I want."

Jane stayed quiet. Mark was finally opening up a little to her, and she needed him to do that. If she just let him talk, she might understand his side of things and somehow find a way to bring the brothers back together. It seemed that Mark wanted that just as much as Peter, though he'd yet to fully accept that himself.

"He's always been the same. Taking charge, insisting his way is the right way, and then when something nice comes along, he always takes it for himself. Ellen, then Jane."

"That's two people you're talking about," Jane pointed

out. "Did they not have a say in matters? Did they want to be with you and not him? Were you sure of that?"

"They probably would have hated me if they really knew me," Mark said with a weak smile. Jane smiled back at his attempt at humor.

"I'm sure they didn't, but did you give them a chance to get to know you at all?"

Mark's expression changed again. "What did I say about it not being your business?" he barked. "Go and do your silly chores. Leave me alone, sick and weak."

Jane shook her head. "Stop that," she said firmly, remembering Peter's words that Mark responded best to those who told him plainly how to behave. "Stop feeling sorry for yourself. If you want things to change, you need to work to make that happen. If you want to get well, you need to eat and you need to move, just as the doctors told you. If you want to mend things with your brother, you need to talk to him and stop making excuses and taking it out on me because I simply happen to be here."

"You're all I have," Mark said simply, a little taken aback at her outburst.

"No, I'm not. You have a brother who cares for you. I meet him every single day to tell him how you are getting along. You pushed away a perfectly good friend because he works for that brother, and he would visit you often if only you'd let him. And you have a sister-in-law who cares for you enough to stay here and care for you, even though you have been rude and ungrateful and you lied to her from the very first."

Mark stared at her. "Miss Brown?" he asked as what she'd said sank in and he realized the truth of the matter.

"Mrs. Algood. Jane Algood," she corrected him. "You never asked for my last name. In truth, you never even seemed to notice I had one. Mark, your brother misses you more than you can imagine. It cut him to the quick that you did not come to our wedding, that you sent the invitation back to us."

"Miss Brown," he said again, softly to himself. "Peter said you were pretty. I was just so scared you would hate me. Everyone hates me once they get to know me, even Peter."

"Peter doesn't hate you. Not at all. He loves you."

"I was so mean to him."

"Yes, you were. But he'll forgive you."

"I wouldn't if I were him. I couldn't ever let go of my anger about him taking Ellen."

"What actually happened there?" Jane asked, intrigued. Peter was still confused by the revelation that Mark had feelings for his ex-fiancée. It puzzled him greatly.

"I met Ellen first. She was quiet and liked numbers, like I did. We played chess together. But then she met Peter and Harry, and suddenly she didn't want to play chess or do number puzzles anymore. She stopped talking to me and started to do her hair differently and wear different dresses."

"You thought she liked you?"

"I know she did. But Peter and Harry were so much more interesting than me, I suppose."

"And she thought herself in love with one but ran away with the other?"

"Yes, I suppose so."

"Do you think she regrets that choice?"

"I don't know. But I've never found anyone else like her."

"But you'd like to?"

"Yes, maybe not to marry, but to play chess with and do number puzzles. I'd like that. But I don't like living here alone, either. I enjoyed Wilbur living here because he was good at chess."

"Would you like Wilbur to come back?" He nodded. "And perhaps a housekeeper? Someone to take care of you and keep the house clean?" He nodded again. "Well, I can certainly arrange the latter, but you may need to apologize to Wilbur before he'd consider coming back. You hurt his feelings quite badly."

"I need to apologize to Peter, too, don't I?" Mark asked softly. "I've thought only of myself. He always did so much for me, and I never realized until he was gone. He gave up all sorts of things for me. He made a vow after Ellen, but I never thought he'd keep it so long." He chuckled and shook his head. "I must confess that I find it rather funny that to get me to see sense you practiced a deception on me, just like I did in the hope it would make you like me more."

"It is hard to like someone when you never actually meet them, Mark. Sometimes, you just have to be brave enough to show up."

He nodded thoughtfully. "I'm glad he has you."

Jane paused for a moment before she spoke again. She didn't want to push Mark too hard, too fast. But it seemed the perfect moment. "So, why don't we get you dressed and take a little walk to the coffee shop around the corner. I was going to meet your brother there, but I know he'll be delighted if you join us."

"You truly think he'll be happy to see me?" Mark asked anxiously.

"I do," she assured him. "He raced here as soon as we knew you were unwell. He wanted to be by your side."

"And he sent you, knowing I'd never answer the door to him."

"Exactly that. So, do you want to mend things? It is always best to do these things before you can give yourself a chance to talk yourself out of it."

He nodded and pushed himself up to his feet using the table to support himself. "I think I might need those canes you keep trying to get me to use. I can't just shuffle around holding onto the walls if we're going outside."

Jane ran to fetch the walking sticks he'd been refusing for weeks. He took them and used them surprisingly well to walk along the corridor and up the stairs without her assistance, though he did call her to come and help him dress once he reached his room. She handed him soap and a clean wet cloth so he could wash himself, then helped him put on a clean shirt and pants.

He bravely tried to take the stairs more quickly than he had before and beamed when he managed it more easily than he'd thought he would. Jane smiled. Side by side, they walked along the sidewalk and around the corner. Peter was waiting outside the coffee shop for Jane, and his eyes widened in surprise when he saw Mark by her side. He hurried forward to help his brother. Their eyes met. No words needed to be spoken as they enfolded each other in a brotherly embrace that brought tears to Jane's eyes.

EPILOGUE

CHRISTMAS EVE, 1894, EAGLE CREEK, MONTANA

ane put the last sprigs of holly on the mantel and stood back to admire her work. The new house was so much bigger than her little cottage had been, but she was determined that it would still have the cozy feeling that she had loved about her first real home. Everything looked very festive. She wondered if she'd brought too many branches and boughs in from the outside to decorate the inside, but then she decided that such a thing could not be possible.

She stroked her slightly swelling belly tenderly. "Well, little one, isn't it wonderful that we'll soon have a full home, full of everyone we love?"

The front door clicked open, and Peter called out to her. "We're home!"

She hurried into the hallway and beamed at the people standing around her husband. Mark stood to his left, Cable and Wilbur to his right. She hugged them all. "I am so happy you could all come."

"After Peter told us all about the Christmas Eve party here, we couldn't say no," Cable said. "And he said something about the finest cook in the land making dinner tomorrow." He kissed her cheek. He looked as spritely and full of mischief as ever, though he'd taken to using a cane to support himself now, not just for the aesthetic of it. Naturally, his cane was a striking black ebony with a shiny silver fox's head at the top.

"Are you well, Wilbur?" Jane asked. He seemed to have gained another six inches since she'd seen him last, and he'd been gangly enough before.

I am very well. I have met a girl.

"Well, that is wonderful news," she said. She kissed his cheek. "Peter will show you up to your rooms."

She hung back a little with Mark. "How do you feel about Wilbur and his girl?" she asked him once everyone else was out of earshot.

"She's very nice. She plays chess," he said with a grin. "And she is better at it than Wilbur. I've said they can still live in the house when they get married, and I've asked Peter if he'd sign over a share of the house to them."

"That is very generous of you."

"She is easy to be around. And she cooks very well."

Jane laughed. Once you understood Mark, he really was very easy to please. "I'm glad I have this moment with you alone because I want you to be the first to know. You're going to be an uncle, Mark."

He stared at her as if he didn't quite understand, then looked delighted. "I'm going to have a nephew?" He picked Jane up and whirled her around.

"Well, it might be a niece, but you mustn't tell anyone. I've not even told your brother," she said. "I thought I'd tell them tonight, at the party, but I wasn't sure if you'd want to be around so many people all at once, and I didn't want you to find out after everybody else."

He puffed up with pride that she had wanted him to know first. "I do want to come, but do you think people will mind if I don't stay for very long?" he asked her a little anxiously.

"Not at all. I've told everyone that you are quite quiet and a little shy. Stay as long as you can bear, then just come home."

"I'll stay until you tell everyone," he assured her. "I want to see Peter's face."

A few hours later, Jane handed out fur hats and mittens to the newcomers and showed them where they could find blankets and furs, in case they needed them through the evening. All of them assured her they would survive, but she and Peter shared a knowing look as they pulled on their coats to go to the party.

The rest of the town was already outside, enjoying the huge bonfire and dancing to the band. Peter put his arm around his wife's shoulders as they walked along Main Street, introducing Mark to people. Cable and Wilbur greeted everyone as if they were old friends, having met everyone at the wedding. It seemed everyone remembered them both fondly, and nobody seemed to have a problem with Wilbur's rapid scribbling conversations. Jane watched happily as Jake Graham and Walks With The Sun took Wilbur under their wing and headed off with him to join the other young people.

When they found Marianne, James, and Cook near the bonfire, Jane felt her stomach churn a little. It was a nice feeling rather than an unpleasant one, but she was surprised by it. She'd not expected to be nervous about telling people her news.

"Would you fetch Wilbur for a moment," she whispered to her husband, who looked at her quizzically but didn't question her.

When he returned with the boy, she looked at each of the faces in front of her, amazed that she was able to call them her family. She, who'd had nobody, now had the most wonderful people all around her.

"Everyone," she began tentatively, "I have something I want to say." Cable looked at Wilbur and raised his eyebrows. She tried to ignore them and looked at her husband. She took his hand between her mittened ones. "Peter, God has given us the very finest of gifts this Christmas, the gift of having our family all around us. But he has blessed us even further because you are going to be a father."

Peter looked stunned, then delighted. He picked her up and whirled her around. When he set her back on her feet, she glanced over at Mark, who was beaming at his brother's reaction. Quietly, Cable handed Wilbur ten dollars, while Wilbur grinned delightedly.

Jane laughed as Cook folded her into her arms and hugged her so tightly she could barely breathe. "Now, chile, this is what I came all the way to this icy cold place for," she cried happily.

Marianne and James both hugged her tightly before Peter claimed her once more. "Mrs. Algood, you have made me the happiest man alive. Though I'm not sure I should be condoning you deceiving me this way. How long have you known?"

"Just a week or so," she said with a grin. "But it was you and your brother who taught me the value of a little deception. Without it, I'd not have you, would I?"

The End

OTHER SERIES BY KARLA

Sun River Brides

Ruby Springs Brides

Silver River Brides

Eagle Creek Brides

Iron Creek Brides

Faith Creek Brides

CONNECT WITH KARLA GRACEY

Visit my website at www.karlagracey.com to sign up to my newsletter and get free books and be notified as to when my new releases are available.

Printed in Great Britain
by Amazon